Jilted in Greece

A Romance Novel

Tania Park

ISBN: 978-0-6455254-3-4 (Paperback)
ISBN:978-0-6455254-4-1 (e-book)

A catalogue record for this
book is available from the
National Library of Australia

NATIONAL
LIBRARY
OF AUSTRALIA

Tania Park Publishing
For enquiries, write to rights and permission via goldpark3@gmail.com

Dedication

To write a book takes many hours. The first draft is the easiest. It's when editors and fellow readers get a hold of the final manuscript, the real work starts. You get back a manuscript covered in suggestions. You wade through those suggestions and make changes. Sometimes the changes are nothing more than a spelling error. Other times it requires and entire chapter re-write.

Thank you to all those who have made suggestions. I appreciate every comment. I don't always agree with you but let's hope the finished product is readable and enjoyed by those who read it.

Pure romance isn't my favourite genre. I prefer a bit of action, crime, tension. So my romance novels also include those aspects. I'm not a mushy writer but I'm told if it's two protagonists who end up together – it's a romance. So here is a romance novel with other bits included.

Other Titles by the Author

The Only way I Know – 2011 - Biography
Mistaken: 2015 – Crime/mystery/romance
Retribution: 2015 – Crime/mystery
Blind Justice: 2016 – Crime/mystery
Commended 2016 Christina Stead National Literary Awards.
Road Trip: 2016 – Adventure/mystery
The Swan: 2018 Crime/mystery/romance
Finalist 2020 The Wishing Shelf International Awards.
Stalked: 2019: Psychological Thriller
Long listed 2020 Davitt Awards.
Double Cross: 2020 – White collar crime
Long listed 2021 Davitt Awards
The Chest: 2021 – Mystery/crime
Beloved Intruder: 2022 – Romance
Third place – Romance Writers of Australia – Sapphire Award.
Workshop Workings: 2023 – A collection of winning short stories and poems created in writing workshops.
Redemption: 2024 – Crime/Mystery
The Price of Freedom 2024 - Romance

One

'Excuse me, but I think you are in my seat.'

Even though the deep voice was nearby, Phoebe Jackson ignored the man because no way could he be referring to her. She was in the correct seat. Must be the seats in front, she thought while she continued to stuff a novel, puzzle book, peppermints and a pen into the pocket of the airline seat in front of her.

A hand touched her shoulder. She jerked around, lost her grip on the pen. It slipped from her fingers and dropped to the floor with a little *splat*.

'Shoot,' she hissed under her breath as she bent to retrieve it.

'You are in my seat.' The voice was louder and more insistent. The hand had moved to her back and tapped.

Stuck halfway to the floor and twisted like a contortionist in the tiny space, she attempted to reach the elusive pen. The hand tapped again. She turned her head to see the nuisance for she was in her designated seat for this leg of her journey to Athens from Singapore. The man must be wrong.

'I think you have made a mistake.' Her breath stalled. A massive man towered over her crunched position but what snagged her attention were the features on his face. Deep brown eyes glanced at his boarding pass, up towards the lockers and settled on her with one hoicked up eyebrow. A shiver wove down her spine.

'Either we have been given the same seat or...' he removed his hand from her shoulder and pointed to the next seat, 'the window seat is yours.'

1

With a lump of lead low in her innards, Phoebe searched the seat pocket for her boarding pass, slithered out what was now a crumpled mess and smoothed it out. Before she had a chance to check the numbers, the paper was whooped from her fingers. A grin of triumph spread across the man's face before he pointed towards the window. Heat rose in her cheeks.

'I'm so sorry.' There was no doubt the heat had risen higher for an incinerator burned inside her cheeks. They must now glow like a red neon sign. They always did. To hide her obvious embarrassment, she kept her head down while she wriggled and squirmed to get upright. Free, she hefted her backside up and over the console and without a pause or glance began to empty the pocket of the middle seat and transferred every item to her pocket. At least next to the window she would have a tad more room to shove her pillow against and she could pretend an intimate study of the sky as an excuse to not talk for the next twelve or so hours.

The chuckle as the man settled into the seat she had vacated, didn't ease her chagrin one iota, but it sure increased the level of heat. 'It's not funny,' she quipped under her breath, but had to bite her lip to prevent any more words from escaping. Please don't let him have heard her smart comment. Somehow she always spoke her mind before putting her brain into gear and often regretted her hasty words, a habit she was determined to overcome.

He laughed. 'Sorry, I wasn't laughing at the mistake in the seat, it can happen easy enough. I have managed to do the same myself except I was in the wrong row.' He shoved a black bag of the laptop computer variety, under the seat in front of him. As his hand rose, he swung it in her direction. 'I believe this belongs to you.'

Two long fingers with neat, clipped nails gripped her pen. Not the grime she always had to pare from under her torn excuses for nails. Not sure how clean her nails were, she

2

grabbed the pen with curled fingers and glanced up. Her breath caught. My, but up close he was a hunk. Black hair cut short, eyes almost as dark and a straight nose over the most gorgeous mouth she had ever seen on a guy: one with permanent smile creases curved around the edges. The dark tinge of his complexion enhanced his appeal. Again, her heat level rose but this time started at her toes and crept upwards. No single man should have so many hot, sexy attributes. It took her too long to realise she was staring and wondered if her tongue hung out as well. To make sure it wasn't, she ran it along the inside of her lips. Yes, mouth is closed and no drool has escaped.

'Err, thank you,' she said and ensured her lips were super-glued together in case it appeared she was gawping, until she remembered he had laughed at her. 'What was so funny?'

Another chuckle escaped those gorgeous lips when he smiled the kind of smile created to draw her in like a magnet. 'You, when you blushed with such innocence. Very becoming.'

There was no way Phoebe could stop her hands from flinging to her cheeks to hide the heat which flared into an inferno once again. She yelped and winced when the pen she still held, stabbed into her cheek, further increasing her humiliation at being such a klutz. Far out, how bad can things get? Embarrassed yet again, she shoved the weapon into the seat pocket and twisted her head away to stare through the window until the heat dissipated and her body quit the spurt of adrenalin.

All over the tarmac, little carts dragged luggage to and from various sized planes. Hoses hung from sockets and snaked to larger vehicles: jet fuel, she figured. Maybe water as well. She could sure do with some water right now. With lots of ice blocks. A large van with a colourful logo of a catering firm, rolled from the side of their jet, now empty after it had despatched better airline meals than normal, she hoped. Fat chance.

'No don't feel embarrassed,' came from her left seconds before warm fingers cupped her chin and forced her head around to face Mr Hunk. 'It's so rare to see a woman blush these days. I like it, so don't hide.'

Is this man for real? Phoebe searched for adequate words: words which didn't exacerbate her mortification. 'It's all right for you - you're not the one who blushes with such ease. It can be such an embarrassment at times.'

'Well, I like it and since we will be in close proximity for the next twelve or so hours I will do my best to not embarrass you again.' He held out his right hand. 'Nick Kalameides.'

'Oh, err, Phoebe. Phoebe Jackson.' The moment she grasped the proffered hand she regretted it. A shaft of electricity shot from his fingers into hers. Heat flooded through her body, up to her cheeks for the third time in as many minutes. She snapped her hand away when a sense of guilt rose, for she had no right to even think about this man or for her body to react with such awareness.

'Phoebe?'

'Oh, please, don't. I've been teased about my name all of my life but it is the one I am lumbered with.' It irked a tad when he laughed again.

'I like your name. It suits you. Since you have a Greek name and are headed towards Greece, does it mean you have Greek heritage?'

'Good grief, no.' When hurt flickered across his eyes, Phoebe realised she sounded as though she didn't like Greeks and with his name and features, he must have Greek blood although the distinctive Australian twang said otherwise. 'Sorry,' she reached out, placed her fingers on his wrist, but tugged her hand back when another spark of awareness hit. 'I sounded like I'm racist but I'm not – in any way. I'm a true-blue Aussie; about four generations I think. My dad is the arty kind and had a love of the ancient Greek culture, in particular, the architecture. When I was born, he named me. Phoebe Helena.'

'Your father named you? Your mother didn't get a say?'

'My mother died three hours after I was born.'

'Oh, I'm sorry.' Nick leant towards her; his expressive face changed to concern in an instant.

'It's okay. I never knew her. You can't miss what you never had.' It wasn't quite true. In fact it held not even a hint of the truth. She had missed the presence of a mother since she was old enough to figure out not all kids had a single parent and since then she had envied all her friends who had a special mother – child relationship.

'I'm afraid I don't believe you.'

With a will of its own, Phoebe's head shot around to stare at the man. Was he a mind reader? 'Excuse me?'

'I find it impossible to believe a young girl wouldn't miss her mother.'

Yes, had to be a mind reader. 'I missed having a mother but didn't miss my mother since I never met her. My dad worked from home so had no problem in caring for me. I was never once left home alone when he had to go out to sites since there were nannies, housekeepers and babysitters until I went to high school.' When she realised she had revealed way too much about her personal life she bit her lip and turned away, willing her tongue to stay still while she concentrated on the bustle of activity on the tarmac, except the bustle had turned into a ghost town. Most of the vehicles had gone, along with the ground personnel.

'You are uptight about sitting next to me aren't you? Why? I'm just a man.'

There was no *just* about it. He was one of the sexiest men she had ever encountered and why she'd had such a reaction was beyond explanation for she had never re-acted this way in her entire life. In the course of her father's business she had met hundreds of men, had studied and worked with a majority of males since she'd left high school, so why she now acted like a naïve teenager was beyond her.

'Sorry, it's not you, I'm a bit... the past few weeks have been hectic.' Stupid, stupid woman! Why did she reveal personal details? Now he would want to know why her life had been so hectic and she didn't want to talk about – not yet – it was too hard.

A sigh of relief escaped her lips when an announcement came over the intercom about hand luggage in lockers and under seats, the closure of doors and take-off procedures. More than thankful for the usual but necessary information, Phoebe snapped her seat belt into place, yanked it tight and re-organised her bits and pieces in the pocket into a much neater fashion than the shoved in mess she had managed to achieve in her haste. To fill in even more time, she fidgeted with each item until she was certain they would be within easy reach during the long flight. It was imperative to have tasks to do to keep her mind from the constant repetition of the past couple of weeks and the sudden loss of her beloved dad. She eyed the fat book of puzzles and the latest crime thriller she found on the shelves in the airport newsagency. Still desperate to waste more time so she would appear to be pre-occupied, she removed each item, clipped the pen into the inside cover of the puzzle book, and took utmost care to re-arrange every item next to each other yet in easy reach. The result didn't look much different from the first effort.

At the commencement of emergency procedures, Phoebe searched for and found the card outlining exits and studied every word and diagram even though she knew the details by heart. She should since she'd flown often enough.

'There won't be any words left on your card if you keep staring at it.' Nick reached over seconds before he removed the card from her hand and slipped it in the very back of her pocket. 'The demonstration is over and we have begun to move.' He wavered his open hand towards the window.

6

They were indeed backing out from the terminal. Now why hadn't she noticed? Probably because this man had her more flustered and super-aware than she had ever been before. And she had close to thirteen hours crammed next to him. Thirteen hours to avoid a single touch unless she wanted to be zapped each time. Thirteen hours to not peek at the hunkiest man she had ever seen. And darn it, he smelt so yummy. All male with spice undertones from some super male aftershave, or maybe body wash. Far out, this journey was going to be torturous.

'And since we have a spare seat on the aisle, I will move over when the seatbelt signs go off so we can both be more comfortable,' Nick added.

'Thank you, God,' she muttered under her breath.

***

All he received in response was a quiet, 'thank you,' over her shoulder. It amused him how Phoebe kept her head turned towards the window. Nick studied what he could see. There was nothing remarkable about her but she was a beautiful woman in a natural sort of way. Long brown hair was caught back with plain white elastic in a ponytail at the nape of her neck. The neck was long and graceful with a visible pulse above her collarbone. No make-up, which was unusual. Not often did he come across a woman who wouldn't be caught dead without layers of precise artificial enhancement. Natural was good, he decided. No, better than good. Legs clad in blue denim were long and slender and he wondered how tall she was. A simple red, collared T-shirt, which seemed to be a little baggy, left tanned arms bare. Her skin appeared smooth and silky. Was it as smooth as he thought? He was tempted to find out but figured by the easy way Phoebe blushed and the way she had reacted to him, she wouldn't appreciate another touch, whether accidental or not. And it sure wasn't appropriate to touch a stranger, but it was oh, so enticing.

Even as the plane accelerated along the runway, Phoebe didn't move. It was as though she had turned into a marble statue. His body pushed itself back into the seat as the huge jet rose from the ground. At the same time, Phoebe raised a hand and... sweet mercy, she was trying to be surreptitious in wiping away tears.

He forced his body forward against the G-forces, reached over and swiped away a tear. Lord but her skin was like velvet. 'Why the tears?'

She sniffed, paused, bit her bottom lip, which quivered in an obvious attempt to gain control. His heart managed to somersault at the despair etched on her face. This was one devastated woman. As though a dam wall had been blown apart, moisture welled over the lower edges of her eyes and tumbled down her cheeks.

'Phoebe, what on earth is the matter?' He couldn't help himself when he swept his arm around her shoulders and drew her as close as the restrictive seats and belts would allow. When he realised how inappropriate it was to hug a woman he had just met, he yanked his arm back. Lord, but he would be accused of sexual harassment if he kept this up. But a sense of helplessness filled his innards when Phoebe dropped her head into her hands with floodgates open wide. She cried and cried some more. He had experienced women in tears before, often of the crocodile type to gain his undivided attention for some inane reason. Since he couldn't abide needy women who used pretence to gain attention, the relationship was brought to a gentle but polite end soon after such displays of artifice.

But these tears were real. Gut instinct told him this woman had held back this deluge of despair for way too long and needed to release her agony. He glanced at her left hand, caught sight of the drips of salty moisture but there were no rings and no pale mark where a ring had sat - so maybe not a romantic break-up. She mentioned a father. Was he ill? Was she on her way to Athens to meet her father? But her voice hadn't cracked when she mentioned him.

'Phoebe?'

'I'm sorry,' she whimpered between two huge sobs and a sucked in breath.

His heart managed another tumble-turn. 'Don't be sorry. You can cry as much as you like. You sound as though you need it.'

With one hand he reached out to grasp her hand in comfort while attempting to slide his other hand in the pocket of his jeans to retrieve the clean handkerchief he had shoved in at the last minute before the taxi took him to the airport. It was impossible to even get his hand in the pocket in the tight confines, so he unclipped his seat belt despite the fact the plane was still on a steep climb. He levered his hip upwards, stretched his leg out into the aisle until he was able to straighten his hip and yank the handkerchief out. He hated these tiny seats to the extent he preferred to travel business class but at such short notice, this was all he could get. Economy class seats were not built for men his size.

'Here, use this,' he said. He shook the cotton square from its folds and stuffed it into her hand which grappled the hanky, screwed it into a tight ball and swiped at her tear-streaked face with one vicious stroke. Her other hand grasped his as though it was the last scrap of driftwood in the ocean and she was desperate to cling on. Her grip was so strong it hurt. Not that he minded. It had been a while since he'd had the pleasure of a beautiful woman in his arms. His crazy workload for the past few months had given him little time to even ask a woman out, let alone spend a few hours over a romantic dinner.

'Th... thank... you,' she stuttered and pulled away with her head half turned away while she put the handkerchief to good use. She swiped and blew and swiped some more. 'I

9

am so sorry,' she began but paused when she studied the crumpled state of his handkerchief.

He grabbed her hands. 'Phoebe, it's okay. It's a square piece of cotton and will dry in no time. I have plenty more. Keep it.'

When she lifted her eyes they were red-rimmed and haunted. Dark half-moons under her eyes now stood out like deep bruises, which gave him the notion a decent sleep hadn't been on Phoebe's agenda for quite some time. What could be so bad to cause such pain? One way to find out.

'Since I am the recipient of so many of your tears, can I know why?'

'I am so sorry. I didn't know it would be so difficult to... to... to say goodbye.'

'Say goodbye to what?'

'My dad.' Tears leaked again. 'I buried him a week ago.' The dam wall erupted and overflowed. He recognised these tears as grief – the kind that stole over a person and sucked out the soul. He had seen it before in his mother when his father died. Nick flung up the console between them, snapped open her seatbelt, dragged the devastated woman against his shoulder and wrapped her into a cocoon. He would handle the harassment issue later but somehow he doubted Phoebe was in any state to even think about the inappropriateness of his actions. Right now all she needed was another human to give her the comfort it was obvious she hadn't had to date. How could she when she now had no parents. He figured it was possible she'd had no-one to share her grief with. It would be a tough call to deal with the trauma of the death and burial of your sole parent when you were all alone.

Two

A strange scent, pleasant and spicy, tickled Phoebe into awareness before a sudden movement under her cheek shocked her awake. She opened sleepy eyes and saw brown leather. It was threaded through... blue denim? Jeans? A belt? A man's belt. Memory surged and she shot upright.

Whack! Her skull connected with something hard.

A muttered string of words in a foreign language hissed into her ear while she rubbed the top of her head and tried to rise. Even though she didn't understand the words she had no doubt they were not meant for public ears. Within a split second her backside slid downwards until it jammed.

'Careful,' was followed by a deep chuckle.

She turned her head towards the voice. Uh oh. It was him. Nick, the poor guy she had slobbered all over like some wimpy two-year-old. Embarrassment hit and dreaded heat rose. Had she fallen asleep with her head on his lap? Oh, far out! She knew the answer and the heat boiled over. He must think she was a total idiot and, good grief, she hadn't met this man before today and her head had been in his crotch. Way to go, Jackson.

Large hands settled under her armpits a second before she was hoisted from between the seats with so much ease it was as though she weighed no more than a feather when she knew she was no lightweight. And the darn man dared to laugh again.

'I can't see what is so funny,' she blurted a second before her backside settled onto the seat.

'You shot up as though you were a cannon ball.'

'Well, wouldn't you if you woke up to see...' Her face burned.

11

He laughed again, a deep throaty sound. 'If I woke up to find my head in your lap, I am sure I wouldn't want to leave it quite so fast. Oh, sorry, I should not have inferred... God, so inappropriate.' He rubbed a hand down his face, which had taken on a pink tinge. 'Phoebe, I want to assure you, I am not the sort of man who would ever take advantage of a woman, any woman, especially one who is grief-stricken. At a guess, I would say you were exhausted in both the physical and emotional sense and needed the sleep. Am I right?'

All Phoebe could manage was a shy nod.

'I did ensure there was a pillow under your head at all times as well as one under your shoulder to give a bit more support.'

Mortified, Phoebe swept both hands to cheeks which had turned into a mighty hot incinerator from the inside. 'How did I, why did you... oh, shoot, why didn't you shove me away?'

'When I enjoyed your presence so much? Not a chance. You needed sleep, I let you sleep.'

'How long have I... you know...?'

'Been asleep with your head on my lap? About twelve hours.'

Her head whipped around to stare at him. 'Twelve hours?'

'Almost. We arrive in Athens in about thirty minutes.'

'Arrive? I slept the whole way? But I never sleep on planes.'

He chuckled again. 'Well you did this time so you must have needed it. I must say you look heaps better than you did when we left.' He brushed a finger under each eye. 'The bruised smudges have gone. Now your cheeks are a rosy pink.'

It was called a red-hot blush of embarrassment she wanted to say but didn't dare. But what could she say without digging herself deeper into the mire of utter embarrassment? A sudden message from an overfull bladder

12

told her she needed to visit the conveniences. Was it any wonder since she had slept so long? A second thought followed in an instant. If he had been forced to sit there the entire time he must need... oh, even more embarrassment. 'If you will excuse me, I need...'

He eased from the seat before she had a chance to finish. 'I'm surprised you lasted this long. From my experience, women tend to...'

'Don't say it,' Phoebe hissed. It was then she remembered the little bag of essentials the airline had handed out when she first boarded the plane. A dig in the pocket and she tugged them out. 'Don't you think I'm embarrassed enough?' She squeezed past him, eyed up and down the aisle to see which end was closest, and sped towards the rear, thankful there was no queue and a little green *vacant* light shone.

Most people still watched monitors; a few were asleep in the most awkward of positions while others had open novels or played games on electronic gadgets. Airline pillows and blankets, along with plastic wrappers, cups and water bottles, were strewn all over the place and the enclosed space smelt kind of musty. It reminded her of a time she stayed over with a friend when she was a teenager. The room had been a write-off and had taken them ages to tidy after the mother had seen the devastation. They giggled the entire time, which didn't speed up the cleaning frenzy but it had been a fun night. Not like right now when she had *slept in a complete stranger's lap!*

In the tiny cubicle, which was a poor excuse for a bathroom, and had a strong urine stench, Phoebe dared a peak in the mirror. Dear, God. Her hair was a tangled mess so she pulled the elastic free, finger-combed the long strands and tied it back again. The little travel pack contained the teeniest toothbrush ever and a tiny tube of paste, which she put to effective use. With her hands she washed her face and patted it dry on paper towels. Face dry, she studied her

13

features. The worry lines had disappeared and there was a tad more colour to her face after the best sleep she had managed in almost three weeks.

Her father's sudden illness, a minor stroke, had seen her frantic rush home from Italy at his doctor's phone call. She spent hours by Dad's bedside with her heart in constant pain while she talked, coaxed and sent out acres of love while he recovered from the initial stroke. The doctors had been optimistic about a full recovery when a second stroke, a massive one this time, claimed his life in an instant. One second they were in fits of laughter over a story about a prank her father had been a party to in his teenage years. A split second later he stuttered, jerked, gasped - and was dead.

Every atom of her insides tightened and twanged at the vivid memory. It had been such an awful shock. In one sense she was glad she had been there when he passed away but it had been so horrific; an experience it was unlikely she would ever forget. Phoebe fought back a new bout of tears. To stave them off, she huffed several quick short breaths and fanned her cheeks with her hands to gain control. No way would she show any more weakness to the stranger she had blubbed over with such abandon. Heavens, how could she ever live down the humiliation but at least she would never see the man again after they landed.

When she returned to her seat, she noticed two blankets were still draped over the window seat. The armrests had been lifted and pushed back while the two pillows lay on the floor. Nick must have arranged all those. But how, without her waking, for she was such a light sleeper? Not game to touch him again, she stood to the front. He rose and stepped aside to make her entry to her seat as easy as possible – which was never easy in the economy seats. There was never enough room, she thought while she wriggled her body and grappled the two seats in front, careful not to grab hair strands of the elderly couple who still emitted soft snores with their heads together. So cute.

Before sitting, she lifted the blankets onto the middle seat and wriggled over to the window. Nick settled back into the aisle seat and sent her a smile. Head down, Phoebe folded the two blankets and shoved them under the seat in front. Entrenched good manners meant she needed to thank this man for such generosity.

'Thank you for... everything.'

'You are more than welcome.'

'I apologise for you not able to roam around during the trip.'

'Oh, I was up and down several times. I even managed thirty-minute intervals down the back where I could stretch my legs and do a little exercise. You were so tired you didn't move each time I lifted your head.'

'I am so embarrassed.'

He reached over and gripped her hand. 'No need. Do you want to talk about your dad? Or is it too painful?'

'It's very painful but I'm fine - I think. It's not like me to lose control the way I did. Please accept my humble apology.' She dared a peek at him. His shirt was rumpled and there was a mark which had to be a dried patch of tears. Oh, wow, how bad was she? Thank goodness she hadn't worn any make-up.

'I don't want to hear another word of apology. You appeared as though you were grief-stricken. At a guess I'd say you haven't allowed yourself the time to grieve. A few tears are understandable and I believe, necessary in cases like this. You loved your father a great deal, didn't you?'

'Yes, he was my best friend and an amazing dad. The best. His illness and death were so sudden.' As Phoebe related a few details she was surprised she didn't have to fight back more tears like the ones she had forced back since the first phone call about his sudden stroke. No way had she let Dad witness her heartache at his illness, but instead she feigned and forced constant smiles. Maybe her untimely release was what she had needed.

15

'Why were you overseas?' Nick asked.

'The intention was to travel Europe for eight months. I design gardens and outdoor areas for businesses and homeowners. I wanted to see famous gardens as well as different types of plants and gardens typical of the countries. I was in Italy when Dad had the first minor stroke.'

'So why Athens?'

'Greece was next on my list. I was in two minds about continuing but with Dad gone, I was at a loss and needed to get away from home. It was too hard to wake up in the morning to the emptiness without Dad. Too many times I got up, went to the kitchen and began to prepare breakfast for two before I remembered Dad wasn't there any longer. I miss him so much. It was impossible to face to task of packing away his clothes and… so I closed up the house and booked this flight. Plus, I need to collect the gear I left in Italy with a friend. I still have three months before I need to return to fulfill bookings.'

'Have you ever been to Greece before?'

'No, but Dad visited several times. He has a close friend who lives in Athens. Someone I need to visit in person when I break the news.'

'I think you will like it, in particular some of the less tourist-popular islands. Try to explore some of the local villages.'

'I had intended to, the inner Cyclades in particular, for those islands were Dad's favourites.' She wondered if she dared ask a few personal questions. Why not since he had asked about her life? 'You have a Greek name and appear to have Greek heritage but you sound so Australian.'

He chuckled. 'Born and raised in Australia. Dad was Australian, born to Greek immigrants but Mum is a Greek woman he met on a holiday while he visited relatives. I have dual citizenship and spend about six months in each country. When Dad died several years ago, Mum returned to Greece to be with her large extended family. My older sister was already married in Australia, where she still lives. I have an older brother who completed a degree in forensic science not long before Mum returned. He went with her, along with my younger sister. Alexos had intended to stay for a few months but found a job as a forensics investigator with the Greek police force. He still lives in Athens and has married a Greek woman. My youngest sister also stayed in Greece and became engaged to a local a few months ago.'

Further conversation ceased when landing procedure announcements began. Phoebe took a few minutes to fill out her disembarkation card, collected all her unused bits and pieces and stowed them in a small backpack, which was still shoved under the seat in front of her. So much for keeping busy during the flight.

***

The waft of vanilla teased Nick's nose when he stood behind Phoebe in the queue of passengers anxious to disembark. Now they were both upright together, she reached just over his shoulder. Perfect height. God, what was he thinking? But why not find out where she was staying? He wanted to since no woman had intrigued him this much for a long time. Phoebe Jackson was like a breath of fresh air compared to his usual dates. He hesitated but the queue began to move and two other passengers squeezed in front of him. The opportunity had gone.

The moment he stepped onto the passenger runway he quickened his stride to catch up. 'Phoebe, wait up.'

She paused mid-stride. 'Yes?'

'Would you like to share a cab into the city?' A taxi ride would give him the opportunity to ask a few more questions.

'Thank you but no. My fiancé will be here to meet me.'

Fiancé? Where did this fiancé come from? He grasped her left hand and tugged her to a halt. 'A finger with no signs it ever held a ring?'

17

A red flush rose up her neck. She turned away but not before he noticed a brief wave of hurt wash over her eyes.

'He didn't… we decided not to waste money on a ring.' Phoebe dragged her hand from his grip.

Somehow her explanation and the brief wave of pain he spied, sounded not quite right. 'We, or he, decided?' A sudden deepening of the pink gave him the answer. 'If you were my woman there would be a ring on your finger so fast, you wouldn't be able to blink. A man should be proud to show the world you belonged to him.'

Her face paled before she flicked her eyes away as though she knew they gave away her inner turmoil. 'You don't have a right to speak about someone else's personal things.'

Way too defensive. He guessed there was a deep-seated hurt, for her actions indicated something was wrong. 'Maybe what you say is true but how I see it, even a token ring to show the man's pride in your partnership wouldn't break the bank if money was the issue.'

The very fact she broke away on the run told him the lack of a ring cut deep or maybe he had hit a sensitive target with his words. The supposed fiancé was a callous moron. The man didn't love her. Well, he had no right to talk since he didn't even believe in the notion of romantic love. He enjoyed women, without a doubt but in all his thirty odd years he had never felt so crazy about a female, he would give up his lifestyle for her. There was no problem about marriage and family, they were fabulous institutions and he would like to marry one day. A family would be wonderful but mutual respect and close friendship were the only strong emotions needed to maintain a good relationship. He had seen too many of his friends who had married for love and the union had lasted no more than a few years with bitter break-ups and fights over custody, money and possessions. All had left painful heart-ache – so what did it say about this so-called love?

When he reached yet another queue at the passport counter, he searched for Phoebe. She stood with her head down, her passport and entry document were in her hand. The small but stuffed backpack she carried was slung over one shoulder. The knowledge he had hurt her, snagged at his conscience. He wanted to apologise but with a Greek passport he was headed for a different exit line.

After he'd managed to pick up his luggage and had cleared customs, Nick hurried towards the taxi rank, glad to leave behind the loud ruckus of a thousand voices, intercom messages and wheels of luggage and over-stacked trolleys. While he wove between the hordes, he twisted his head in all directions in search of a bright red T-shirt but Phoebe must have already gone for there was no sign of her in the vast foyer of the arrivals area. With a shrug of his shoulders, he stepped outside to be greeted with relative silence, a blast of putrid summer air and a heavy waft of exhaust fumes from the snake of idling vehicles. The heat felt damn good after blustery wet Sydney, but it always did every time he stepped foot on Greek soil. But he knew, after a few months he would begin to hanker for Sydney. He had a lot of Greek blood in his veins but Sydney was home.

The queue for taxis was much shorter than the line at the luggage carousel, which had delayed him longer than normal. Another reason he preferred business class for the luggage always came off first. He was next in line when a flash of scarlet caught the corner of his eye. Phoebe. She paced along the glass walls with an anxious frown across her brow. So the loving fiancé hadn't been waiting in eager anticipation. The thought reinforced his notion that all was not happy in the relationship. Although it wasn't any of his business, his conscience wouldn't allow him to leave her stranded. He stepped out of line, waved the next passenger ahead of him and headed in Phoebe's direction.

'Phoebe, do you need a ride?'

She jerked up straight and spun around. Those expressive eyes gave away her inner turmoil but he decided not to comment. He had already been too personal and stirred up too much unpleasantness.

'No, Brad promised he would be here so I will wait.'

'Would you like me to wait with you until he arrives, to make sure you have a ride?'

Her hesitation told the story but a tentative smile crept out. 'No, I will be fine. He emailed me the hotel he's in so I know where to go.'

'Why don't you phone him?'

'No sim card yet and a flat battery.'

'Give me his number.' Number given, Nick dialled, waited but the phone rang out. 'He didn't pick up.'

'It's possible he's caught in traffic but he often forgets to take his mobile with him when he goes out, which drove me nuts because he often asked to use mine. Oops, sorry, too much information.'

'I can wait if you want.'

'No, I'm fine. He'll get here.'

'If you are sure?' He paused, thought and decided it would be a good idea to give her a contact number in case she got stuck. He drew out his wallet, searched through one of the pockets and found a business card for his Greek office. It was a bit tattered but gave all the relevant details. 'Here, contact me if you need even the slightest help or advice. This is the address of my office, which is right in the centre of the city.'

Phoebe hesitated, swung her glance between him and the card three times before she took the card and slid it into the pocket of her jeans. 'Thank you. I'm sorry I…'

He cut in. 'Another apology, Phoebe? Please, it is not necessary for you made a long journey far more pleasurable than normal. To have a woman sleep in my lap more than compensated for not being able to get business class seats.' His grin was cheeky. 'I must try it more often.'

A shy smile crept from the corners of her mouth.

'And please contact me if you need anything.'

'Thank you. Would you be offended if... um... if I gave you a thank you hug?'

Her request surprised him but he wasn't about to forego the sensation of this woman in his arms one final time. 'Definitely not.' He opened his arms and stepped forwards, ensuring the hug was long. This woman had touched something deep inside and he was more than sorry they had to part company but he wasn't about to poach another man's woman. It wasn't the way he operated. Had she been unspoken for he would have wangled her contact details. He couldn't resist the kiss he dropped onto her head seconds before she drew away.

Within minutes he was in a taxi on his way to the city to sort out yet another crisis, a hesitant wave from Phoebe his last glimpse of the intriguing woman.

Three

Phoebe glared at her watch for the umpteenth time. Two hours. So far, she he had waited two interminable hours. A constant stream of people from many different nations had passed but not one of them had the distinctive features of Brad Evans. There had been a few blond-headed men: one, a squat man with a paunch, another tall and lanky, a couple way too old and three too young. A desperate call over the public address system resulted in an embarrassing wait at the enquiries counter. Eyes appraised her, followed by whispered words behind less than discreet hands. The call had yielded no Brad.

Frantic, worried and with a tad amount of anger, she figured she needed to phone him. She searched the pocket of her backpack and tugged out her mobile. It wasn't until she pressed the on button she remembered the flat battery and how she had removed the Australian sim-card before she left for the airport. It had taken her the first week of her travels to figure the enormous cost when you used a mobile phone overseas with an Australian sim-card. A local sim-card was needed but would be useless with no battery power.

After another half-hour with no sign of Brad, a niggle of doubt about his commitment to her began to claw at her innards, not because Nick Kalameides had commented on her lack of a ring but also because of the thoughts she had mulled over while at home. No way did she dare voice her disappointment about Brad's excuses for not giving her a ring when Nick mentioned it but it had reinforced her thoughts when Brad had proposed two days before she flew home to Australia. Even a ring carved with love from wood or one of woven hair would have been acceptable. It wasn't as though Brad was poor. He'd always had sufficient money for a meal and drinks at the many taverns and cafes they had frequented over the months of their journey - although they always split the bill and paid their own way. Hmm, come to think of it, he had never paid for a single one of her meals when she had often shouted him a meal. Another niggle of unease swept through her at the thought. But he wore an expensive watch and brand-label clothes so there must be money somewhere. They had never spoken about money apart from the deal they'd made before the onset of their journey. Now, Phoebe was glad she insisted they always pay their own portion of bills. But maybe she should have brought the topic up more often during the four months they'd travelled together. Regret surged for not having delved a little deeper before she accepted the proposal. Why did she even consider his proposal? But it had been so sudden when her brain was in over-drive with worry, she hadn't had the nous to think. Sure she had travelled with him for a few months and had known him for the month before they left but it didn't mean she knew him well enough to marry the man.

When another glance around revealed no sign of Brad, she leant against the glass panel and thought more about the time they met. At the opening of one of the gardens she had helped design, back home in Australia, Brad had snagged her immediate interest but romance wasn't a consideration since her eight-month study holiday was already planned and booked. She had been more than surprised when Brad rang her the day after the event and asked her to dinner. The trouble he had gone to, to track her down meant he was more than interested so she had agreed and enjoyed the night a great deal. Brad had appeared to be knowledgeable, was a great conversationalist and a lot of fun. They hit it off straight away and it wasn't long before she had been enamoured with him but she still had reservations about the relationship since she was about to leave the country for so many months. When Brad suggested he join her, she had been more than surprised, and wary, but after a few long discussions, she agreed with conditions. Each was to pay their own costs and if one decided they no longer wanted to travel together, they would part company and go their own way. Their travels had gone well with a few downs and a lot of ups which was normal when you explored new places but his sudden proposal had rocked her for they had never slept together despite Brad's obvious hints it was what he wanted. But Phoebe wasn't one to fall into a man's bed just for the sake of physical release. Been there, done that and it was not one of her better moments. After such a bad experience she decided the physical union of a man and woman needed to signify a deep emotional commitment. With Brad, she had never felt such a level of commitment from him – until he proposed, which had come out of the blue.

While at home with her father, those niggles had turned into strong jabs of unease. But they spoke on the phone yesterday before Phoebe left for the airport. He said how much he had missed her, how eager he was to see her again, although, come to think of it, he never mentioned the word love. So where was he?

Visions of smashed cars and mangled bodies edged into her thought bank. Maybe he was caught in a traffic jam caused by an accident – it wouldn't be the first time such a thing had happened while they'd been together. They were stuck in a real doozy of a snarl for several hours after a motorway crash in Belgium. Maybe he was in some hospital bed, unable to contact her. Her heart began to palpitate.

She yanked her arms out of the backpack and scrabbled around for her purse to count out how many euros she had. Because she wouldn't need much cash, she hadn't bothered to bring much with her. All of her Australian currency was at home. All she had with her were the euros she had in her purse before her emergency flight home. Thirty-seven euros. Maybe it was enough for a cab. She had a Cashcard filled with plenty of money but needed a compatible ATM to be able to withdraw cash. She knew most people nowadays used their credit cards for every purchase but she'd already learned how easy it was to overspend if you didn't keep track of every cent and the banks charge exorbitant exchange rate fees so she'd put her holiday money into a special Cashcard account. Every time she needed cash she took out enough for a week for with a restricted daily budget, she preferred to use cash. So much a day, with a little left over made it much easier to keep track.

Phoebe strode to the taxi rank and waited in line until it was her turn. She spouted the hotel name Brad had given her and asked how much but was met with blank eyes and a frown. Terrific. She had to get a driver who didn't speak English. With one hand held out, she said, 'Athens. How much?' and shrugged her shoulders before spreading out her arms with palms up in the universal gesture of a question.

'Fifty euros,' came back in a heavy accent followed by the stench of strong tobacco. Phoebe reeled back. No way would she go with this driver, she thought so stepped aside to let the next passengers take the cab. She could go inside and search for an ATM but public transport would be much cheaper so to avoid any more delays she searched for the signs that indicated bus or rail transport, which were always cheaper but often longer. It was another hour before she was seated in a bus, jam-packed with bodies and suitcases of all descriptions, headed towards the city.

While the bus sped along the freeway, she studied the scenery as it flashed past, surprised to see Australian eucalyptus trees growing in mass profusion on the banks of what appeared to be a newish modern highway. There were no ruts in the bitumen and the concrete kerb held no cracks or weathering. A vision of the many olive groves back home came to the fore – so why not import eucalyptus trees when

Greece had the ideal climate for them. It made a whole lot of sense.

The reflection of white from the hundreds of houses was so bright in the hot summer sun, the glimmer hurt her eyes. In the background, vociferous dialogue she didn't understand, indicated the Greek people were far more outgoing than back home, where passengers gave the impression it was mandatory to remain mute whilst on public transport. Well, except for those rude enough to have mobile phone conversations loud enough for everyone in the enclosed space to overhear.

After another hour, Phoebe stood on the pathway at what appeared to be a major bus station. Traffic of both the vehicular and human kind was chaotic. She had no idea where to go next so sought out an information booth. There was no booth to be seen but there was a ticket seller who stood next to the open door of a bus. She gave the name of the hotel Brad had sent her.

'Not this bus.' At least this woman spoke English.

'I can walk but can you tell me where it is?' A hand waved, twisted, flapped and twisted a few more times at the same time a long list of turn this way, two blocks, turn left, turn right, three blocks were garbled out at a blistering pace. A few, *too far*, *long way* and other scary instructions were added for good measure. It would be long walk but Phoebe wasn't afraid of the distance. She had almost walked through Europe before she'd flown home. All she needed were precise instructions.

From the pocket of her pack she pulled out a pen and small notepad she always kept handy to jot down plant names and sketch garden layouts. 'Would you be kind enough to draw me a map?'

Ten minutes later when she had a rough sketch, names of roads and landmarks to guide her, Phoebe set off. It didn't take long before perspiration dripped from all sorts of body parts and her shirt, along with underwear, stuck to her skin. A desperate thirst reminded her she'd had no food or drink since Singapore. She turned into a small food market and ambled the aisles while deciding the cheapest way to quench both thirst and hunger. The smell of vine ripened tomatoes enticed gastric juices to flow as did the array of fresh cheeses but she opted for a banana, an apple and a litre of bottled water. They were cheap, healthy options, could be consumed while she walked and the rubbish easy to dispose of.

Exhaustion, plus a desperate need for a bathroom, had set in by the time she spotted the large silver letters of the hotel she needed. Phoebe pushed open the glass doors, stepped inside and paused on a sucked in breath of surprise. The cool air was most welcome but this place held too many upmarket features for her budget. She had saved a certain amount for her adventure after working out an average cost per night for basic accommodation, a food allowance for each day and a little bit extra for the occasional luxury, emergency or must have purchase. This place, with its faceted glass, or were they crystal chandeliers, shiny marble floors and columns, intimate groups of plush lounge seats and a classy eatery graced by well-heeled patrons was way beyond her budget. There was no need to ask the room-rate to know she would never have booked into this hotel. She could afford it for one night but it would mean she'd have to scrimp for the next week if she wanted her travel budget to last another three months.

This can't be the place, she thought on a slow three hundred and sixty degree spin around to study the vast room. When she noticed a small sign on the far wall, she headed in its direction. At least she could use the facilities and make her body comfortable before she made enquiries. No-one would know she wasn't a resident. If anyone questioned her all she needed to do was tell them she hadn't booked in yet. Bladder empty, she washed her hands and face and patted them dry on fancy cloth towels. She withdrew the printout of Brad's email to check the details. Right hotel and correct street name meant it was the right place, so why had her stomach clenched into a tight ball of apprehension?

One way to find out for sure, she thought with a new determination. Straight back, head, high, she vacated the exquisite facilities, another reason she knew this hotel was priced beyond her budget. Marble benches and real soft cloth handtowels didn't equate with budget accommodation.

Apprehension gripped at every step towards the shiny wood reception counter. As she neared, she slowed, for tense nerves tightened her stomach muscles into large knots. The three male receptionists were dressed in smart charcoal grey suits and wore identical blue ties. The two patrons at the counter were dressed in impeccable outfits while she had on blue jeans and a T-shirt which had definite deep crumples and dark wet patches of perspiration. It was possible it stunk of body odour as well.

She huffed up at a stray strand of hair, tucked it behind her ear before continuing a walk which felt like she was about to head for the gallows. With the two patrons still either booking in or out, she paused to wait about a metre behind them.

'Can I help you?' a middle-aged man asked. His face wore a deep frown, the opposite to the friendliness of his invitation.

'I'm not sure.' Phoebe stepped right up to the counter. 'I am supposed to meet my fiancé. He said this was the hotel he is booked into.'

'His name?'

'Evans. Bradley Evans.' When the man screwed his lips in an unpleasant scowl, a shimmy of apprehension snaked across Phoebe's shoulders. The man hit a few keys on a keyboard, glanced at her, turned away and pulled a couple of folded papers from a pigeonhole.

'And your name?' The tone was curt and cold. Her apprehension shot to panic stations. Why this coldness? What had Brad done?

'Phoebe Jackson.'

'Miss Jackson, these are for you.' He held out two separate folded papers.

Somehow Phoebe knew she would not like what was written on these pieces of paper but she took them. Her heart was in panic mode with thumps bigger than a big bass drum when she opened out the first. It was a bill. Her eyes boggled for the amount was enormous.

'What is this?'

'Mr Evans departed this morning. He informed us you were responsible for his accommodation costs.'

'Excuse me?' With no control over her body, Phoebe's voice managed to climb several octaves and several decibels on the two words. Further words defied her. She paused, gulped, tried to speak but had to gulp again since her brain seesawed as though on a frantic, death-defying roller-coaster ride. 'Do you expect me to pay for someone else's accommodation when I wasn't even here?'

'You said you were his fiancé.' It might have been uttered as a question but it felt more like a statement of fact. Judgement had been passed. She was guilty as charged.

'I must have amnesia because I'm certain I didn't ever agree to such a... such a ridiculous thing. I wasn't even in the country until a few hours ago. I did not stay here, was not a party to this agreement and I will not pay this ludicrous amount of money.'

'You will have to.'

'Excuse me?'

'Someone must pay and our instructions are that you were responsible for all payments.'

She leant over the desk. 'Who informed you I would pay?'

'Mr Evans.'

'Did he now? And is it normal practice for you to accept the word of a patron that a third party will pay for a person's costs without confirmation of the details? Especially when the third party isn't here to agree to such nonsense? Did you bother to check with me to see if this was in fact true?'

'Mr Evans showed us a letter, which you signed.'

'What?' The word exploded from her mouth.

'Hush, you cannot disturb the guests.'

'I will not hush,' she yelled even louder. 'Show me this so-called letter.'

'You already have it,' the man said in an exaggerated whisper with one finger pointed to the sheets in her hand.

More than angry, Phoebe's hands shook when she peeled the top paper away from the second and read the scrawled message. It was signed with her name but the handwriting wasn't anything like hers. And it wasn't Brad's writing either, although it was possible he could have tried to disguise his scrawl. She peered closer. Was there an F starting her first name? *Feeby?* A choked laugh caught in her throat. Whoever wrote this didn't have a clue how to spell Phoebe so it wasn't written by Brad.

Her body had managed to shoot out so much adrenalin she wondered if she might have a heart attack. Desperate to calm, she drew in a couple of long breaths, paused until her nerves settled enough she could face this little problem without losing her cool. On a final huffed out breath, she placed the sheets on the counter. A third folded page fell to the floor. She scooped it up and opened it out.

I can't marry you. I met someone better.

Someone better? Her knees buckled and she began to slide downwards. She managed to grab a hold of the counter to prevent an ignominious fall.

'Are you all right?' The voice from behind was female. A hand grasped her upper arm.

No I am not all right, Phoebe wanted to say but couldn't find the strength to open her mouth. Her head dropped to arms which still managed to grip the countertop and keep her upright. A wave of moisture washed over her eyes but she fought it back. The scumbag wasn't worth tears. All she could see in her mind were those words – *someone better*. He could have said – *someone else*. But no, he had to rub acid into a fresh gouge and say – *someone better*. The words cut deep, more so since the word sorry was nowhere on any of the papers.

'Miss, are you all right?' This time it was the man who had imparted this wonderful news.

Phoebe eyed him and glared. 'What do you think? I fly into this country to be greeted by an obscene bill I didn't incur and which you demand I must pay. I have been handed a callous note to say I have been jilted and you want to know if I am all right?' An indelicate snort escaped. 'No I am not all right and I will not pay a bill incurred by someone else,' she yelled.

'But you have to,' the man had the gall to say.

'No I don't!' Phoebe yelled back and sent him and even fiercer glare. 'I never stayed in your stupid hotel and I...' she stabbed at the so-called letter of permission, 'did not write this letter.'

'You will pay if you want your backpack.' The man dared to snigger.

It was the first time Phoebe had even thought about all her clothes and bedding in a large backpack she had left with Brad so she didn't have to cart them all home. The sole reason she had come back to meet with Brad was to regain her possessions. It had taken a lot of thought and mental kicks up the backside, while with her father. to figure out her agreement to marry Brad was not only the wrong thing to do but one of the stupidest things she had ever done in her life.

'Are you daring to blackmail me?'

For a split second he appeared to be chastened or was it guilt which swept across his face before he straightened and schooled his features into a determined stone mask. 'What I am saying is, unless this bill is paid by you, we will keep your backpack until you do.'

'So even if someone else,' she turned around in search of anyone else, and was taken aback to discover a large semi-circle of people, all with luggage, and all absorbed by her predicament. She waved her hand to indicate the lot of them and turned back to her tormenter. 'If any one of these people paid this ridiculous bill, you would still refuse to give me my backpack.'

The man huffed. 'That is not what I meant.'

'But it is what you said.' She searched the ceiling for inspiration and as a way to snatch a few moments to gather together frustrated wits. 'I did not write this note – see here,' she pointed to the signature, 'whoever wrote it can't even spell my name. This is not my handwriting and I did not stay here so was not the person who incurred these costs so please explain to me why I should pay another customer's bill?'

'You are this man's fiancé.'

She snorted. 'Not anymore.' She spread out the third sheet of paper. After the man had passed a cursory glance at it, she leaned forwards. 'So, since I am not the person responsible for this bill, nor am I his fiancé, can I please have my backpack?'

'No!'

P hoebe had never been one to give up a fight when she knew she was right but three muscle-bound security officers, with less than discreet bulges which she guessed were either guns or tasers, held unbeatable odds against her. So here she was on the pavement in front of her worst nightmare after being ousted from the premises. What the devil was she supposed to do now? With anger and frustration on the verge of explosion point, she glared both ways up and down the hilly street while her mind scrabbled for some sort of coherent plan. She needed her phone but didn't have enough cash to buy a sim card. Therefore she needed cash, which required a bank. She searched the street for such an institution. Of course, there were none.

Traffic was more congested than it had been when she'd arrived, to the extent it was at a standstill ninety-five percent of the time and crawled a few metres the other five percent. She turned her wrist over to see the time. Peak hour, which meant nightfall was imminent and she was hungry, dirty and thirsty with nowhere to bed down for the night, nor any clothes other than a spare pair of knickers, a thin jacket and one clean T-shirt stuffed into the small bag she had brought with her. Fat lot of good they will be unless she was game enough to change her underwear in public. Toiletries consisted of an airline emergency pack of comb, toothbrush and a weeny tube of toothpaste, which had already been used on the plane. Thank goodness she hadn't tossed it in the bin. Since she needed money for a hotel room, and the stupid sim-card, she decided a Cashcard friendly bank was to be her first port of call. If she could get into one for many overseas banks had their cash machines in a locked room able to be opened only by an accountholder who had the code to get in.

Decision made, she headed uphill, back the way she had come earlier. With her eyes searching she scanned both sides of the road for a bank. Even though it would be shut, she would be able to withdraw funds from an ATM – she hoped for in her brief travels she had discovered not all foreign banks accepted these new-fangled Cashcards at the ATM's. Often she had to go inside to a teller and she didn't like to recall the number of banks where you had to go through a security check first. Then there were the numerous banks where you had to use a numbered code to even get into a special room where the ATM's were located.

At the next intersection she spotted a bank on the diagonal corner across the road. While she waited for the lights to change she slid a hand in the pocket of her jeans and felt a foreign object she didn't remember putting there. When she withdrew it, she remembered Nick Kalameides and the card he had given her. If all else failed she could contact him. But, she recalled, her mobile had no damn card and a stupid flat battery. Just dandy. It seemed the world was against her today. Well, never mind, once she had cash she could remedy every darn negative and turn them into positives. A hotel room has electricity, a bed and a shower. It might be a problem to purchase a sim card after hours but there was always tomorrow. Ah, most hotel rooms had a phone, albeit an expensive way to make a call.

Before she could think of another solution, the lights changed so she scooted across on the diagonal and managed to incur the wrath of a motorist who indicated he wanted to turn right. Too late, she remembered she was not in Sydney where the walk signal indicated for everyone to walk – not just those moving with the flow of traffic. She shot her hand up in the air to acknowledge her apology and increased her stride to the bank, confident for the first time since she had been caught in the wrong seat on the plane. All she needed were a couple of hundred euros and she would be able to find a hotel for the night; and it would not, under any circumstances, no way, no, no, no, be the one she had just been marched out of in utter humiliation.

It took more than a few seconds to search for the card she hadn't used for almost four weeks. Well, it was her second card because she had misplaced the original one in her rush to get home. It had got caught up in her clothes when she packed them in her backpack is such a frenzy and she hadn't had time to unpack and search for it.

She poked the plastic card into the slot and followed the instructions when each blinked on the screen. The luggage mess could be sorted out in the morning. Maybe a visit to a police station might be the answer – at least she would be able to explain the situation and learn her rights in this country. There was always the Australian embassy – if there was one in Athens. Must be one in Athens since it is the capital city.

Lights flashed; words came up – *Insufficient funds*. Huh? She blinked to clear her eyes, certain there was dust in them, which made them all blurry. But despite a swipe down her face with one hand and a vicious glare at the machine, it still said the same thing.

'No way!' she yelled. 'This can't be right.'

To make sure, she cancelled the transaction and began to press buttons again, much slower this time to ensure there was no mistake.

Insufficient Funds blinked right back at her.

'Well, shoot,' she mumbled and tried for a third time but for a lesser amount. When it came up with the same words she withdrew the card and glared at the machine. It cannot be right, no way – she had a tad over ten thousand euros still in the account. Her earlier frustration, which she had managed to shove away, stormed to the forefront once again. She didn't dare have another go for often more than three attempts saw your card get eaten by the machine. To get it back would be a nightmare, as if she wasn't already slap-bang in the middle of a scary nightmare.

Now what am I supposed to do, she thought. Furious, she shoved the card back into her money purse and yanked the zipper closed. She did a quick calculation of her cash, subtracted the cost of her earlier snack and the bus fare. Enough for a meal but not a hotel room unless she came across a backpackers building. And of course, her travel guide was in her backpack locked away in a swanky hotel, held as ransom by a brute and three, armed security guards.

Confused, frustrated and more than angry, Phoebe stalked towards the main city centre along the same route she had taken to reach the hotel. Despite the hour, it was still hot with a dusty, dry aroma in the air, enhanced by copious exhaust fumes and unpleasant body odour, most of which was her own. There were few trees or shrubs along the streets, which went a long way to enhance the intensity of the heat. So different from Sydney where greenery abounded but at least the humidity was low, unlike Sydney in summer.

When she passed the store where she had purchased her snack, she paused, the aroma of spices and cooked meat snagging her attention. Her stomach rumbled in complaint. She was hungry and to go without a decent meal for the sake of a few scant euros was not sensible so she stepped into the small eatery next door to the store. Greek food at home was one of her favourites but Sydney restaurants never smelt this good.

A pudding of a woman in a plain brown dress covered in a white starched apron, smiled as she approached. '*Kalispera,*' the woman said with an even wider smile. She pulled out a chair at the nearest vacant table.

'I don't speak Greek,' Phoebe replied, with a smile.

'Ah, English, welcome.' A menu was taken from the table and held in front of Phoebe's eyes.

'No, I am from Australia.'

The woman's smile widened. 'Then you must enjoy the best we have. This, I have just made so it is fresh and tastes…' she kissed the tips of her fingers and flung them in the air. The pleasure that radiated from the woman's face showed she took pride in her cooking.

Phoebe studied at the indicated words written in Greek but had *meatballs with tomato sauce* handwritten underneath. At least she would know what was on the plate and it was the kind of food needed to fill an empty stomach. She peeked at the price and was surprised. Six euros sounded too cheap but made the selection even more appealing.

'Thank you, I would love to try the meatballs,' she said and sank onto the proffered seat but had to lean forward again to remove her backpack. The woman bustled away but was back within a minute with a carafe of icy water and a glass. The glass was filled, the items on top straightened and cutlery wrapped in a paper serviette set against the placemat which caressed the plastic tablecloth adorned with a regular pattern of bunches of grapes and wine carafes. There was no doubt this woman loved her job. Phoebe had the impression this was a family run eatery and this woman had to be Mamma. Even if she wasn't, it felt right so Mamma it would be in her mind.

The plate set in front of her a few minutes later, was piled high with a rich orange tomato sauce poured over a generous portion of tablespoon-sized meatballs and a swirl of spaghetti. A decent slab of garlic bread was set in a cane basket alongside a small dish of pungent fresh grated Parmesan. Her mouth watered when she drew in the rich aromas. Basil was strong, as was the garlic. She tucked in and savoured each delicious mouthful.

Not game to think about what she could do after the meal, Phoebe lingered, enjoyed the noisy chatter and friendly camaraderie of the patrons and staff. Bouts of loud jesting followed by hearty laughter brightened a day she would never wish on her worst enemy, even though she couldn't think of any enemy she had – well maybe Brad at this point in time. Shoot but she had been suckered in. She drank down the last of her water, searched the room and followed the discreet sign so she could make use of the bathroom facilities. On the way out she paid the small bill and stepped into the dusk. Her stomach felt bloated after eating so much but since she wasn't sure when her next meal would be, she didn't dare leave a skerrick of food on the plate.

Lingering warmth wrapped around her arms and caressed her skin as she stood on the edge of the footpath and wondered what the heck to do. After a quick search of the area she noticed across the road a large group of people were gathered, all with their backs to her. The silence intrigued her so she waited for a break in the traffic before racing full pelt across the four-lane road. Unable to see what held the group's attention, she wove her way through the crowd until she was closer. It was some sort of memorial with four men dressed in uniforms she knew to be old traditional, undertaking some kind of ritual of precise steps. High straight-legged kicks, heavy stamps of wood-soled clogs with curved toes, stiff-arm movements and gun manoeuvres reminded her of the changing of the guards in London. But this was far more intriguing. She recalled an article she'd read about the dirt-coloured costume of pleated skirt and tunic with a fancy red, round hat. Black pompoms dangled down the calves from garters around the lower legs which were covered in thick white leggings all the way to the top, or at least, as far as she could see. Traditional soldier outfit if her memory served her well. She watched until two soldiers were left, one each side of the stone monument and another two marched away accompanied by a soldier in a regular modern uniform. Fascinating and now most of the crowd had moved away, she could get a better view and figured this was some sort of important war memorial.

When an ancient couple vacated a nearby wooden bench, Phoebe took their place and settled down to watch and contemplate her predicament.

The entire day replayed through her mind in vivid detail over and over. What surprised her the most was her reaction to Brad's defection. Sure, she was beyond angry at how callous, cruel, and nasty he had been. There were a few more adjectives she could think of to describe him, none of them pleasant and none ladylike. His scrawled message was one of a nasty coward, much like someone getting dumped via a SMS message like one of her friends had. It was her inner reaction which required deep reflection. Pain simmered in the sense he was such a jerk but instead of a painful ache in her heart the way it did about the loss of her father, emotion-wise it was more a deep sensation of pure relief which told her the hesitancy about sleeping with him had been right. Gut instinct had told her all along - this was not the man for her. Her fondness had been pure infatuation brought on by the mere fact a man had wanted her for who she was and the way she was. It had never been about love; she was now convinced. So maybe a little snippet of positivity had come out of the day. She laughed at the thought.

Happy with the decision, Phoebe became more aware of her surroundings. She didn't have a clue how long she had wallowed in self-pity but another change of the guards had taken place. Now she had to figure out what to do about finding a place to sleep. With little money it would have to be outdoors, which she didn't relish but it wouldn't be the first time. She had slept in the open many times back home but it had always been out in the country, with no-one else around except for her father who enjoyed sleeping under the stars as much as she did. She had also slept on the beach in Italy but Brad had been there along with a couple of other backpackers.

Now she was in the middle of a densely populated city with oodles of people around and if it were like any other city in the world some of those people would be unsavoury. She glanced around. What safer place to bunk down than under the guard of soldiers? She eased upright, stretched out kinks and numbness while she assessed the area. She strode across a patch of grass to the left of the memorial and glanced around in search of some kind of shelter. The neat mown grassed area sloped downwards. Hmm, it would hide her from the view of passing pedestrians. It was ideal. In the shadow of a large tree, she dropped to the ground, pulled her jacket from the backpack, wriggled her arms into the sleeves and zipped it up almost to the top. With the backpack as a pillow, she settled down for a night under the stars in Athens.

While lying there, she was aware of the presence of people nearby. Some stopped for a while, while others passed on by. Soft murmurs reached her ears, as did the scrapes, scuffles and clicks of footwear on the pavement about ten metres behind her. After twelve hours of solid sleep on the plane, Phoebe lay wide-awake staring at the sky. The sun had made its final dive below the horizon and now there was the vast area of dark space above her with a scattering of stars determined to shine despite the glow of city lights. It was different from back home. There was no Southern Cross to indicate the way direct south and the constellations winking back at her were not so familiar.

Sleep eluded her since constant recall of the events of the last few weeks wouldn't give her mind a moment's peace. A picture of her father had settled in the forefront of her mind when she sensed the pressure of eyes on her. She raised her head and searched the area. A soldier dressed in the regular uniform stood a couple of metres to her side.

'*Ti kanis?*' he asked.

More than a little hesitant, Phoebe sat upright. 'I don't speak your language.'

When he took a step towards her, his shadow emitted a threatening sensation. 'What are you doing?' he asked.

She thought it was pretty obvious but to tell the truth might not be such a good idea. What if this man shuffled her away? Where else could she go? 'Studying the stars,' she said and swung her legs around before folding them in a loose cross. At least it was the truth; even though her study of the night sky was because she wasn't in the least bit tired.

He took another step closer. 'Why?'

To hide the sensation of fear which managed to engulf her in an instant, she smiled up at him. He was tall, very tall and there was something familiar about him. When he squatted on his haunches, the closeness threatened her even more. Her muscles tightened in readiness for flight.

'Because the stars are different from back home. Weren't you one of the soldiers in the fancy get-up who stood guard over there?' She waved her hand in the vague direction behind her towards the memorial.

'Yes, my time is up and I can return home. Where is your home?'

'Sydney, Australia.'

'So you are a visitor to my country.' His English was excellent with an accent less pronounced than those in the little eatery across the road.

'Yes.' Keep it simple, her brain whispered, to avoid the need for involved explanations.

'It appears you have settled in for the night.' He indicated with a hand where she had been stretched out.

Guilt hit but no way would she tell the truth. 'How else can one study the star formations if they aren't prostrate?' Shoot, but was she glad it was dark and her face was shadowed for it was on fire. Telling porky pies didn't sit well with her, especially since she could never get away with it when her face flamed neon red with such ease.

'So, where are you staying?' He reached out and grasped her chin. She knew it was to prevent her turning away but

43

the sensation of danger grew ominous. Why did he even dare touch her, but then again she wasn't in Australia.

She gave the name of the nightmare hotel without a nervous blink while staring back into his eyes and prayed he couldn't read her guilt. It was the one hotel she knew the name of so at least she didn't lie about the name. Well maybe a teeny, tiny white lie.

'You shouldn't walk alone.' Thank goodness he released his grip and moved back a fraction.

'Why, isn't your city safe?'

'As safe as any big city,' he smiled, 'and as unsafe as any big city,' he added. 'I wouldn't allow my woman to wander alone after dark.'

What is it with these Greek men? Rings and walking alone and why were they all so darn tall and good looking? A wistful need centred in her chest. Why couldn't the man she had agreed to marry have been this concerned about her welfare?

'I will catch a taxi. Thank you for your concern.' When the man stood, a wave of relief skated through her body. But he lingered as though not certain whether or not to leave her there, which managed to dissipate the relief in an instant. Was he suspicious of her motives?

To get rid of him, she rose, leant over to collect her pack to prove she had intended to leave. 'I was about to go in any case.' To convince the man, she wove her arms through the straps, spun around and headed towards the road. Her heart skittered seconds before adrenalin spurted through her veins when she sensed his presence next to her. What did he want with her? How could she get rid of him? 'I might have a hot drink before I leave,' she said with her hand pointed towards the eatery where she had eaten earlier. She would be safe amongst other people.

Her elbow was grasped, which sent her body into panic mode with nerve ends on alert and her stomach managing to somersault. 'I will join you.'

44

Before she had a chance to open her mouth to remonstrate, she was ushered across the road and into the eatery. When her arm wasn't released until she was seated, the frisson of unease which had sent blood thrumming through her veins, turned into outright fear. This hunk of a man might be a soldier but it didn't mean he could be trusted to not have unsavoury intentions and at this point in time her level of trust for the opposite sex was at an all-time low, well maybe except for Nick Kalameides who had been kindness personified.

The arrival of a waiter broke her reverie. 'Coffee?' asked her companion.

'No, coffee will keep me awake. Black tea, please.' While the order was given, Phoebe began to muse about how best to escape her guard.

He sat back and eyed her. 'Why are you in Athens?'

'To meet a friend.'

'Male or female?'

'None of your business.' A rat gnawed at her stomach. Too personal – too invasive. To sleep by the memorial was now out of the question and if he wanted to walk her to the darn hotel – well what then? What if he insisted on taking her right inside? What if she was bundled into a car and driven to some bleak spot. And he was so huge – far bigger than she could handle. There was no doubt he was a fit man. Had to be since he was a soldier.

She shoved more than one option through her mind but discarded them all. Better to act nonchalant for a while. When the drinks arrived she took a sip, gasped and spat the still boiling liquid back into the cup. The roof of her mouth and tip of her tongue tingled from the scald.

'Excuse me, please, I need cold water on my tongue.' S stood, grabbed her backpack and wove her way amongst the tables to the rest room.

After she managed to drown her tongue under a constant stream of cold water until the sting eased, she made use of the facilities but hesitated before returning to the restaurant area. What if the soldier meant her harm? Maybe she could escape now. Terrified he might wait for her, she creaked the door open a few centimetres, poked her head into the narrow passage stacked with cartons of what had to be bottles of wine, beer and soft drinks, and searched both ways. A grin broke out when she spied a door which appeared to lead to the rear of the premises. She searched the area again to ensure nobody watched and sped towards the door, turned the handle and grinned again when the door opened. She stepped outside and jolted. Three men sat sprawled on wooden chairs around a small square table graced with a glass carafe of red wine and three half-full glasses. By the white aprons tied around their waists it was obvious these were workers on a well-earned break.

When all eyes turned to her, her tell-tale heat rose but she thanked the heavens for the bare low-voltage light several metres away, which would hide her blush. 'Err, can I get out this way?'

The men stared for a moment as though they had a desperate need to know why she was at the back door. She didn't blame them. Maybe they thought she was about to skip out on the bill. 'A man... in there,' she wavered her hand in the direction of the inside. 'He won't leave me alone and scares me. I need to get away.'

One man nodded as he rose. 'This way.' His English was faultless with no more than a hint of accent.

Phoebe paused for a moment when an idea struck. She stepped under the single light and groped in her pocket for Nick Kalameides' card. 'Can you give me directions to this place?'

The man took the two steps needed to reach her, read the card but shook his head. 'This place is not far but will be closed.' He stabbed at the address. 'It is a business.'

'I know, but I need to find it early tomorrow.' She groped around for a reason, any reason. 'I start work there

46

tomorrow.' Guilt rose for all the untruths she had spouted. It wasn't a habit of hers to tell lies. Her father had drummed into her at an early age the importance of honesty, even when to admit guilt meant she would have to suffer the consequences. Somehow she figured Dad would forgive her for all of tonight's transgressions if it meant her lies kept her safe. Besides, she'd admitted to her dishonesty hadn't she? Surely an admission counted as owning up. She was more than relieved when the man began to sketch a plan and directions on a paper serviette. Finished, he studied it with half shut eyes. Maybe he wanted her to pay her bill. After a long hesitation he nodded and handed the serviette to her.

'Go down this lane, turn left. It will take you out in the next road. This,' he pointed to a cross on the serviette, 'starts from there. It is not far – ten minutes to walk.'

'Thank you.' Phoebe gave the man a quick hug, then embarrassed by her stupid impulsive gesture, strode away.' Why was she such an impulsive person? Did she have no common sense?

'*Kalinichta*,' the man called after her.

The words sounded as though they meant good night. She turned and repeated, '*Kalinichta*,' as best she could before increasing her speed.

Five

'Yeoww.' Startled awake, Phoebe shot upright with a loud groan at an excruciating pain in her side seconds before another kick pounded into her ribs, accompanied by a string of words she couldn't understand.

'What the…' was all she got out before another hefty kick stabbed into her lower leg.

'Ouch,' she yelled and quickly rolled over onto her knees and swung her arms up to defend her body from further attack. 'What are you doing?' she called.

'Get out,' a heavily accented female voice screamed back at her.

Finally able to get her eyes focused, Phoebe stared up at a face wearing a serious scowl. Venom shot from almost black eyes. The young woman had a large handbag held over her shoulder ready to beat Phoebe to a pulp. Her scrambled mind, still fuzzy with sleep, began to sort itself out and come to grips with reality. It was morning and by the heat of the already high sun, much later than she had intended to sleep. But then again, sleep had been scant since she had been too scared to close her eyes for way too long into the night.

'Get out of here.'

The bag began a rapid descent towards Phoebe's head. To ward it off, she grabbed at the side and yanked. Her aggressor lost her balance and stumbled towards her. There was a brief tug of war before Phoebe released her grip so sudden the woman staggered backwards and had to grab a hold of a portico post to prevent a painful fall onto the pavement. Another string of incomprehensible expletives was flung at Phoebe. Somehow, she figured they were not the politest of words. The tone alone indicated she was being cussed at.

'Calm down,' Phoebe said with her raised hands to indicate submission.

'Get out.' A finger pointed to the left.

'I'm waiting for Nick Kalameides,' said Phoebe.

The woman's eyes popped. Her mouth opened and closed three times but no sound came out. At least Phoebe was in the right place, since it was obvious this woman recognised the name. There were long seconds of silence. Phoebe figured the woman's mind had to be turning over but for the life of her, Phoebe couldn't figure out what the problem was. Why was it such a problem? This was Nick's office and she wanted – no, needed to see him for a few minutes.

'Nick not here. He in Australia.'

The heavily accented statement in poor English gave Phoebe a definite message to ruminate about for Nick was not in Australia. So why would the woman lie?

'This is his office?' Phoebe pointed to the blue painted wooden door, the same bright azure blue that covered almost ninety percent of Greek doors from what she had seen so far. Window frames and flashing around the roof seemed to attract the same colour by the bucket load, or should she say the tin load since paint came in tins.

'Yes, but he not here.'

'You work for Nick?' Suspicious, Phoebe inspected the woman who now stood on the pavement with the bag again raised ready to be used as a battering ram. A black skirt was so skin-tight the only way the woman could have put it on was to be poured into it. Thick black hair was a fluffed-up twist held in place by a large, gaudy silver clip. Stray tendrils poked out all over the place but Phoebe knew shabby chic was fashionable. Not Phoebe's favourite look. She preferred neat and tidy with shirts tucked in although right now it was possible she gave the impression of being a hobo.

50

Bright red lips stood out on the over made-up face but the most startling feature was the bright green blouse cut so low, large breasts almost spilled out over the top. To top it all off, four-inch stiletto heels were wedged onto feet a size bigger than the shoes with bulges of flesh over the top. Phoebe winced for the shoes had to hurt. The woman was dressed for seduction. Oh, Nick was here in Greece all right, and his assistant was ready to stake her claim. She was welcome to him. Phoebe was off men.

'When will he be here?'

'Soo… next week,' the woman blustered.

Bingo. So he would be here soon. When Phoebe glanced at her watch it was a shock to see how late it was. Already a quarter to nine. She guessed nine o'clock was starting time but she had discovered how a lot of European businesses opened later, in particular those that didn't close until late in the evening. But this was a business and not a shop so maybe the wait wouldn't be long since the assistant was here – if she was the assistant. Might be a girlfriend. The thought sent a shiver across her shoulders. Poor Nick if this woman was a girlfriend. Logic told her Nick would be here soon but there was no way she would be able to get past Miss Protective. Phoebe was up for a game.

'I will come back.' She bent to retrieve the backpack she had used as a pillow. A sharp twist of pain indicated how stiff her joints were. Muscles, cramped in a half crouched position, protested at the hours spent in the unusual pose, but hunched in between two posts with the indentation of the side of the small portico used to lean on, was the only way Phoebe was able to remain hidden from the view of the vast number of people who had wandered by until the wee small hours. She was now convinced no-one in Greece went to bed until at least three in the morning.

She grinned when she noticed the woman shudder when Phoebe sidled past. She supposed she could be taken to be a tramp since she had worn the same clothes for two days –

without a shower. Her nose wrinkled in distaste at the mere thought of her appearance and for a brief second she was tempted to sniff her armpits but thought it neither couth nor wise. To give the impression she was leaving she strolled along the footpath.

At the echoed slam of a door, she turned. The woman had disappeared and the blue door was shut. She wondered if it had been locked from the inside. Possible. Deciding to play the woman a bit more, Phoebe continued to the corner where she waited, leant up against the fence with one eye on Nick's office. At five to nine, a car drove into the rear of the building. From the size of the driver, Phoebe figured it to be Nick, although she couldn't see clear enough to make out any features. She waited ten minutes before she turned towards the blue door and retraced her steps.

Much to her surprise the door opened when she twisted the brass knob. Phoebe stepped inside and peered around. A typical reception desk, minus the receptionist, took up half the wall opposite the door. To the right sat a low table with a neat stack of magazines in the centre. Two serviceable armchairs stood at each side of the table. A small square rug glowed with the only bright colours in the room and sat under the furniture while the rest of the floor was polished wood. What were old but excellent quality polished floorboards were the most appealing feature of the room.

Phoebe approached the chest high reception counter and dinged the little silver bell. It was a full two minutes before the sound of a chair being scraped across the floor indicated someone might come. A door to her left opened. A head came out. It wasn't Nick. The woman from her earlier encounter frowned, glanced back into the room and set her face into a determined mask before she stalked towards Phoebe. The way she slithered from the room and firmly shut the door gave Phoebe a clear message. Nick was in the room. It was obvious the woman attempted to be sly but it made her actions even more ridiculous.

Phoebe smiled but received a haughty glare in return. 'Nick not here. Go away.'

It was what Phoebe expected. She eyed the woman. 'May I use your toilet?' She indicated to the sign on a door in the far corner.

'Not for you. Only workers. Go.' A finger painted to match the harlot lips, pointed to the front door.

Phoebe raised her eyebrows. 'So customers can't use the toilet when they come here.'

'You not customer, go.'

'How would you know I'm not a customer? You never asked. I need to speak with Nick so will wait here until he arrives.' Phoebe ambled over to the cosy nest of table and chairs, made a dramatic show of pulling out a seat, sat and reached over for a magazine. Her lips twitched at the hiss of disapproval, but she ignored it. Instead, she flicked a couple of pages and paused as though interested in an article before she flicked over a few more.

'I call police,' the woman hissed in an undertone. It was so darn obvious she didn't want Nick to hear, Phoebe had to twist her head to hide a grin.

Instead, she waved a hand. 'Go ahead, call them.'

The sound of dialling was interrupted by a gruff voice from the other room, 'Tina, we have to hurry.'

Phoebe grinned at the bang of the slammed down receiver followed by frantic movements as the woman headed for what had to be Nick's office. Tina's face had paled, even under the layer of make-up.

'Nick!' Phoebe yelled moments before the door closed. There were muffled raised voices. The door opened again. This time Nick came out. He took one step and paused. Wide eyes stared as though he couldn't believe what was in front of him.

'Phoebe?'

She fumbled when she tried to get out of the oversoft but comfortable chair but managed to straighten and strode

53

towards Nick. 'You said I could contact you if I needed help.'

He moved towards her. 'Of course.' When he eyed her up and down she imagined what he must think if her appearance was as bad as she thought.

'What happened?'

Hmm, worse than she thought, huh? Without the benefit of a mirror she wasn't able to inspect her appearance. 'It is quite an involved story but first I need to use your bathroom if I may?'

'Of course.' He gestured towards the door she had been denied entry to a couple of minutes ago.

Phoebe grinned at the derision on Tina's face. She stood, hands on hips, in the doorway. She was going to pay for her perfidy. 'Your assistant said it was for workers and not customers,' Phoebe shot over her shoulder loud enough for everyone to make out as she sped towards the door of the tiny room.

'Excuse me?' she managed to hear Nick say before she closed the door.

She stuck her head back out the door. 'By the way, according to Tina, you are still in Australia.' She couldn't make out what was said after her little aside but from the rumble of raised voices she gathered Nick was not happy with his assistant. Well, that made two of them.

The moment she stepped out of the room, after she'd tugged her hair into some sort of order with the tiny airline comb and washed off the worst of the grime, Nick took Phoebe's arm.

'I have an important meeting to attend and am already late. Come with us, you can tell me what happened while we drive.'

She pulled to a standstill. 'I don't want to intrude.'

'You're not intruding; in fact, I could do with an outsider's opinion.'

'An opinion of what?' she asked when her arm was taken and she stumbled alongside Nick through a rear doorway of the building. The door slammed behind her when it was yanked hard by Nick.

'You will see when we get there.' As they approached the sedan Phoebe had surmised earlier belonged to Nick, there was a rapid *clack, clack* of heels. Tina rushed past, grabbed the front passenger door, and flung it open with the same amount of force Nick had just used on the door to his office.

Wow is she peeved, thought Phoebe.

Nick halted with a frown across his brow. 'Tina, I would appreciate it if you sat in the rear so Phoebe and I can chat.'

The woman glared at Phoebe but smiled such a sweet smile at Nick. 'I not mind,' she simpered in such a sugar-sweet voice. Phoebe had to suppress a smile at the way Tina tottered all around the car and eased as ladylike as one could in tight clothes, into the seat behind Nick.

Oh, she minds but what Phoebe couldn't figure out was why Tina acted so jealous since neither had been introduced to each other. It left her to wonder what Nick had told Tina – if anything.

'Now tell me why you are still wearing the same clothes as yesterday and why you were camped on my doorstep so early this morning?' Nick asked as they waited an interminable time to turn onto the main street. Traffic had built up all of a sudden but pedestrians were still scarce. There was a mixture of old single storey buildings and more modern high-rise, the majority now business premises but Phoebe spied a few which still had the appearance of residences.

She figured Tina had mentioned Phoebe's presence but she bet she had been referred to as some homeless tramp of the worst kind. Phoebe spent the next few minutes relating the important points of her story in an undertone, hoping Miss Jealous in the back couldn't overhear the details. It was

55

childish to be so miffed but hey, the woman had started this by kicking Phoebe awake and treating her like trash. A quick glance in the rear-vision mirror showed Tina perched on the seat with arms folded and a sullen pout on her face. She was one irate woman. Maybe it was because Tina's plans for seduction had gone so awry. Must be it.

'He left you his bill to pay?' Nick exclaimed, bringing Phoebe back to the conversation.

'The hotel is holding my backpack as ransom.'

'They what?' The car jerked when Nick turned to Phoebe. He said something in Greek which sounded like a swear word, quickly straightened the wheels and slowed a fraction.

'If I don't pay up they keep my backpack.'

'You know they can't do such a thing.'

'Well they did and to make sure I got the message I was shown off the premises by three, armed security guys.'

'So where did you stay last night?'

Nope, no way did she dare tell the truth. 'I found somewhere cheap.' It wasn't much of a lie so guilt didn't flare about her response – well, not much.

'Why somewhere cheap?'

Darn it, she would have to relay the rest of the events of her sorry day but if she didn't give him all the details Nick wouldn't understand why she was so desperate for help, so she outlined what had happened at the bank.

They pulled up in front of a building which must still in the throes of construction with skip bins lined up outside. 'Would this man have stolen your money?'

'Pardon?' Shocked by the insinuation, Phoebe swung her head and shoulders around to see his eyes on her, Nick turned off the engine. The sudden silence in the car was profound.

Nick twisted his body so they were eye-to-eye. 'Is there any way he could have accessed your bank account while you were back in Australia?'

'No, he wouldn't steal from me.'

56

'Are you sure? After what he did to you yesterday he has shown what a lowlife he is so is there any way he could have accessed your account?'

'No way.' But a sudden thought came to her. Could he have done? Would he have stooped so low? 'Maybe but I hope not. When you get these Cashcards you are given two, both with different Pin numbers. I lost one the day before I flew home.' Her stomach churned at the surging memories. When she couldn't find the card which she always kept in the same pocket in her money purse, she had racked her brain for details of when she had last used it and couldn't figure a time or place where she hadn't put the card back in its little slot. Was it possible Brad had stolen it? God, she hoped not.

'Lost or misplaced?' Nick reached out and lifted her chin so they were eye-to-eye. 'Or maybe stolen while you were asleep.'

'Shoot, I don't know. Maybe. It could have been possible. But why? Why would he be so mean?'

'Think back. When you couldn't find the card, had you already made plans to fly home?'

She trolled through her memory bank to sort details into a rough timeline. 'Had to be after because I used the card to pay for the ticket. We went out for dinner that night, where I used it again. It was the next morning when I couldn't find it.'

'You didn't report it stolen?'

'No, because I thought it must have got caught up in my clothes when I stuffed them into my backpack. I had to hurry to catch my flight and after I arrived home, well, I had so much on my mind I had no spare time to even think about it. With Dad so ill, he was all I could concentrate on. But surely Brad would have needed my Pin-number, which I never tell anyone, not even Dad.'

'He could have watched you at any time during your travels while you punched in keys. How easy is it to sneak a peek over someone's shoulder while they concentrate on their transaction? To me it sounds like he planned this. You know, to ditch you, leave the bill, and steal your money. I bet he kept sweet with phone calls and emails while you were back home so you wouldn't suspect anything was amiss.'

'Yes, but why would he be such a lowlife when he asked me to marry him only a day before?' Phoebe pulled her chin free. 'No, impossible. I cannot believe it was him.'

Tina interrupted them in a string of Greek. Nick acknowledged then turned to Phoebe. 'We have to go. I'm late for a meeting.'

Phoebe gazed through the windows to try to figure out exactly where they were supposed to go. 'Go where?'

He pointed towards the building. 'In there. This is what I do to earn a crust. I buy old buildings and if they are sound, I restore them. If not, I demolish the structure and either sell the site, or rebuild, whichever turns me the best profit.' He opened the door and eased out but bent over and stuck his head in the opening. 'This one has been turned into home units – four on each floor. Two more luxurious units on the top level.' His head disappeared. Tina climbed out the back and *click-clacked* after him, almost on his tail while Nick mounted white marble steps which needed a good scrub. He opened an unpainted wooden door with ornate mouldings. Phoebe gathered she was expected to follow since Nick had mentioned his need for an outsider's opinion.

Inside, the entry was large. It featured a double set of lifts, one each side of the front entrance doors. There was a door to the right, one to the left with two more opposite the lift wells, either side of a staircase in the middle. Phoebe assumed the doors were the main entrances to each unit and the stairs went all the way to the top to be used by those who enjoyed the exercise or when the lifts failed to work. She walked towards the open door from where the sound of voices emanated.

One step over the threshold she came to a sudden halt, taken aback by the appalling décor. The three colours in what appeared to be the main living area, clashed so bad it was an abomination on her senses. With the smell of new paint in the air, she figured the unit had been recently painted but whoever had chosen the colour scheme had got it very wrong.

'What do you think?'

Phoebe spun sideways at Nick's voice. With his hands on his hips his eyes weren't on her but scanned around the room, a frown across his handsome face. What was she supposed to say? Did he want praise or honesty?

'Umm, what qualifications does your interior decorator have?'

'Tina?' Nick asked.

'You saw pictures,' said Tina.

'I saw one emailed picture of a living room. I asked you to check her out.'

'Her house good.' Tina straightened but a flash of fear shot across her eyes before she glanced away.

'Did you check her qualifications?' Nick sounded frustrated as he sidled from one wall to the next, his hand sliding over the paint.

Silence followed, which Phoebe broke. 'How could she check when this woman doesn't have any qualifications.'

'You not know.' Tina's voice had the stridency of tense nerves.

'Well if she does, she needs to go back to college to learn the basics all over again.' Phoebe strode to the outside wall. Her sensibilities had been shaken to the core. No-one with an ounce of training would do such an appalling job. 'None of the basic rules of design have been followed. Take this, for instance.' She ran a hand down the wall. 'This room has three paint colours but none of them have the same base tint. This wall has a yellow base. This,' she bent and pointed to the wooden skirting boards, 'has a blue base and this,' she walked across the room and tapped on what was supposed to be a feature wall. It was a feature all right but for all the wrong reasons. It screamed bad taste. 'This has a red base. They were never going to blend together. And the carpet is wrong. A good designer starts with the floor coverings and tones in the paint and soft furnishings to match the carpet. This room has been done back to front therefore the carpet will never tone in with the paint. To be honest, this has to be the worst co-ordinated room I have ever seen.'

'You not inside decorator,' Tina yelled.

'No, but my father was.' Having let her temper run amok, Phoebe blew out a long breath. She paused to ease in a couple more. 'Sorry, I shouldn't have been so blunt.'

'I'm glad you were because I agree with you.' Nick ambled over to the window and fingered the drapes. 'These are the colour of mud.'

Phoebe agreed for it was an apt description. He turned to Tina, who had somehow managed to creep around to the front door as though ready to bolt.

'Why didn't you do a background check on qualifications and references like I asked you to? And where is the woman?'

'She not here, yet.'

'Obviously but we are supposed to have this floor ready for display in just over two weeks. I can never show this.' His hand swept around the room. 'How much of the unit has been completed?'

'Whole floor.' Tina sounded scared and well she might if what Phoebe suspected was true. Tina was too defensive of the creator of this mess, which gave Phoebe the idea that maybe it was a friend of Tina's or, at least, someone she knew.

'No wonder Costas urged me to come earlier. I'm glad he called a halt to the tiling in the other units.' Nick's hands ran through his hair in frustration. He spun around and stalked into the next room. Phoebe followed. It was the main bedroom and not much better than the first room but here if one took down the curtains and repainted two walls and the skirting, this room could be redeemed.

Phoebe studied the walls, the floor, the ceiling and settled her eyes on the drapes. Too many colours clashed and once again the base tones were wrong. It was okay to have the two rooms with different décor but there should have been some feature to tie them together. Here there was not a single hint of co-ordination. She screwed her eyes as she studied the drapes. To her they didn't appear to be new. She crossed the floor, took a firm hold of the fabric and rubbed it between her fingers. She lifted the dull sateen to her nose and breathed in. Chemical fumes caused her to choke. 'These curtains aren't new.'

'What did you say?' Nick joined her.

'Smell. They have been dry-cleaned and up there.' She dragged the drapes away from the window and pointed to the tapes through which the metal hooks had been threaded. 'They don't even make this tape anymore. These curtains have to be at least ten years old.'

Nick reached up to get a closer look. 'Are you sure?'

'Positive.' She turned to Nick. 'How much has this woman charged you for this?'

He gave a figure as outrageous as the hotel bill.

'Have you paid it?'

'No, thank, God.'

'Don't. Was there a written contract?'

'Yes... well I think so. I have a standard contract form but make specific changes to suit the occasion. I remember I typed in the changes and emailed it to Tina but I don't recall if I signed the final agreement.'

'Contract not be broken,' interrupted Tina. 'You not know.' Phoebe received a contemptuous scowl from behind Nick's shoulder.

Oh, how wrong you are, Miss Secrecy. 'I have been writing design contracts for over ten years, both for my

61

father's work and my own. If you let me study the contract I can figure out where you stand, but if it is like contracts back home, this woman hasn't delivered, especially since she has used second-hand items.'

'Unit finished; you must pay.'

Ignoring Tina's demand, Nick dropped the drapes and they both stepped back. 'How do you know so much?' he asked in an undertone.

Glad this conversation was private she also kept her voice low. 'From a young age I would sit on my father's knee while he put together colour palettes, matched fabrics with tiles and carpets, selected wallpaper – you name it, I learnt it. He used to explain why he chose one over another. I guess you could say I had a lifetime apprenticeship.'

'But you didn't follow in his footsteps.'

'No I preferred to get my fingers dirty and work in the outdoors so I studied landscape design while Dad designed the insides.'

'How good was he?'

A smile crept out. Her dad had been sought after by the well-to-do of society. 'The best. He never advertised for jobs. Never had to. The work came to him to such an extent he had to turn half of it down. I could show you some of his work on the Internet.'

'And how good are you?'

Phoebe's cheeks warmed. One of her creations won a design award but she wasn't into blowing her own trumpet. 'Not bad. Dad and I used to have competitions. He would give me a room, sometimes an entire house, to design as I saw fit. He showed both his and my designs to the customer. If the customer preferred my design, Dad had no qualms about going with it. I seemed to do better with the more feminine side of things.'

'Wait here,' he said to Phoebe, as he turned away and called Tina to follow him as he went outside. Tina grinned in triumph with nose in the air as she tottered after him. When he came back, Nick was alone, carrying a laptop computer. With no furniture in the room, he set the computer on the floor. It took a few minutes to fire up. He indicated with his hand. 'You said you could show me some of your father's work.'

'Commercial projects or smaller houses?' Phoebe sat cross-legged on the floor, brought up her father's website and winced in pain. She hadn't thought about deleting the site since his death. She hadn't had a chance to think about it but it would have to be deleted soon. A sigh of regret hissed between her teeth while she scrolled.

'Since this is a large project, show me some commercial buildings.' Nick squatted beside her.

His body heat sent a sizzle of awareness along her nerves to the extent her fingers were unsteady as she pressed keys and waited for the photo files to come up. She flicked through a few before settling on one. A press of a key and a tiny picture enlarged until it filled the screen.

Nick gasped. 'Your father was responsible for the décor of this hotel? I've been in there several times. It's fabulous.'

'Yes, but I chose this one to show you because,' she brought up another picture. 'This suite in the hotel is my design. It won an award.' During the final inspection with the hotel owners, Phoebe had been proud of the way this particular suite turned out. It was one of the deluxe suites on the top floor and received high praise.

'You did this? Your father taught you well.' Nick reached out and turned her head around so they were once again eye-to-eye. 'What I can't figure out is why you didn't follow in your father's footsteps for you have his talent.'

Shoot but she hated it when this sort of thing happened. Sure, she liked the accolades but a wodge of discomfort settled in the pit of her stomach when it was this close up and personal. To her it was no big deal. She suggested what she thought would work and she worked with what she knew but it was her father who had passed on his knowledge. 'Thank you but I prefer to work outdoors and in any case, with Dad I often got to do both.'

Nick stood. 'Okay, I'm convinced. Now all I want to know is if this place can be saved.' He swept his arms around the room.

'It will take a lot of work but whatever you do has to be better than what is here now. You almost have to redo to entire unit.'

'How would you tackle it?'

'Me?' Phoebe shot to her feet.

'The inspection of this floor has been well advertised with a list of people anxious to make an inspection but I will be a laughing stock if potential buyers see this mess. So right now I am a little desperate. I don't have time to advertise for interior decorators and from past experience it takes a lot more than two weeks to decorate an entire apartment, let alone a complete floor. So I am asking, sorry, more like begging if you will take it on.'

'Me? But I don't have the qualifications needed.'

'How old are you?'

'Almost twenty-six, why?' Why on earth would her age be relevant?

'I am more than happy with someone who has had a twenty-six-year apprenticeship under a master. You couldn't make this place any worse than it is now. If you say yes, you will have an open chequebook and a team of any workers you need. I will pay you well if you can make some magic happen here.'

'In two weeks? Impossible.'

'Not two weeks, you have nineteen days.'

Oh, whoopee.

'What about if you concentrate on this one unit?' Nick added.

Phoebe left his side to take herself on a complete tour of the unit, her mind already clamouring with ideas. It could be salvaged – anything could be salvaged given the money and time but two weeks was an enormous stretch. She stopped dead when she stepped into the bathroom.

'Good grief,' slipped from her lips in shock. It was black. The tiles on the floor and all the walls – right up to the ceiling were black. The ceiling was painted glossy vivid white and the fittings were in shiny chrome. Sure black, white and chrome had been a minimalist trend but this gave the impression she was in some cheap, nasty brothel of ill repute.

'Oh, hell.' Nick cannoned into her since she had stopped so abruptly and it was so dark. 'Sorry. This must be why Costas was so concerned. No wonder he urged me to come and see.'

Phoebe turned. 'Who is Costas?'

'The architect who designed the layout of the units. He has been my site manager while I was back home. I hadn't planned on coming to Greece until two days before the opening but he rang me and, well, I'm glad I took heed. A groan rumbled from deep in his chest. 'This is downright... I can't find an appropriate word. We'll have to rip all these tiles off and start again.'

'You said the tiling was stopped in the other units, does it mean there are no other black holes,' she wavered her fingers around but doubted they could be seen, 'in the other units?'

'Thank, God, yes, so maybe we should work on the other three-bedroom unit.'

She peeked into the toilet behind the privacy wall. It should have had the same tiles as the bathroom but this was all white with a different style of tile. The way every room was so different gave her an idea as to what had gone on here.

'I think I know what this woman has done here.'

'She made one hell of a mess, is what she has done,' snorted Nick.

'Granted but if my guess is right, she bought a whole heap of those interior decorator magazines which show off finished rooms and has picked out a bathroom from one, a bedroom from another and so on. They never show the entire house for this very reason, so nobody can copy a designer's intellectual property.'

'You think, but none of these rooms work even if taken alone.'

'No, because she doesn't have a clue about interior design and how colours go together.' Phoebe crossed the room until she stood in Nick's line of sight. 'I bet if you went to see this house Tina was so wrapped in, you would find the same mistakes. She might have lucked out on the lounge room you saw a picture of but she has no credibility to call herself an interior decorator.'

'That goes without saying.' Nick leant up against a windowsill.

Phoebe had to shift position to get rid of the glare from the outside light. Nick's scowl showed his displeasure. 'If I take this on, I will need two days to run around to suppliers and you will have to come with me to pay bills since I don't have a line of credit here. I have someone I can phone to tell me which suppliers are best. He is a retired interior decorator friend of my father's. He lives here. I think I might have mentioned him to you on the plane. I was going to call in and see him in any case. He knows I'm due here so expects me to visit sometime over the next couple of weeks.'

She began a second tour of the unit, her ideas now coalescing into an overall plan for the entire floor. She could never figure out why or how this happened but once she picked a colour theme, the scheme seemed to fall into place in her mind. Here, by using the already laid carpet as the base, she could turn this unit into a far more elegant place. Get rid of the mud-coloured walls and curtains and the carpet would take on a gold tinge. She knelt on the floor and bent low to inspect the fibres of the carpet. At least this was wool and decent quality. Gold. Gold would be the feature to link the units on this floor.

'So you will do it?' Nick squatted in front of her.

'Yes, but I can't guarantee it will be completed by your deadline and I have two conditions attached.'

Nick grinned then sobered. 'Anything - if it is within my power to make it happen, it's yours.'

'I need you to come to the hotel to help me get my clothes and I need to borrow some money so I can afford to find a place to stay and buy food.'

Nick smiled. 'Done. Let's go.' He strode away without another word. Left flummoxed for a few moments, Phoebe shrugged her shoulders, stood and chased after him.

Six

When she reached the car, Nick had his mobile phone at his ear and jabbered in Greek into the mouthpiece. Tina seemed to have vanished. He waved his hand to indicate Phoebe was to get in the car.

'Where's Tina?' she asked two minutes later when Nick settled into the driver's seat.

'I put her in a taxi to go home and change her clothes. She was dressed like a prostitute.'

An unbidden chortle bubbled from Phoebe's throat. 'She was trying to seduce you,' Phoebe managed to get out between gasps of laughter.

'What did you say?' With his mouth agape, Nick's eyes flared into a shocked stare.

'Tina has the hots for you and was desperate to impress.'

'Dear, God, she's nineteen. I would never go out with one so young and am not even interested in her.' A hand swept across his face. 'Hell, are you sure?'

'Oh, yes.'

'How can you tell?'

'Well, let me see.' She counted on her fingers. 'One, there were the stiletto heels she had trouble walking in because her feet were bigger than the shoes. They must have hurt a lot. Two, she wore a skirt so tight it's a wonder it didn't come apart at the seams. And I can't believe you missed the beacon red lips and nails of the same colour which screamed, *come and get me*. There was the over-the-top make-up and, in case you weren't already seduced by her efforts, there was the oh, so low sexy neckline to display all her womanly assets. How could you miss the message?'

69

'Lord, no wonder she wasn't happy when I said her clothes were those of a hooker.' Nick turned the key and the engine purred into life.

Phoebe laughed. 'I don't suppose she was in the slightest bit happy. So her subtle hints didn't work?'

'Subtle. Give me strength. What on earth would potential customers think if they came into the office and saw her dressed like a hooker?' Nick pulled out onto the road; a grimace of distaste marred his handsome features.

'You run a brothel?' Phoebe laughed. A scowl and groan were her response.

The journey to the hotel took much less time than the hike Phoebe had undergone the night before. Nick had no qualms about pulling to a standstill in the zone set aside for guest embarkation and disembarkation. When Phoebe remained in her seat after Nick had climbed out, he ducked his head down. 'Are you coming?'

'After yesterday? No way. Can't you just go in and collect my luggage?'

Nick grinned. 'Chicken. Come on, I promise you will come to no harm. Besides, I called the police.'

'You did?'

Nick moved around to the passenger side of the car and pulled the door open. 'It helps to have a brother who works for them.' He glanced away as his name was called. 'Here's Alexos now.'

With the law on her side Phoebe didn't feel so uptight; after all, she had intended to contact the police, so she eased out of the car. She could tell the two were brothers with similar height and features but Alexos appeared to be darker skinned and a little leaner. They were both as handsome as sin. More than one female passer-by gave them long glances of appreciation. It was no wonder Tina had the hots for Nick.

After brief introductions, Phoebe related the details of the worst day of her life and handed over the three sheets of paper, her cheeks an inferno at the sense of shame which surged about being duped with such ease.

'Come,' Alexos said with a hand on her shoulder. He had to nudge Phoebe forward.

Nick on her other side gave her courage but inside her stomach did tumble-turns at the prospect of meeting up with the reception staff again. And it was the same man. Oh, shoot. 'It's the same receptionist,' she whispered under her breath.

'Can I see your register, sir,' Alexos said in a very officious English voice with his badge held out.

Phoebe didn't understand a word of what was said. She watched Alexos scan pages in the register. He asked for her passport, which she handed over after a scrabble through her pack. Why did the one item you wanted always have to slide right to the bottom?

After another few minutes of argument in Greek, Alexos turned to Phoebe. 'Did you spend any nights in this hotel?'

'No.'

'Nick, can you verify this woman was on the plane with you?'

'Yes, for sure, I sat next to her all the way from Singapore.'

Alexos held the open passport in front of the receptionist and from what Phoebe could gather, the man was asked to confirm she was the same as the picture when eyes flicked from photo to her and back again. Alexos thumbed through the pages and pointed to the customs entry stamp, which on close inspection had the date of Phoebe's entry into Greece. Thank you, God, thought Phoebe with a glance skywards while the incomprehensible conversation rattled back and forth.

It was such a shock to her when her backpack was hauled from a back room and dumped at her feet. Stunned, she stared at it, lifted her face and eyed Alexos, unable to believe the bag had been handed over with such ease. Anxious to leave, she bent to retrieve it but Nick beat her and picked it up with a loud grunt at the weight.

'How do you manage to carry such a heavy weight on your back?'

Phoebe laughed and turned. She couldn't get out fast enough. They strode across the room towards the front door. 'It's not so heavy once it's on your back.'

Outside, they waited in silence until Alexos joined them. 'It appears your boyfriend had another female with him.'

She had suspected as much so wasn't surprised.

'She signed in under your name.'

'She what?'

'But the young woman, with a French accent, couldn't spell Phoebe. Your passport verified who you were and your story was true. The hotel has now lodged an official complaint against your fiancé, which means I can begin an official search for him.'

Phoebe held up her hand to stop Alexos. 'Please don't ever call him my fiancé. I don't even want anyone to ever mention the scumbag's name again.'

Nick grinned and moved to the rear of the car where he stowed the backpack in the boot. 'There is every chance he has left Greece by now.'

'It will be easy to check,' said Alexos. 'There will be a record of his departure if he left the country but at a guess I'd bet he is on one of the islands. If he is, I will find him.' He stepped forward and loomed over Phoebe. His shadow blocked the sun, giving her a sinister sensation.

'Now, Nick tells me your bank account has been cleaned out. If you let me have the details of the account and your Pin numbers I will see what I can find out about your missing money. If your... um... the scumbag, has stolen it, there is a good chance we will be able to retrieve most of it and he might find himself locked up for a while.'

'You can arrest him?' This surprised her since Brad was an Australian citizen.

'Of course. If he broke laws of this country, and he has by not paying his bill, we can and will arrest him. He will be detained in a prison cell until a court hearing, unless of course, you want to post bail for him.'

A shiver snake down her spine.

'I figured not,' Alexos continued with a wry smile. 'Now, if there is nothing else, I need to get back to work but keep in touch with Nick so I know where to reach you.'

'Not a problem for Phoebe is now on my payroll,' said Nick with his hand on the passenger door for Phoebe.

When Alexos scowled, Phoebe's innards tightened into a knot. 'She doesn't have a work visa, only a tourist visa for thirty days.'

Nick paused on route to the other side of the car. 'Phoebe, do you have an accessible account other than this one which has been cleaned out?'

'Yes, but I don't use it when I'm overseas as it's too expensive with fees for the currency exchange. Besides, there is a low limit on my card. It's only there in case of a dire emergency. All the rest of my money is in a savings term deposit.'

'Alex, what if I pay Phoebe from my Aussie account so no money leaves the country but instead will come in? Besides, she won't be doing any actual physical work. I will have my usual gang to undertake the work. I'll just use Phoebe's excellent design skills to fix up the mess a local has made to my building.'

'I didn't hear this from you and know nothing about it.' Alexos clapped his hands over his ears in such a dramatic fashion it was comical. His wide grin eased the tension which had built up again inside her. 'I'll catch you two later.' He strode off but turned back. 'I'll need your card details.'

It took mere minutes to find the second card and write down all the details.

'Problem solved.' Nick joined her in the car.

73

'It doesn't sound legal to me,' said Phoebe. They joined the stream of traffic. This yo-yo of tension had created havoc with her equilibrium and she still didn't comprehend how, when and where she would be paid.

'I don't see a problem. If anybody in authority asks why I give you money I can say we are together.'

'Pardon, did I hear you right? Together, us?' The flutter in her chest region had to be because the idea was ludicrous. Men were off the agenda for a long time.

'Technically it would be true. We will be working together and if you take me up on my next suggestion…'

Phoebe didn't like where her mind took her. 'Which is what?'' The flutter changed into a pound that was so hard she glanced down at her chest to make sure it wasn't vibrating.

'I suggest you stay with me until we can sort out your finances. I have a large three-bedroom townhouse with plenty of space, although there is only one bathroom, which has never been a problem before since I have been the sole resident to date.'

'But, but…'

'Let's go there now so you can see for yourself. I figure you could do with a shower, a change of clothes and since you slept the night on my doorstep, a meal is on the agenda.'

Heat surged. 'How did…?'

Nick laughed. 'I didn't for sure but now I do.'

'Shoot,' Phoebe mumbled.

Seven

It seemed like forever but less than an hour had passed. Phoebe wriggled to get more comfortable at the small glass-topped dining table. Its best feature was how it overlooked the Acropolis and part of the city. The magnificent columns of the Acropolis stood tall in shadow, giving them an eerie appearance. She couldn't work out if her skin tingled from the vicious scrub it had received from a flannel or from the thoughts of the ancient Greeks who built such a pleasing-to-the-eye edifice. The proportions were so perfect she put an intimate close-up study of the ancient structure on her to-do list while she was here. Now, she understood why her father had been so enamoured by ancient Greek architecture. She had seen pictures but the real-life structure far exceeded what any two-dimensional picture could show, even from this distance.

A cold drip plopped onto her hand. The chill startled her mind back to the present. To ensure no more water found its way onto the table, she brushed a hand through her hair, which hung in combed wet strands down her back, and, joy of joys, her skin wallowed in the sensation of fresh clothes. An embarrassing rumble of her stomach was too audible from the aroma of roasted herbs and spices.

'It's not much but has enough goodies to fill an empty stomach and give you adequate nourishment.' Nick placed a plate overflowing with a vegetable-filled omelette on the table in front of her. Delicious aromas wafted. 'I haven't had time to food shop. Alexos' wife left me a few basics.'

Phoebe didn't care what *basics* meant. The moment, Nick sat opposite, she tucked in and savoured the soft eggs when the first forkful hit her tastebuds. 'I did eat a substantial meal last night,' she said after the mouthful slithered down her throat and settled in an empty stomach. A glass of juice landed next to her plate. Beads of condensation began to roll down the sides from the ice-cubes that chinked against the glass.

'Which was over twelve hours ago.' Nick lifted his cutlery, sliced off a wodge and put it in his mouth. The smile was wry. 'Now, fill me in on what you need to get started with this job.'

Between mouthfuls, Phoebe detailed where she needed to go for supplies. A phone was produced so she could speak to her father's friend, George Chalmers, which resulted in a time and place to meet as soon as they could get there.

From then on it was a frantic rush to meet with George and journey through the suburbs to find the suppliers he recommended: aided by the list George had helped to compile and most precious of all was his gift of a paint manufacturer's colour wheel, which gave samples of every colour available in the company brand – organised in the all-important base tints.

By the time they arrived home late in the afternoon, the car jam-packed with samples, Phoebe's head spun from exhaustion along with the deluge of information about colours, fabrics, tiles and a myriad of ideas. Her brain whirled in overload mode. It took almost an hour to unpack the car and spread dozens of samples out on the sitting-room floor, the table nowhere near big enough.

'Now I need a floor plan with the dimensions.' Arms akimbo, Phoebe stood amidst the organised chaos.

'Dinner first,' said Nick.

'Can we order take-away?' asked Phoebe. 'I don't have time to eat out. I have to calculate floor and wall areas and sort a palette of colours before we can buy correct paint quantities, followed by tile areas. I assume the carpet is the same colour throughout the first floor.'

Nick brushed a hand through his hair. 'To be honest, I don't have a clue.' Shoulders lifted on a long exhale of breath. The sag around his eyes gave the impression he was as exhausted as Phoebe. Her lack of sleep the night before along with jetlag, had caught up with her so she imagined Nick was in a similar state. Light-headedness from fatigue had beset her more than once during the day. A couple of times she had to lean on benches or cupboards to keep her body upright but she didn't mention her lethargy. It wasn't in her nature to complain.

'We need to go back to the units, don't we?' Nick added on a groan as he rubbed a hand down his face.

Eyes closed, Phoebe tilted her head back, sucked in a long deep breath and eased it out between clenched teeth. This was a nightmare but the process for preparation was always the hardest part. To sort out colours and quantities took as much time as getting them onto surfaces. And the colour of the carpets was critical. To ease the tension, she pressed the fingers of one hand into the knotted tight muscles of her neck and opened her eyes. 'Yes, we need to be sure.'

'Okay, so why don't we pick up some food on the way? We can dine while we wander. I am certain there are two sets of floor plans in the units. I can take a calculator. We can compute while we eat. Is it always this exhausting?'

Phoebe managed a sarcastic-type laugh. 'Under normal circumstances I can spread out this process over weeks, not hours. If you want this done in nineteen days don't expect to get much sleep.' She headed for the front door, turned back and grabbed her small backpack. If she dared sit still any longer she suspected it would take a front-end loader to get her up again. 'Let's go. The sooner we get there the sooner I can come back and fall into bed. And we need a decent tape measure,' she called over her shoulder.

'Slave driver,' was muttered into her ear as Phoebe stepped onto the landing step outside. Little did he know once she got started on a project, rest would be a figment of the imagination.

The journey in the car was silent while Phoebe jotted down ideas in her ever-present notebook. She worked from memory of the brief foray of the unit she would no longer decorate. 'Is the other three-bedroom unit the same layout?' she asked without lifting her eyes from the pad.

'Yes, but the opposite way around. The layout is the same on every floor except the top floor. Two, three-bedroom units face the front and two, two-bedroom units in the rear. All have two bathrooms.'

'For this small mercy, I am thankful.' Phoebe kept on with her pencil to sketch out ideas. Even when Nick left her in the car while he purchased hot food, she jotted down notes and added more and more items to the detailed list of what they had to buy. All the while, an overall plan came to fruition in her head but it all depended on the same coloured carpets through all four units, which in itself, was a problem. Who in their right mind would want the same colour carpet as their neighbour? The trick would be to design each unit so the carpet appeared to be different because of the colours surrounding it. Well, it was her theory. Whether or not she could pull it off without her father to offer suggestions was another matter. 'Dad, how I miss you,' she whispered seconds before the driver's door opened, Nick climbed in and dropped two plastic bags of take-out on the rear seat. Her stomach rumbled at the delicious waft of scents.

'What are we eating?'

'Surprise. Wait and see.'

'Meanie.

He laughed.

When they pulled up in front of the skip bins, Phoebe hoisted lids open and searched the contents with her eyes until she came to the one with carpet remnants. She grinned. All the same colour.

'What are you doing?' Nick pressed against her side and peered in.

She reached into the bin but had to stretch and wriggle her stomach over the edge until with a final lurch, her fingers managed to grasp a largish roll of carpet. She tugged the carpet free, hefted her body from the rim of the bin and landed on her feet. 'Tra la,' she chirruped in triumph with the scrap held up. 'There is only one colour in the scrap bin. I need this to match up colours and fabrics.'

'So we can go home?' Nick took the roll from her hands and stowed it in the boot of the car.

'No way. I still need the floor plans and it's easier to work out areas if we are on site.'

Nick groaned, went to the back seat and held up the large bag of takeaway containers in the air. 'So it's to be a picnic on the carpet.'

***

Two days later, Nick stepped through the front doorway of the units and stopped dead. The entry walls had been painted two different tones in soft gold – the upper half lighter than the bottom. The change was remarkable but he hadn't anticipated any work in the entry since he expected a single unit to be decorated. To his right was a long trestle table on which stood the sewing machine he borrowed from his mother at Phoebe's insistence. Because of the short timeframe, she purchased ready-to-hang drapes, which required hems to altered to fit the windows. It was obvious by the pile of fabric on one end of the table, Phoebe had been busy.

He snorted. She hadn't stopped. The so-called picnic on the first night had consisted of him cross-legged on the floor for about five minutes flat. Phoebe had been like a worker bee flitting from window-to-window, wall-to-wall, room-to-room while she collected measurements and honed the numbers onto the set of plans he found spread out on a bench in the unit he now referred to as *the black hole,* after Phoebe's apt description. Every time he managed to grab a forkful of food Phoebe had him move to another wall to hold one end of the tape measure. Phoebe's picnic had consisted of her stopping long enough to shovel food in her mouth. She chewed while she worked.

He strode across the still bare concrete floor of the entry, mystified as to why muffled thuds came from the unit they weren't supposed to be working on while whirrs and bangs emanated from the other. When he reached the unit door, he shoved with the flat of his hand. 'What the devil?' A painter with a roller on a long pole had just begun to apply paint – dark red paint.

'What are you doing?'

The painter paused mid-stroke. 'Painting.'

'But the colour. Who chose it?'

'You told us to do as Phoebe asked.'

Nick lifted his hand in the stop sign. 'Just hold it for a minute. I need to check with Phoebe.' He glanced around. 'Where is she?'

'Across the way in the other unit.'

'Why the devil is she in there? This is the unit we need to get finished.'

The man hadn't moved. The roller was still pressed up against the wall and the red stain had begun to spread. 'Which is what I was about to do. Can I continue?'

'No, this colour can't be right. Let me fetch Phoebe.'

'Very well but you need to hurry if you want a smooth finish.' He eased the roller from the wall and wrapped it in plastic film.

'What are you doing?' Nick pointed to the plastic-clad roller.

'This keeps the paint wet so it doesn't harden on the roller.'

'Oh.' It seemed logical although he'd never seen it before but he supposed it was the way it was done since his team of painters were professionals. Nick retraced his steps across the foyer. 'Phoebe.' The answer he received was an almighty crash. With his heart bouncing from his pelvis and back up into his throat, Nick sped up, afraid Phoebe had come to grief. 'Phoebe,' he yelled, grabbed the door handle and twisted. He flung the door open to find the room empty.

'Not like that,' Phoebe yelled from the bowels of the unit. Panic set in. He ran through the unit in pursuit of what sounded like glass being swept along the floor.

'Now you have to remove those as well,' Phoebe growled seconds before he reached the doorway to the black hole.

Phoebe stood with her hands on her hips, scowling at two men who were hunched on their heels picking up pieces of broken black tiles.

'What on earth is going on?' Nick yelled over the ruckus.

When Phoebe's spine stiffened, he figured she was not in the best of moods. There was a definite hiss as though she sucked in a long breath and blew it out again. Her shoulders rose high then slumped in rhythm to the hiss. It took a few seconds before she twisted her head his way, opened her eyes and stared. He expected an outburst.

'What does it look like?' The tone was too quiet. 'And why are you here? I thought I suggested you stay away for a few days.'

She was mad and was about to be even madder. 'The tile supplier rang.'

'Give me strength,' came out so quiet it was difficult to make out the words. 'Which tiles can't they get?' she added.

'No, they have them all.' Nick paused, a little afraid to impart the rest of the message.

'So what is the problem?'

'They are on the way. Delivery should be in about twenty minutes.'

'So?'

He didn't like the way her voice rose so high on one simple two-letter word.

'Um, all of them.' Phoebe had been assured they would arrive in four separate deliveries so they had time to lay tiles in between.

'Please tell me you mean all the tiles for the one unit.' Her hands turned into tight fists on the end of rigid arms planted down the side of her jeans.

'Umm, no - *all* of them.'

'Are you kidding me?' she yelled. 'Where are we supposed to store them? Can't anybody get things right in this stupid country?'

Uh oh, it sounded like this wasn't the first disaster for the day. How to placate her? 'I can get the men to cart some upstairs.'

'Which means we'll have to cart them all down again, and we don't have the time to take men off the jobs they have already started.'

Guilt stabbed when Nick remembered he had stopped the painter from his work. 'Can you come with me for a minute? I have a couple of items I need to discuss.' Nick paused. 'Why are we working in this unit?'

'*We* aren't. Your so-called tilers are.'

Well at least he now knew who had made a blunder. Still, he had to ask, 'Why?'

Phoebe's hands rose to her hips again as she squared off her body so they were eye-to-eye. Her eyes didn't blink. 'You,' she pointed right at his chest and stabbed hard with one rigid finger, 'called them in to work today.'

Obviously, a mistake on his part but he was not game to ask why it was such an issue.

'Since there were no tiles for them to lay, they needed to be occupied so I suggested they begin to remove the black tiles I didn't want.' She paused. 'With utmost care,' she added in a pointed tone. Now he knew what they had done wrong. The crash must have been tiles falling.

82

'But I thought we were supposed to take them all down.'

'We're not. I worked out a design where we can keep the black on the floor and some on one wall.' She turned and pointed to the two men who still picked up tiny shards of black marble. They were remarkably silent and concentrated really, really hard on every last sliver. 'They didn't listen. Maybe you can translate for them and tell them in Greek how I want one tile taken off at a time and to *not drop any on the floor.*'

Nick could not, for the life of him, prevent a grin when the two men flinched. He didn't need to translate. 'I think they understand now,' he said with a sweep of his hand to indicate Phoebe should follow him out. She glared at the two men, spun around and stalked as though a crazed maniac was after her. The way she stalked; no maniac would dare approach her. On tenterhooks, Nick followed but called Phoebe to a halt before she entered the other unit.

'Phoebe, before we go in there, can I ask why this foyer has been painted?'

Her sudden stop said a great deal. She straightened and oh, so very slow, turned around. Her eyes were like the shards of shattered black tiles – cold and rigid. Big mistake, Kalameides.

'You want to sell these units?'

'Of course.'

'Every businessman worth his salt knows you have one chance to make a good first impression. If you stuff up the first chance it takes seven more attempts before your clients come around to your ideas. What do you think is the first thing your prospective buyers will see when they walk through the front door?' She pointed to the still unpainted main door.

He didn't need to be told. 'I see your point and under normal circumstances we would have completed the foyer but I figured with such time constraints we wouldn't have time.'

'I will make time. Now is there anything else?'

'There is just one more point I need clarified.' And there was no way he wanted to mention it now. With Phoebe so keyed up he had no doubt he was about to suffer severe consequences. To waste time, he moved towards her, slid his hand in the small of her back and began to lead her towards the red splotch of paint. 'I just want to check this colour is right.'

They came to a sudden standstill inside the door.

'What, may I ask, is wrong with it?' came so soft he knew he had made a monumental blunder.

'It seemed so... red.'

The pause was palpable. 'Burgundy,' came out as a hiss. 'And it is the key colour for this unit.' She turned. 'You saw all the samples. You agreed with my ideas. Not once did you say anything negative or suggest you didn't like any of the colour schemes. So now we have bought every item and the men have begun to apply the paint, you decide you don't like it.' She paused again, hissed in three long breaths, blew each out. 'You know what? I am out of here.' She turned and stalked across the foyer.

Nick's blood ran cold. She can't leave now. His entire body tensioned as he took a step. She turned. Please say you aren't leaving.

'You have seventeen days to pull all this together. Have fun.' She spun around and yanked on the front door handle.

'Phoebe, no, please, you can't.' When his stunned muscles found out how to move again, Nick chased after her. 'I'm sorry, Phoebe, I just wasn't sure.' He reached her, grabbed at her arm, and managed to tug her to a standstill. Please let me find the right words to say.

'Please, let us discuss this. Yes, I saw all the samples and agreed with all of your ideas. To be honest, I was so darn confused after seeing so many colour combinations my mind felt as though it was in the midst of a force seven tornado. It was a shock when I saw the paint go on the wall. It seemed

84

so dark but hell, I don't have a clue.' When he realised he could be hurting her he eased his grip and slid his hands up her arms in hopes he could ease the pain he had inflicted. 'I am sorry. I trust your judgement.' He smiled and batted his eyelids, hoping to get some sort of response.

'This is why I suggested you not come in for a few days. Most people see the one colour in front of them when the first paint goes on the wall, whereas I can see the completed picture in my mind. I knew this would happen. Shoot, it almost always happens.' She brushed her hand across her face: one which was drawn with exhaustion.

'So you will stay? Please?'

'I made you a promise and I always keep my promises.' A tentative smile on her, eased his tension. 'As long as you promise no more interference.' She stalked back across the room and into the unit. 'Paint,' she hissed rather too loud at the poor man who had been leant up against the wall. He shrugged, grinned at Nick, which made him feel even more like an idiot. Now he wondered how his position as boss stood.

Nick followed Phoebe, terrified of bringing up the subject which had brought him here in the first place. 'Where do you want the tiles?'

'Damn stupid tiles,' she muttered but she turned around with a deep sigh and turned it into a half smile. 'Maybe the best place will be in the units on the kitchen floors. I will stand at the entry and direct each carton to the respective units. We can get everyone to help to make it quicker.'

Even though he was supposed to be somewhere else, Nick stayed to cart tiles. A brief phone call to Costas to explain the delay was met with a frosty reception for it meant two other people would be put off their schedules as well and it also meant Nick would be home late.

They had passed boxes of tiles from one person to the other for about twenty minutes before Nick realised one of the tiling team wasn't present. 'Where is Stephanos?'

85

The stillness and profound silence was so sudden it screamed out an alarm of doom. He searched everyone's face to be met by downturned faces and a shuffle of feet. He replaced the carton of tiles he had been about to hand to Phoebe at the same time as all seven men vanished into various doors.

'Okay, Phoebe, since you are the only one left here, spill the beans. What happened to Stephanos?'

'I told him to get the hell out of here,' she mumbled into her chest since her head was hung so low.

'Can I ask why?' Nick closed the gap, cupped her chin and forced her head up.

'Ask the other tilers since they thought it was a huge joke.' Phoebe's eyes glittered but whether it was from anger or because she was on the verge of tears, he couldn't fathom.

'My question is to you since it's obvious whatever happened before I arrived has put you in a foul mood.'

'He made a pass at me.'

There had to be more since Phoebe's cheeks began to burn bright red after the colour had risen up from her neck in a flash. 'What kind of a pass?'

She dragged her face away, stalked across the room. 'He grabbed me from behind, shoved his hands around my chest and squeezed my boobs. He was... you know...' she said over her shoulder.

'Aroused?'

'Damn it, yes.' She spun around with a mortified face but it was obvious she was about to lose a battle against tears, but at least he now knew why her temper was about to erupt like Mt Vesuvius had so many years ago.

Shocked at the gist of her words, Nick didn't know what to say. The young man was family. He came from a strict Greek heritage where such behaviour would never be encouraged. 'Are you sure you didn't lead him on?' Nick

86

took a couple of steps towards Phoebe but paused mid-stride when he saw the anger erupt on her face.

'Typical male. You all blame the woman. She must have asked for it,' Phoebe parroted. 'She must have wanted it, she must have led the man on,' she ranted before she stormed across to him and jabbed him in the chest. 'I didn't even know who he was. We hadn't been introduced and I am not into making out with strangers, especially young kids. All I did was draw a line on those blasted black tiles to show which ones I wanted taken down and the punk grabbed me and…' she added with an extra hard punch to his chest, 'those other men came in and laughed.'

When Phoebe turned away as though she was about to run like she always seemed to do when insecurity hit, Nick grasped her shoulders and dragged her against his chest but instantly regretted it for it felt too right to hold this woman against him. He eased away. 'Hell, Phoebe, I am so sorry. Let me be clear, I don't think for one second you asked to be treated with such disrespect. I need to know all the facts so I can confront Stephanos. He is family – a cousin and is the breadwinner for his mother and sister. His father passed away about twelve months ago. Lung cancer. He was a very heavy smoker.'

'Being family doesn't give him the right to be sexually abusive to any female who happens to cross his path,' Phoebe ranted against his chest while she struggled to pull away but Nick held tight.

'No, it doesn't and his mother will be more than shocked when I tell her. In fact she will be downright furious.' Nick allowed her to get arm's length away. 'I am sorry.'

'You have nothing to be sorry about.'

'Yes, I do. Stephanos is in my employ, which makes me responsible for his actions when he works on my sites. I promise to have a long talk with him along with all of my men. Unfortunately, harassment regulations are not quite as strict in Greece as they are back home and many men aren't used to taking orders from beautiful young women.'

When Phoebe yanked free and turned her back, Nick wondered what he said to upset her yet again. 'Phoebe, what's wrong?'

'I'm not beautiful,' came back so quiet he had to strain to make out the words, which were so humble and apologetic it was as though she believed them to be true, which shocked him. Why on earth did she believe such nonsense?

He moved around until he stood face-to-face. 'You don't honestly believe that do you?'

'I'm just an ordinary plain Jane. I don't wear, or even own, fancy clothes and am more than uncomfortable with make-up plastered all over my face and I never wear ridiculous heels on my feet. I like to dig holes in the dirt and get soil under my fingernails which can never be described as elegant since they are always torn and ragged. I prefer to wear jeans and T-shirts to lacy fripperies. There is nothing beautiful about me.'

Nick couldn't help but laugh as he drew her close again. 'Oh, Phoebe, you are so wrong. The first thing I was attracted to on the plane was your naturalness. You don't need make-up and fancy clothes. You have a gorgeous feminine body and classical beautiful features so I'm not surprised Stephanos acted so out of character. He was attracted to you but because he is so young, it's possible he has no idea how to handle his youthful hormones. I doubt there has been any romance in his life. He's only nineteen and has had to be the man of the house for three years.' When Phoebe stiffened he added, 'But it doesn't condone his actions and I promise I will make sure it doesn't happen again with any of my men – I promise you.'

He dropped his hands but was shocked when he regretted the loss of her touch. He had to force himself to step away. 'Now I have to go. Because I stayed so long, I delayed a meeting, which means I won't be home until about seven tonight. So, will you catch a cab home?'

'I can't?'

'Why not?'

'When I took on this job I asked you to agree to two conditions.'

'Which were?'

'I knew you'd forget.' She raced into the next room.

Nick followed with his brain on fast speed in an attempt to remember. One came to mind. 'I said I would get your luggage, which I did.'

'Was one,' Phoebe said with a distinct frostiness.

'Please remind me of the other so I can fulfil my promise.'

'I asked if you could lend me…'

'Some money.' He hit his brow with a fist. 'Why didn't you remind me?'

'Because I never nag. I only ever ask once.'

'Oh, Phoebe, sometimes it doesn't hurt to offer gentle reminders, especially when it is so important and don't forget we've had rather a lot to absorb over the past couple of days. I'm surprised either of us can even remember who we are.' He removed his wallet from his back pocket and opened it out but frowned after he eased out the three notes. 'I have fifty euros on me at present.' He held them out and pressed them into her hand when Phoebe refused to accept them. 'I can get more cash during the day. This should be ample for a taxi – and make sure you negotiate the price before you get in the cab. For the distance it shouldn't be more than five or six euros.'

Eight

A tired sigh slipped out. Desperate to ease the ache in her legs, she shuffled from one foot to the other. A head stuffed with cotton wool from sheer exhaustion didn't help slice the vegetables without cutting the tip off her finger. When the onions and garlic sizzled in the pan and sent up an aromatic steam, the capsicums, mushrooms and tomatoes were less of a hazard to her welfare. Strips of marinated beef waited on a plate in the refrigerator but doubts plagued as to whether the chilli flakes were a good idea but there were no other spices in the pantry. Nick's kitchen was modern and well-fitted out, far more up-market than the one back in the home she had shared with her father all her life but there was an absence of the fresh herbs and spices she loved to gather from her garden to use.

A quick peek at the clock, in went the tomatoes and were stirred. The pungent odour shot up and caused her saliva glands to spurt. Since she hadn't had time to take a lunch break, hunger pangs gnawed. She grimaced. Already five past seven. Nick would be home any time soon and dinner wasn't ready. A smile broke out at the recollection of his reaction to her insistence they take turns to cook the evening meal. It was one of the conditions she made if she was to stay. He hadn't liked it but had lifted his hands in submission and smiled.

Happy the sauce was ready, she scraped the hot, juicy mixture into a metal bowl and withdrew the meat from the refrigerator. A dash of olive oil – wait for it to sizzle - tip in the meat strips - level them out with a spatula. Two minutes later she turned them over and added the other sliced

91

vegetables. After popping on the lid, she pulled two large plates from the cupboard and set them on the bench. She lifted the lid, eased the sauce in a circle over the meat, swirled with the spatula until all the goodies had combined. Lid back on, she turned down the heat and brushed sweat from her brow.

The key in the front door clicked. 'Phew, made it in time,' she muttered under her breath. Nick would never know how long she had remained at work after the men left. Just because the guys had regular hours to work, didn't mean she had to follow suit and when Nick said he wouldn't be home till late - it was a wonderful opportunity to get in a couple of hours with the sewing machine to shorten hems on curtains.

Footsteps neared, Phoebe turned and forced a smile. 'Evening, dinner is ready.'

Nick scowled and came to a sudden standstill. 'Sorry, but I'm eating out tonight.'

A wave of disappointment turned to frustration in an instant. She wouldn't have bothered to cook if he wasn't going to be here. 'You could have told me,' was all she could manage to get out.

'I would have done if you answered the phone.' His hand indicated the wall phone next to her. 'I've been trying to phone you for the past couple of hours.'

Guilt flared. How could she get out of this without letting on she had worked so late and hadn't been home to hear any darn phone? 'I would never answer your private phone. What if some woman is on the other end? How am I supposed to explain my presence?' She knew by the way the heat had risen inside her cheeks, they turned red yet again.

A puzzled frown settled over his face before he smiled. 'The only woman who phones me at home is my mother and she knows you are here and why. So answer the landline anytime. What about your mobile? You do have one, I presume.'

'Yes, but there hasn't been enough time to search for a local sim card yet. I took the Aussie one out before I came.'

'Maybe you should make it a priority so we can contact each other at any time.'

'Of course, I will get one tomorrow.' As if she would have even a spare second and who needed a mobile phone in any case when the two places she would be for the next two weeks was here in the house or at the units?

'Sorry about dinner but tonight is important.' With no more explanation, Nick strode towards his bedroom, pulling off his shirt as he went, which gave Phoebe an eyeful of toned muscles. And they had to flex and ripple along well-honed biceps and bare back before he disappeared from view. The second lot of heat that swept up her body wasn't from anger. Darn, but Nick was all man and way too handsome, with a body to match.

She shook her head in disgust. How could she let his sexy body affect her this way. 'You'll be gone in two weeks,' she said aloud to convince her brain romance was not on the cards. 'You're here to a do a job,' she added to the stove with a vicious twist of the knob to kill the heat. 'He's not for you,' she demanded to the covered pan.

The thought of eating alone while Nick was out with some other woman, sent her hunger pangs into purgatory. She paused, leant against the bench. Why should she be so darn uptight? Sure, she enjoyed the couple of meals they had shared to date. Nick was a great conversationalist and laughed with ease. He was intelligent, thoughtful and always found conducive topics of conversation.

Determined to get over any thoughts of romance with Nick, she put away the two plates and paused with her hands on the cupboard door. He was also the one man she had met with whom she felt at ease. It was more common for her to be on edge in the company of a male in case she made some awful social gaffe or he realised she was no prize catch in the physical beauty or dress department. Hadn't she been humiliated enough for one lifetime?

Another glance towards the bathroom from where the sound of water gushed. A hunk of a man stood under the shower - butt naked. Shoot but the vision stuck in her mind was way too erotic. 'Nick Kalameides is not for you, Jackson,' she muttered while headed for her bedroom where she flung her body onto the bed. To get her mind back on track she sent visions of Nick on one side of a dinner table and some gorgeous leggy blonde opposite, to the forefront of her mind.

'I'll catch you in the morning, Phoebe,' accompanied by a rap on her door, brought her back to the present.

'Have fun,' she called back but doubted he heard since the front door clicked shut at the same time. 'I hope she's a bitch, and the meal tastes terrible.' She slid her legs to the floor, straightened and made her way to the bathroom. A shower was needed, followed by bed to sleep so she couldn't think about him.

The room was still steamy with a glaze of condensation clung to the shower screen and mirror. A clearer patch had been wiped in the centre of the mirror but Nick's damp towel hung straight on the rack and the vanity bench had been cleared of his toiletries. So darn considerate. The man never left a mess anywhere. Another big plus. Apart from the steam, the sole indication of Nick's recent presence was the spicy aroma of his aftershave. Sexy. His aftershave smelt darn sexy and he wore it to impress some other woman. 'Oh, God,' she groaned and stripped off so quick all of her clothes dropped to the floor.

The shower was quick but she paused in front of the mirror, twisted one way and turned back the other to check out her figure. Too tall and gangly but her figure wasn't bad. She had seen a lot worse. Take Tina for example. Phoebe would hate to have such big boobs. She twisted her steam-dampened hair into a coil on top of her head to see if it improved her features with it up the same way Tina had. No, not really. Disappointed, she dropped the coils and gave it a vigorous brush so it hung on her shoulders. One good feature was how thick it was with a slight natural wave but it never looked spectacular. Maybe she should splurge on a new haircut and get it styled. Perhaps a few highlights or streaks. Would Nick notice her with a changed hair style? Shoot but she shouldn't even think of Nick and her in the same sentence. It would never happen. She was here for a couple of weeks; maybe a month if she found time to explore the city and a few islands the way she had intended.

Determined to not even think about Nick in any terms other than the boss, she shimmied her legs into a pair of briefs, donned her nightwear, a large T-shirt of her father's, and twisted it into place. It wasn't pretty but was serviceable while she travelled, washed well, didn't need an iron and she loved the closeness of it against her skin; more-so now. To have an item of his gave her comfort even though it was faded and a tad tatty around the hem. Dressed, she ambled around the room, set it aright until she remembered the uneaten meal still in the pan. No longer hungry, she figured the kitchen needed to be tidied and the dishes washed. At home she would leave it until morning but good manners drummed into her from an early age meant she would clean away every skerrick of evidence she had been in the kitchen.

The spicy aroma was still in the air. She lifted the lid on the cooled pan and grimaced. The vegetables were a soggy mess but the food smelt good so she fished around and scooped up a strip of beef. It was a bit tough from being overcooked but tasted fine apart from the zing of heat of a few too many chilli flakes. 'A good thing Nick isn't here,' she said to the next strip before she popped it into her mouth. Instead of wasting the meal, she stood at the stove and used fingers to eat the better bits. The rest got tossed into the bin when her stomach sent a message of satisfaction.

95

After the room had been restored to its normal pristine tidiness, Phoebe ambled into the lounge where she channel-surfed on the television but gave up when not one programme caught her interest or she could comprehend because of the language. Many countries she had visited to date had plenty of English-speaking channels. Greece didn't appear to be one of them, or, at least, not tonight. To get her mind rid of Nick, she collected her sketch pad and pencils. Too restless to sleep, she plumped up two cushions on one end of the soft sofa, settled down with her legs outstretched along the length of leather and opened up to a new page in the pad. Without the aid of a ruler she divided the page into lots of tiny squares and began to design a pattern for the tiles on the floor of the entrance hall. The measurements were easy to remember since the area was a perfect square, ideal for any designer to work from, but it rarely happened.

***

A strip of light glowed under the door. Nick figured Phoebe was still awake. He frowned at the glanced at his watch. After mid-night. The woman worked far too hard and should have been asleep hours ago. Especially if she was as tired as he felt. To prove his thought, a wide yawn escaped. God, he was exhausted. He rubbed a hand down his face. The night had been one of the worst he could recall he'd ever had to endure. The meal had been excellent, as his aunt's food always was but not so the evening as a whole. The confrontation with his aunt and cousin had been ghastly, an event he never wanted to repeat. His aunt had been horrified to say the least. He winced at the remembered *thwack* when his aunt let loose with an open hand against her son's cheek. It had been a split-second reaction from which she recoiled in horror at having struck her own son. She apologised a split second after she'd lashed out but followed with a rant about the shame Stephanos had brought to the family.

Nick pushed the door open and stepped inside. 'Phoebe,' he called. His breath stuttered. Phoebe was stretched out on the sofa, fast asleep with her head skewed to one side. As he padded across the carpet he traversed her body from head to toe with his eyes. Damn but she was gorgeous, with long, lean legs that seemed to go on forever. When he reached the sofa, he paused, ran his eyes along the length of soft skin on legs which should never be hidden behind baggy denim jeans. Why did she hide her assets in such a way?

Oh, hell. His eyes became glued to a patch of shiny pink satin that peeked from below the hem of a crunched T-shirt which had ridden up. His libido scorched into instant reaction before he managed to drag his eyes away. What the hell was he thinking? Feeling like some sick voyeur, he turned and raced to Phoebe's bedroom where he yanked the quilt and pillow from her bed He had to pause to suck in several deep breaths in a frantic bid to calm his racing blood before he dared return to the cause.

It was an effort to keep his eyes averted from the source of the hard discomfort behind the zipper of his trousers, but he managed until he draped the quilt over Phoebe's body. He knelt beside her to lift her head so he could slide the pillow underneath until her neck was straightened of kinks. He eased her head into the soft mound, sucked in his breath when she sighed, smiled and turned over. The held breath eased out, long and slow, through pursed lips.

He rose but noticed a book of some kind poked up behind her shoulder: a pad of sorts. Checking Phoebe still slept, he took care to ease the pad up the back of the sofa until it was free. The open page caught his eyes. He paused to study it, noticed the page had become a bit creased but the pattern of tiny, coloured squares emerged when he rubbed the page flat to iron out the wrinkles. He recognised a typical Greek pattern but with a modernised bent. The sketch was good – excellent, in fact. Curiosity got the better of him so he flicked through the pages. Most contained perfect sketches of gardens and plants. An intricate close-up of a leaf caught his attention. The fine tracery of delicate veins was exquisite. He glanced at the creator of these sketches before he flicked over the next page. Phoebe was far more talented than she had let on.

He glanced back at the book and caught his breath. The detailed pencil sketch was of a man leant against a rock wall. Nick couldn't help but smile at the enigmatic joy radiating from the man's face. A frown replaced his smile. Was this the jerk of a fiancé? He prayed it wasn't for the man in front of him gave the impression of being far too polished and personable to have been so callous.

Nine

'Is this the fiancé?'

'Far out.' Phoebe jerked around from the sink at Nick's voice, sloshing milk from the carton. She'd been deep in thought about how she could get back at him for his non-appearance at the previous night's dinner. 'Now look what you made me do,' she muttered but paused when she spied her sketchpad held high in the air. She wasn't too sure she liked the amusement on his face.

'Where did you get that?'

'It was on the sofa.' When he stepped towards her she noticed he pointed to a sketch she had drawn while in Italy. 'Is this the fiancé?'

Phoebe made a vain attempt to grab the pad. 'It's none of your business.'

Nick took a step back with the pad held higher, out of her reach. 'I know but the sketch intrigued me. Who is the man you've drawn so well?'

'No-one in particular.' She jumped again but Nick flicked the pad away.

'So if it's not the fiancé, I'm glad.'

Now he had her attention. 'Why?' To give the impression she wasn't in the least interested, she handed him a coffee, turned to take out plates from an overhead cupboard and cutlery from the drawer below.

'This man doesn't give the appearance of being a jerk.'

Surprised by the comment, Phoebe turned back to see Nick flick the open pad across the table. 'He was a stranger but he reminded me of my father.' She ran a finger down the length of the sketch.

'In what way?' Nick's voice had softened. He dropped sliced bread into the toaster and carried butter and spreads to the table. It surprised her to discover Nick ate the more traditional Australian breakfast rather than the Greek style.

'He watched over his two young sons while they built sandcastles on the edge of the water. He allowed them the freedom to explore and create without the constant nagging of, *don't do this* and *don't go there*. Yet the father praised and clapped when either child made some small achievement. One boy waded a little too far into the water and was swamped by a wave. The father said nothing while the boy struggled until he reached the sand. I could tell by the tension in his body, the father was ready to run to the rescue but instead he gave the lad a chance to solve his own problem before he praised his son for his bravery while he surreptitiously checked the boy was okay.'

Phoebe settled into her chair. 'My dad was the same. He gave me enough rope to get myself into and out of my own predicaments yet always kept close enough to ensure I didn't come to harm. It taught me to be independent from as far back as I can remember.'

'You loved your father a great deal, didn't you?' Nick placed a plate with two pieces of warm toast in front of her.

Phoebe reached for the marmalade and began to spread a thin layer of gold over the browned surfaces while she fought to keep tears at bay. Mention of her father caused the grief of her loss to resurge. But it appeared, despite her best efforts to keep her stress hidden. Nick must have noticed for he dropped into the chair opposite, reached over and lifted her chin.

'I know how it feels to lose your dad. The pain never goes away but it does ease over time. My father has been gone for over five years. The pain of his loss is still raw but I try to focus on the good times we had and tell myself Dad would never have wanted us to dwell on his death. I am sure if he were here now, your dad would tell you the same.' He gave her a sappy grin. 'Now, tell me about this other picture.' He flipped over a couple of pages in the pad and pointed to the myriad of squares she had spent so many hours anguishing over the previous night.

Deep down she knew Nick was attempting to get her mind away from her deep sadness so she forced a grin. 'Do you like it?' she asked and munched off a corner of toast.

'Yes, you have captured a couple of traditional Greek motifs in a...' He paused, his head to one side, 'a modern sort of way. But why all the tiny squares in so many different colours?'

'It's a design for the tiles on the floor of the entry hall.' When she caught his eye, there was surprise in them.

'Why so elaborate? I'm certain we don't have time for this.' His hand swept across the page.

'Your team of tilers will be flat out with the wet areas but George Chalmers mentioned he could call in any one we need. I thought I might phone him because I need to ask his opinion on a couple of other ideas as well - if it's all right with you.' All of a sudden, doubt set in. Had she gone too far to suggest outsiders? The dreaded warmth flared in her neck and zipped upwards. To hide what must be bright red cheeks she dropped her head and began an assiduous attack on her toast, even using the tip of her forefinger to mop up the crumbs.

'Phoebe.'

She didn't dare catch his eye so instead drew the jars of preserves towards her and screwed on the lids. A hand landed on hers.

'Phoebe, look at me.'

She couldn't. The hand released her fingers, lifted into the air, gripped her chin and drew her face around so she closed her eyes. They jolted open when his fingers ran down her cheek, cool and soft against her overheated flesh. Shoot but she shouldn't enjoy his touch so much. She wanted to melt into his hand but instead stiffened and forced her body to still.

'I told you there was an open chequebook to get whatever you need. If you feel another team can create this masterpiece you designed, go for it. I trust your judgement.'

'Are you sure?'

He smiled. 'Yes and if the entry hall is completed it will make a far better impression on inspection day. My concern is if it will be finished on time.'

'I think so. It was one of the questions I wanted to ask George Chalmers. May I use your phone?'

Nick frowned. 'You don't need to ask. Of course you can.'

There was no, *of course* about it. Her father brought her up better. To use anyone's anything without permission, he would have grounded her for a month. With a wodge of discomfort stuck in her throat she didn't want to ask for another favour but there was no way she would step foot in Nick's building without some sort of armour. The incident with Stephanos had put the willies up her. Not only had she been mortified but also petrified. When those men laughed at what Stephanos did, she thought she was about to be gang raped.

'Thank you, I can phone him now but before I do, there is one other request. Do you have an old, and I mean old as in ready for the ragbag, long-sleeved shirt I can use to protect my clothes? I haven't got any real work clothes with me and don't want to get paint, plaster and glue on the clothes I do have.' Scared Nick wouldn't believe the reason, she garbled it all out without a breath. It had taken her ages to come up with a plausible reason to use one of his shirts.

'I think I have some old shirts in the wardrobe,' he said with a smile. He gathered the plates and stacked them on the sink. 'I'll search while you make your phone call and don't forget to take the time today to buy a sim card.'

Ten minutes later Phoebe grumbled while she folded back the cuffs over and over again so her hands hung free of the navy and white striped sleeves. Dad's shirts were never this big. Happy with the sleeve length she slid buttons through their respective holes but left the smaller collar button undone. Too far up would look ridiculous. To see how much of her body was hidden she spun around in front of the mirror. Not too bad even though the shirt swamped her lean frame and gave the impression she was dressed in an old-fashioned artist's smock. The tails reached halfway down her thighs, which was good. Let them think she was a target for sexual harassment now.

Happy, she grabbed the backpack, slung it over one shoulder but paused to take a deep breath for courage before confronting Nick. She couldn't understand why her darn nerves hitched to awareness since he accepted her reason for the shirt. After forcing her shoulders to relax on a huffed out breath, she opened the door and headed straight for the front entry, not game to seek out Nick.

'See you tonight,' she called over her shoulder at the same time she yanked the door open.

'It doesn't work. All you have managed to achieve is to have the guys more desperate to find out what is hidden underneath.'

The amused voice from right behind her caused her to jump. How could the man be so darned perceptive? It was a struggle to force her lungs to work, but a huff and shrug and she continued on her way, slamming the door to prevent any further comment.

Ten

With hands on her hips Phoebe made a slow rotation to survey every aspect of the almost completed room. When she came to the row of trestles set up on the canvas drop-sheet, she paused to ensure the fabric still covered the layer of thick black plastic the guys had put down to protect the carpet. Satisfied, she ran her hand over the newly sanded skirting boards spread out next to each other on the trestles. It was tomorrow's job to paint them; one she would tackle alone since the men had the weekend off. To be able to paint without the constant need to keep an eye on the hectic activity and without the constant fear of some hormone crazed punk intent on rape, was a day she looked forward to. All day her nerves had twitched at the slightest sound of someone nearby. It had sapped her energy to ensure she knew where every man was at all times despite the stern lecture Nick had given his men to show respect and keep their hands to themselves. None of the men had earned her trust, and she doubted she would be able to give any of them even a minute amount of trust because of the way they had egged Stephanos on. Thank goodness the punk hadn't turned up today for she was certain she would have walked out if he had walked in. She sighed, relieved the day was over but at the same time mental exhaustion simmered and her nerves still twitched.

A quick glance at her watch and she smiled. Time to go. It had been a deliberate ploy to work late so she would arrive home around the time Nick would be in the throes of dinner preparation. Payback time, even though she figured her reactions were childish but heck, he... she didn't know how to finish.

The brisk twenty-minute walk home seemed like a mere two while pictures of how Nick would react flashed through her mind. When she opened the front door, an aroma of fresh onions sent a wide grin from the corners of her mouth. Vegetables were being chopped. Wonderful.

'How was your day?' She headed for the kitchen, eager to see how far along dinner was.

'Hectic,' Nick growled with a quick glance up between slices with a sharp knife through a red capsicum. 'And yours?'

Nerve-racking, she wanted to say but he would ask why and she couldn't answer for she didn't know why she was so uptight, although all her thoughts went back to one word – Brad and the way he had betrayed her trust. Make that two words – add on Stephanos. 'Flat out but some of the rooms are almost finished.' She peeked at the bench. Several bowls held diced salad vegetables. There was a dish of sliced onions on the bench and a plate with two fat steaks which was what she needed to get a hit of iron into her blood to replenish sapped energy.

'Dinner will be ready in about half an hour.' He lifted a washed head of lettuce and began to break off chunks, dropping them onto a small plate.

'Sorry, but I won't be home for dinner tonight.' Terrified, she fled to her bedroom and leant against the door, half expecting Nick to barge in. When there was no knock she searched through her clothes for a more dressy outfit even though she had no idea where she would go but it was Friday night. There would be hundreds of decent eateries open all over the city with plenty nearby, she already knew about, but maybe she needed to go a bit further afield so Nick couldn't find her.

After a search through her clothes she held up a pair of black crepe slacks, inspected them for creases, gave them a vigorous shake and another inspection. Happy, she searched for a suitable top and settled on a filmy soft top with long sleeves and a pretty scooped neckline. It never creased and rolled into a tiny ball so didn't take up much room when in the backpack. Clean underclothes came from a drawer and were added to the little pile on one arm. She paused at the door. Somehow she knew Nick would be on the other side. But she needed a shower.

She twisted the door handle, yanked, ready to run but Nick leant against the opposite wall in a nonchalant pose – between her and the bathroom.

'Can I ask what your plans are?' he drawled as though he didn't care but his body was tense, telling her otherwise.

'You can ask but it's none of your business.' The very second he straightened in surprise she leapt past him and dived into the bathroom with her heart in her mouth. To ensure she took forever, she washed her hair, dried it with a hair drier and brush and took her time to inspect each garment as she put them on. Dressed, she inspected her image in the mirror. Not bad but could be better. To waste even more time, she searched amongst her toiletries until she found a tube of mascara and coated her lashes several times. A touch of blusher was followed by another inspection. Did she dare lipstick? An item she never bothered with. Shoot, did she even have one? She searched and came up triumphant with a grin. A niggle of concern came when she uncapped and uncoiled a tube of coral. The lipstick had been used maybe twice yet was years old. The one time she could recall using it was to a wedding she attended with her father. She sniffed at the tube. Did lipstick go rancid the same as food? It smelt like grease but not rancid so she spread colour across her mouth, smacked her lips together and pouted into the mirror to see if there were any wayward streaks where they shouldn't be. The entire process felt so foreign.

As a final hurrah she picked up a bottle of perfume Brad had bought her in France and dabbed plenty on her pulse spots. Since she'd never had a mother to teach her about feminine frivolities, she'd never been a perfume type of girl. When Brad had given it to her she had wondered if it was a subtle hint she stank of body odour. To date she had never used Brad's gift but maybe it was poetic justice to use it as a means of trying to get back at Nick. Childish, her conscience said. To her, perfume was a seduction technique used by women but tonight she wasn't in the mood to seduce anyone. After recapping the bottle she tossed it into the garbage bin. It was where it belonged since Brad had turned out to be Indian giver – give in one hand and take with the other but he took over a hundred-fold – no, more like a thousand-fold.

Certain Nick would still wait for her in the hall, she stepped out of the bathroom with bravado but wilted when there was no sign of him. What did she expect, the same conscientious voice in her head asked? After depositing dirty day clothes in the hamper she hunted through her bits and pieces until she found the tiny evening bag she bought in London because it was so delicate and pretty – not because she would be the one to ever use it. It was supposed to have been a gift for a work colleague who was one of the few female friends she had. She took out the scrunched tissue-paper from the inside, shoved in the remains of her money, which wasn't much but with the notes Nick had given her, it was enough for a decent meal. As a final thought a folded tissue and comb was added. Not much but all a plain Jane would need.

Nick waited in the lounge. His eyes flared before they took a slow meander up her body. Why did she feel as though she were naked? 'All dolled up, I see.' She wasn't sure if it was a compliment or not. 'Who for I wonder, since you haven't had time to meet anyone since you arrived.'

Her independent streak flared along with her temper which had simmered all day. How dare he? 'I've met plenty of guys. There were oodles of them at the warehouses and all the guys at work.'

Nick's laugh sent a sharp spear stab to her innards. 'Well young Stephanos sure took a liking to you but no way would he dare ask you out and as for the other men, you have two chances of any of them asking you for a date – Buckley's and none.'

His snide remark hit home so hard Phoebe reeled at the pain. Anger and hurt surged, along with the sting of moisture across her eyes. 'I never believed you could be so cruel,' she yelled with a yank on the front door handle. 'I already know I'm not the type of woman men want to ask out, but do you have to be so blunt and rub it in?'

Furious, she slammed the door, jumped to the pavement and ran full pelt. It didn't matter where she ended up as long as it was as far away from Nick as possible.

'Phoebe!' filtered through the rush of blood that already pummelled at her temples.

Without stopping she turned her head and yelled, 'Go to hell!' Tears of hurt welled but she willed them away.

Visions she thought she had locked away for good, rammed out from the deepest hidden recesses of her mind; her senior year school ball - the one formal occasion of her school life. Like everyone else she had been excited about the event to the extent a gorgeous dress had been picked out and hired after a thorough search of many stores. It took as long to find the perfect strappy sandals, which she bought and stowed in the box on the top shelf of the wardrobe. A month before the event a booking had been made to have her hair swept up and professional make-up applied. Even before she had every detail ready she waited - and waited - and waited for an invitation from one of her many male friends, to be their partner. At the time she had been close to several cool, hunky guys in her group, one in particular who always sought her out to share leisure time and study notes. So many of the girls had hinted how Jason had a crush on her and she was kind of keen on him. But he asked someone else. All the guys asked someone else. Even the nerdiest of nerds and creepiest of creeps had a date for the ball. The sole person without a date had been Phoebe Helena Jackson. Devastated, she cancelled the hair appointment, returned the dress and hid the shoes at the back of the top shelf of her wardrobe the day before the big event. For weeks after, she hid away from friends and other students, un-dateable to the nth degree, humiliated and with her self-confidence at the bottom of a deep muddy ditch.

From then on she withdrew from all after-school, as well as weekend sports and social events, to concentrate on study, determined to graduate with high scores. Even in lunch and recess times she hid in the library with her nose in a book. She never told her dad for he would have insisted on being her partner – as if she would have enjoyed the night. When the school newsletter came out with a detailed report on the success of the night, Dad asked why she hadn't attended. It wasn't her thing she scoffed and hid away in her room until the deluge of tears had run dry and her face was no longer swollen and red.

Now tonight, Mr High and Mighty Perfect had to go and tear open best forgotten scars and confirm what she already knew: Phoebe Jackson is not and never had been date material. Even at university she seemed to have oodles of friends of both sexes and socialised in groups at various functions but not one guy had ever asked her out for a one-on-one date. Since she left university there had been a few dates, but not often more than once with the same guy. She didn't have a clue what she did wrong on these dates but second invitations hadn't been on the agenda. Except for Matthew and she didn't want to think about him. Nor her latest fiasco into the relationship world with Brad. God, she was such a loser.

When she became aware of where she was, Phoebe stood smack bang in front of the eatery of her first night. Well, shoot, how did she get here? What if soldier boy was inside? She peered both ways along the street before daring to take a sneak peek inside. An intimate search of all the patrons indicated no soldier so she decided this was as good a place as any to eat since she already knew the food would be brilliant.

Phoebe hadn't noticed the small wooden reception desk last time she'd been here since she had been set upon by Mamma before she'd reached this far. The ancient wood had suffered many scars but had a gorgeous, age-polished patina: the way such wood should be displayed. She ran a hand over the satiny smoothness, delighted in the sensual feel.

'Ah, you return, welcome.'

Phoebe spun around at the remembered voice and smiled at the wrinkled beam from Mamma. 'Yes, I enjoyed your food so much I had to come back.' Her ears burned from the lie.

'You are alone?' Mamma leant sideways and peered behind Phoebe. 'Your soldier was not happy when you left him alone. He made a scene, demanded we find you.'

Shoot, what was she supposed to say? 'I didn't know him and he scared me.'

Mamma frowned for a second but a grin broke out a split second before she grasped Phoebe's hand. 'He came back the night after to ask details about you.'

A shot of adrenalin surged. Phoebe eyed the door and flicked her eyes around the room for a second search to ensure he wasn't there.

'He came back the one night, no more. Come over here.'

Mamma turned and led Phoebe to a table set for four near the middle of the room. Other patrons surrounded her, which gave her a sense of security. It would be safe in here and there was always a taxi to take her home if needed. At least this time she had somewhere to go, along with sufficient cash to get there. Relieved, Phoebe settled into the seat Mamma pulled out for her and glanced at the menu

111

which was thrust into her hand. She gave it a cursory glance before turning to Mamma with a smile. 'What do you suggest tonight?'

Mamma beamed, which managed to tweak Phoebe's heart. 'The roast lamb has just been taken from the oven.'

'Roast lamb it is.' She handed back the menu. 'And some garlic bread, please.'

'And some wine?' Mamma asked while picking up the other place settings and re-arranging the table.

Not a big drinker of alcohol and with work early the next day, Phoebe shook her head. 'No, thank you. Just water please and maybe coffee afterwards.'

When Mamma left, Phoebe gave the room a more intimate study. It wasn't full but appeared to be busy. Small groups chatted amongst themselves while they forked food into their mouths. The hushed murmurs were pleasant and gave the place an easy friendly ambiance which was just want she needed although, she noted with a grimace, she was the one solo diner.

With a chink, a carafe of icy water was set in front of her, followed by a refrigerated glass. A waiter, with a clean folded tea towel over one arm, poured water into the glass with an instant formation of condensation on the outside. He smiled so Phoebe smiled back.

'Thank you.'

He nodded, left but returned within two minutes with a long basket filled with golden garlic bread. Wisps of steam rose from the bread. The aroma was incredible. She sniffed and her mouth salivated in anticipation. She lifted a piece but dropped it onto her side plate when the hot crust singed her fingers. They hadn't spared in the butter for in the brief time it took to move the slice from basket to plate, molten butter managed to coat her finger and drip onto the tablecloth. Phoebe licked her finger. Oh, yum. The intense roasted garlic flavour was unbelievable. She cut a small piece off with her knife and bit into it. Double yum. She was in blocked-artery heaven but garlic was supposed to be good for you and with the amount slathered on, it would negate the bad effects of the butter.

Phoebe managed to devour one piece of the best garlic bread she had ever eaten when a laden plate arrived at the table. Her eyes boggled at the amount of food. There was no way in the world she would ever be able to eat so much. There were no delicate slices of meat to one side but an enormous hunk of golden-crusted lamb was settled into the middle of the plate. Clung to the edges of the plate all around the meat, were crisp brown roasted potatoes and carrots. There were no greens but who cared. A generous amount of rich tomato-based sauce was spooned over the top. Phoebe preferred gravy but it appeared traditional gravy wasn't so traditional in Greece. Tomatoes, tomatoes, almost every meal had tomatoes. It was a good job she loved tomatoes.

She bent over and sniffed in the spicy aroma of rosemary and some other herbs she couldn't name. With two fingernails, she picked off a small piece of crisp skin and popped it into her mouth. She rolled her eyes in delight at the yummy caramelisation of the spiced meat. With gastric juices flowing in utter pleasure, Phoebe sliced off a forkful of meat, swished it in the sauce and placed it on her tongue. The meat was so tender it fell apart as she chewed. She closed her eyes to savour the incredible flavour and didn't allow the nearby scrape of a chair to impact on her enjoyment.

'Ah, my little runaway,' came from so close, Phoebe's eyes flew open, the food flew down her throat and caused her to choke.

Eleven

The soldier lolled back in the chair next to her. One forearm rested on the table, the other dangled over the back of the next chair. Even through watery eyes brought on by her bout of coughing to get the meat down her throat, Phoebe couldn't miss the smug grin, which gave the impression she was the meaty bone given to a puppy, from the way he leered at her. She prayed the after effects of the cough hid her reaction to his presence for her heart pounded and her stomach tied itself in knots in an attempt to expel the meat she'd had so much difficulty getting down.

He wasn't in uniform but wore black trousers and a soft white cotton shirt with the long sleeves rolled halfway up thick muscular arms. It was a shirt she already knew was favoured by the Greeks with a cord laced through eyelets to pull the two sides together. The brilliant white enhanced the darkness of the man's skin. He was one handsome man but he still exuded a sense of menace.

'What do you want?' Phoebe managed to get out. To show she wasn't perturbed about his presence, she regained control of her cutlery, stabbed into a piece of carrot and swirled it in the sauce before she popped it into her mouth.

One eyebrow lifted. 'An apology to start with.'

Yes, maybe he deserved an apology but no way would she give it. She took her time to swallow the carrot. 'An apology for what?'

'You left me alone, sitting here like an idiot.'

The carrot rebelled as much as the lamb but slid down to join the hunk of meat. 'I can't be held responsible for you being an idiot.' She instantly regretted her stupid words, stabbed a small piece of potato and shoved it into her mouth, but it went down whole at his long indrawn hiss. He had already given the impression of anger but now he was a whole lot madder with the insult.

'Look at me when you speak to me,' he growled. One hand shot out and grabbed her upper arm in a painful grip.

She jumped in her seat at the suddenness of his action. Panicked, but determined to not show it, she lifted her eyes to stare square into his face, which was a lot closer now he leant forward. He was so close the heat of his breath brushed against her cheek. Her heart had joined the three pieces of food and was lodged somewhere between mouth and stomach. All four bounced up and down at a frantic pace.

'Let me go,' Phoebe said with a yank to free her arm but instead, he tightened his hold. It hurt - a lot. There would be bruises tomorrow.

'Sweetheart, I am so glad you started without me,' came from behind seconds before a warm mouth planted a kiss on Phoebe's cheek. 'Sorry I am a little late but I got away as soon as I could.' Nick swung another chair close to Phoebe's other side and slung an arm around her shoulders the moment he settled into the seat.

Oh, fabulous. Now she had two macho men to contend with but deep down she was more than overjoyed Nick had arrived. But boy, the night was about to get interesting.

'Care to introduce me to your friend?' Nick asked.

'I would if I could but I don't know this man's name.'

The soldier still gripped hard. The grip tightened and bit into her flesh. 'Stephanos,' the man offered, at which Nick sniggered in her ear.

Sweet mercy, he just had to have the same name as Nick's crude cousin. Two peas in a pod. It was a stupid analogy but she would never, ever, in this lifetime think of the name in terms other than downright awful.

When Nick growled in Greek, Phoebe's arm was released.

'I see no ring to indicate this beautiful lady is spoken for,' said Stephanos. It was scary the way he settled back into his seat as though he had settled in for the night.

'I miscalculated the size of Phoebe's finger. The ring was a little loose and fell off so I took it back to be altered.' Nick lifted Phoebe's left hand and planted a warm kiss right where such a ring would go.

Inside, Phoebe seethed but at the same time relief surged at Nick's ploy. She was more than eager to play Nick's little game if it meant the unwelcome scary stranger left them in peace, so sent an over-sweet smile at Nick. Despite the fact she was no longer a virgin, thanks to the unpleasant encounter with Matthew, there had never been enough dates to master the art of flirty behaviour nor had there been a feminine role model to teach her girlie wiles. So with no practise or skills, she didn't have a clue if her actions were believable. She probably gave the impression of a first-class imbecile.

Nick grinned back with raised eyebrows before he turned to the soldier. 'Now if you will excuse us, all day I have been eager to have the time to enjoy the company of my fiancée over a pleasant meal.'

Much to Phoebe's relief, Stephanos stood and inclined his head. 'My apologies. If I had known the lady was spoken for I never would have interrupted but she did not mention a fiancé when we last met.'

The moment he turned and left Phoebe twisted her head to face Nick. 'Fiancée? Where did this fiancée come from?'

Nick smiled such a supercilious smile. 'This is the second time in two days I have claimed you as my fiancée to save your honour.'

'Excuse me?' Phoebe tugged her hand away from the hold Nick still had on it, not because she didn't like the way he held it. She did like it – which was the problem for she liked it way too much. His fingers were strong and warm but at the same time gentle. Then logic came to the fore. For

Nick to know where she was he must have followed her earlier.

'You followed me.'

'I plead guilty but only because when you left you were upset and I caused your pain by my thoughtless words. But...' he held up his hand to prevent her interruption when she opened her mouth to protest, 'you took my words the wrong way. When I said none of my men would ask you out it wasn't because I thought you were... how did you put it? The *sort of woman men don't ask out on dates.* It was because all the men, apart from young Stephanos, are married. But you took off before I had a chance to explain.'

Mamma, who held out a menu for Nick, interrupted them. Nick glanced at Phoebe's plate, raised his eyebrows in amusement. 'I will have the same as the lady and a litre of house red with two glasses please.'

'I don't think I should have any alcohol,' said Phoebe. 'I need a clear head tomorrow.'

'It is safe to drink a couple of glasses of the house wines in eateries like this without any residual effects. Most often it is a fresh local wine which doesn't have any preservatives and is a lot better taste-wise than expensive imported bottled wine.'

More cutlery arrived, followed by two wine glasses and a glass carafe filled to the brim with red wine. They sure didn't crib on quantity in this eatery.

'I don't appreciate being followed like some wayward toddler,' Phoebe mumbled under her breath as she began her third attempt at eating her meal.

Nick poured the wine. 'I'm sorry, but I was worried you would get lost. When I saw you did indeed have a dinner companion I intended to leave you in peace but just before I turned away I saw the fear in your eyes when the guy grabbed your arm.' Nick lifted his glass, twirled the contents, sniffed and took a sip. 'Hmm - it is very good, try some.' He indicated to her glass.

Phoebe obliged, took a sip and went back for a second when the rich fruity palette hit her taste buds. The wine left a warm, sweet sensation and was very drinkable.

'Your friend mentioned you had met before. When?'

On a long sigh, Phoebe closed her eyes and took her time to replace the glass. Better to tell him for she was certain he wouldn't let the subject drop until he knew all the details. She related the incident between mouthfuls of food, Nick joining her when his meal arrived.

'I think you were smart to leave the way you did,' said Nick.

'Maybe. At the time I felt guilty for I would hate it if someone did the same to me, but I didn't know what else to do. I doubt he meant any harm. More like he was being chivalrous.'

'A man who uses his physical strength to gain a lady's attention is not chivalrous.' Nick reached over and eased up the sleeve of her blouse. He frowned when he saw the already blue marks on her skin. 'It's called physical abuse.'

Phoebe shivered when he ran the pad of one finger over the marks. His touch was so gentle, like the flutter of butterfly wings against her skin. When her entire body trembled in reaction she pulled her arm away and eased the fabric back into place. It had hurt a great deal when Stephanos grabbed her but she didn't realise he had caused such severe bruises for it to be so black already. What would have happened if she hadn't followed her instincts and escaped via the back door the last time? A shudder snaked across her shoulders at the thought.

'It's not so bad,' said Phoebe in an effort to show Nick she wasn't concerned.

'It's called abuse, Phoebe: physical abuse. Only a coward abuses a woman.' The way Nick stabbed at his meat and sawed with his knife indicated he was more than a little angry.

119

Phoebe wondered why since it wasn't him who had been hurt. To change the subject she asked, 'You said you had claimed me as a fiancée twice in the past two days.'

Nick stopped chewing, swallowed and set aside the cutlery. 'Last night.' He paused and frowned. 'It was one of the worst nights of my life, which I never wish to repeat.'

Since she thought he had been out on a date with some glamorous woman, Phoebe was mystified. 'Date didn't go so well?'

'Date?' His face creased into a puzzled frown. 'I wasn't on a date. I dined with my aunt – Stephanos' mother.' He rubbed a hand down his face as though to clean away the memory. 'You have no idea how difficult it was to broach the subject of what her son had done. She was furious to say the least.'

'Why was she furious, she wasn't at fault?'

'This is Greece. Her son brought disappointment and shame to the family. They are traditional Greeks, from the old school. For him to behave in such a callous manner to my woman was even worse. The shame she felt was deep.'

'Now hang on a minute, where did this, *my woman*, come from?' Phoebe pushed her plate towards the centre of the table.

Nick held his hands up in submission. 'I never made the claim but somehow my aunt knew you and I had been on the same plane. I guess since you are staying at my place and also work for me, she assumed I had brought you back with me and we were a couple.'

'But how did she find out any of those details?'

'My mother. I told you Mum knew about you and why you were staying with me. I didn't realise wrong connotations had been put on the situation. Please forgive me for not having explained the situation better.'

Not sure what to think, Phoebe took another sip of wine to give her time to absorb Nick's words. She replaced the

120

glass and, surprised it was empty, pushed it towards the centre.

Finished eating, Nick did the same with his plate. 'Maybe it would be a good idea if we let the men think we are a couple. At least they will respect you as my woman and leave you alone.'

The independent woman in her fired up. This was the twenty-first century. 'I shouldn't have to belong to a man to be given respect.'

Nick sighed. 'I know but we are in Greece and it's a little different here.' He leant back in his chair. 'I had a long talk with my aunt last night. Young Stephanos has been the man of the house for almost three years. Unfortunately, it means he missed the opportunity to just be a teenager. He had to drop out of school to work when his father grew too ill to earn an income and now Stephanos gives almost his entire wage to his mother. I suggested she should give the kid some slack and let him have a normal teenage life from Friday night until Monday morning. Let him hang out with kids his own age and maybe learn from his peers what is and is not acceptable behaviour.'

'It doesn't…' was all Phoebe could get out before Nick interrupted her.

'I know what you are going to say. It doesn't excuse his behaviour. He treated you with utter contempt and disrespect. He understands now and will apologise to you.' Nick leant forwards and grasped her hand. 'I will be grateful if you accept his apology. He will return to work on Monday. If I had another job on I would send him to it, but I don't. In Australia he would have been sacked but I don't have the heart to leave my aunt destitute because of her son's… dear God… his poor lack of judgement. I am sorry. Please accept my apology.'

'You don't need to apologise.' Phoebe felt sorry for him so she grinned. 'Can we go home?'

He smiled back. 'Sure. Have you had enough?' He indicated her half-eaten meal.

'More than I should have but it was delicious. There was enough on my plate to feed three people.'

When Nick went to pay for their food he turned to Phoebe. 'I almost forgot, here.' He pressed a wad of notes into her hand.

Phoebe fanned the money out. 'Oh, no, this is way too much. I need no more than a few euros to get by until I get paid.'

'Take it. Think of it as part of your fee. Heavens but you have already earned it, and more, with all the hours you've already put in.'

Embarrassed, Phoebe shoved the notes into her bag, turned away and ambled towards the front door. The same time she pulled it open Nick came up behind her. He placed his hand in the small of her back as they stepped outside. The heat of his palm radiated through the sheer fabric of her blouse. There were a dozen reasons why she shouldn't enjoy his touch, why she shouldn't feel safe when he was near, but she rejected them all. For a few moments she wanted to absorb and enjoy the nearness of a man she had begun to like a lot more than she should. For the first time in her life, here was a man other than her father, on whom she could lean – even for such a short time. The knowledge warmed her insides.

They stepped outside at the same time. Nick groaned. 'Forgive me,' he muttered in her ear. Before she could ask what he meant, he twisted her around and closed his mouth over hers in a long, hot kiss. His tongue touched hers, lingered, swept and incited, forcing her tongue to follow suit. She began to free-fall from the sky before a parachute opened. She kissed him back, her tongue tasted the wine, the herbs of the meal and a special taste which had to be the man himself. Never before had she experienced anything like it and didn't want it to stop. Her insides spun into fairy floss.

When she thought she would never breathe again, Nick's head lifted. 'Wow, that was...' He cupped his long hands around her face and stared in her eyes. His pupils were enormous. He dipped his head once again, sought out her mouth. This time his kiss was gentler, softer but it still curled her innards into hot coils.

'This should show him,' said Nick when he raised his head.

'Excuse me?' Phoebe recoiled as far back as she could but Nick held her tight, his hands around her waist. 'What do you mean?'

'Your soldier boy is across the road.'

Phoebe's heart dropped all the way down to her feet. 'Let me get this straight. You kissed me to show *him*,' she wriggled her hand towards the park across the road, 'what you said earlier was true?' Unbidden tears welled but there was no way she would let them fall or for Nick to see how much pain he inflicted. 'I never believed you could be so cruel.' She wrenched free of his hold and began to stalk along the pathway.

'No, Phoebe, wait.' Footsteps chased after her. He grasped her arm and brought her to a standstill. 'Why do you have to get so uppity and run off before people get a chance to explain? Okay, the first kiss was to show him but the second... well...' he smiled. 'The second kiss was because the first one was so amazing I had to go back for more. Might I add, I've wanted to kiss you since I first saw you in my seat on the plane. And your cute little mouth sure packs a wallop.'

Stunned, Phoebe gaped while her cheeks seared as much as his kiss had.

Nick turned her around and led her down the street a few metres. She couldn't understand why they were headed the wrong way until there was a *beep, beep* of the electronic lock

123

of a vehicle. Darn man had followed her in his car. The short journey home was silent but the atmosphere intense. So many thoughts raced through her brain, the strongest about how Nick managed to fire up sensations she had never experienced before. Sensations she loved even though she knew she shouldn't. There were less than three more weeks and she would be gone.

As soon as Nick pulled into his allotted parking spot, Phoebe shot from the car but had to halt at the front door when she realised she had forgotten her key in the rush to escape Nick earlier. Shoot, but couldn't she get anything right?

Nick slid his key in the lock but before he twisted it open he turned his head to catch her eye. 'I am intrigued.'

'Intrigued about what.'

'You act as though you have never been kissed before.'

Not like the way he kissed, she hadn't but no way would she admit to her lack of involvement or experience with men. Not ever, no, no would she admit it to Nick. 'I was engaged, remember,' she said instead.

'How can I forget? Get some sleep.' His smile was gentle, but it still sent a warm mushy sensation to her innards. 'Goodnight, beautiful lady,' he added so quiet, she could barely make out the words.

Much to her embarrassment another hot blush rose and erupted. Desperate for him to not see how he affected her, she turned away. 'Goodnight,' she said from her door. Inside, she leant against the closed door with her innards churned into a maelstrom. As if she would ever be able to fall sleep.

Twelve

'Phoebe, Phoebe.'

Startled awake, Phoebe fought to gather the remnants of her dream to keep them locked away safe. The dream had been pleasant, she knew, for a strong sensation of peace settled in her gut. 'Dad?' she called into the darkness; certain he was the one who had called for her.

A loud knock sent the last fragments of her dream to some dark vacuum.

'Phoebe, wake up!' The voice was insistent and it wasn't her father's voice.

Mystified, she reached over, fumbled around in the darkness to find the switch to the streamlined night lamp as dread wound through her body. The last time she had been awakened in the dark, the news had seen her rush home to Australia. Anxious in case there was bad news of some disaster, she shot from the bed, leapt across the room and jerked the door open. 'What happened?'

With a startled face, Nick stood there, hand clenched in mid-air ready to knock again. 'Nothing has happened. Are you okay?'

'If there's no fire or emergency why have you woken me in the middle of the night?' Blood pumped through her veins so hard she wondered if her heart had any left.

'It's almost morning and I hoped you would like to come with me to enjoy a special breakfast.'

Flustered, Phoebe turned her head to glance at the digital clock perched on the bedside table. Sure she had misread the numbers she rubbed at eyes which were still trying to catch up with the rest of her body. 'It's four o'clock!' She turned back to Nick. 'Since when did we eat breakfast at four in the morning?'

Nick grinned. 'Since I decided you needed a special treat.'

'But I have to work today.' And she had been asleep for such a short time. Too stirred up to relax enough to sleep, she had watched the green digits flip over until after one while her mind refused to let go of the sensation of Nick's kisses. Such fire and passion had turned her body to jelly flambé. It sure put into perspective her affection for Brad – or rather how she now knew Brad thought about her. It was now obvious he had never loved her. His attempts to create some spark between them must have been to weaken her resolve to not sleep with him. Oh, how hard he worked to gain the personal triumph of getting her into his bed. Shoot, how many times and in how many ways had he suggested it? At the time she thought he was in love with her and wanted to get her to feel the same. Boy was she an idiot. She hadn't seen his kisses and cuddles for what they were in reality? But darn it, with so little experience with men she'd had nothing to compare them with – until now. Sure, there had been a few one-off dinners, a couple of movie nights and a full four weeks of a relationship with Matthew. And didn't those four weeks end on a brilliant note? So enamoured with Matthew because he thought her worthy of more than one date, she thought it was the real deal – until she slept with him. And what an unpleasant and painful disaster the experience had been. But now she knew what infatuation felt like and she also now knew she could never settle for second best again. For so many hours before exhaustion had dragged her to sleep, she had burned from Nick's touch; her body as aroused as it had been when his lips met hers. She blushed. The thought alone sent her body on fire again.

'And I will be there to help you but first, breakfast.' Nick brought her back to the here and now. 'You need to get dressed. It's still a tad cold so you might need a jacket and wear comfortable shoes to walk in.'

'Huh?' Why would she need a jacket and sneakers if they were going out for breakfast and what eatery would be open at this ridiculous early hour. She knew the Greeks ate at odd hours compared to home, but four. Few eateries opened before eight.

Nick leant forwards and planted a peck on the end of her nose. 'Trust me, you will enjoy it.' With a grin spread wide on his face, he swung away. 'Ten minutes and don't forget your camera,' he called over his shoulder.

After a quick bathroom visit, she yanked on the top item from each pile of clothes in the cupboard and managed to reach the front door in the required time. There had been no time or clear head to see if items matched but who cared when it was still pitch-black outside. Nick leant against the doorjamb with his wrist in the air as though he counted down the seconds on his watch.

'Where are we going?' asked Phoebe after he'd ushered her outside.

'Surprise,' was all Nick said and repeated the one-word answer for the next thirty minutes until he swung his car into a bitumen car park and cut the engine.

'Come on, hurry up, we need to be there before the sun rises,' he urged as he eased from his seat and hurried around the car to open her door.

Phoebe unfolded from the car. 'I will not take another step until you tell me where we are headed.'

Nick grasped her shoulders, swung her around and pointed skywards. 'Up there.'

'Oh, my…' was all Phoebe could say. Eyes boggled and stared at the Acropolis with the Parthenon perched on top high above them. 'Truly?' She turned to Nick. 'Are we allowed to go up there?'

'Probably not, but at this time of the morning who is here to stop us? I've done this before. It is by far the best time to visit. Any other time and you have to fight off thousands of tourists who don't give a damn about you.' He grabbed her hand and tugged her towards the boot, which he opened to reveal a picnic basket covered in a plaid rug.

A buzz of excitement shimmied through her as Phoebe followed Nick along a well-worn path through bushes. They began to climb steep slippery steps of white marble, worn smooth by centuries of feet as they shuffled upwards. Phoebe was awed by the thought of how many people had climbed skywards to experience the aura of such a magnificently proportioned building. It wasn't until they reached the top she realised just how huge the structure was.

'Oh, wow.' She wandered around studying the enormous pillars, unable to resist rubbing her palm over the fluted marble. How many people had touched this same stone? 'How come there are patches of different coloured marble?' she asked Nick who spread out the blanket in front of one pillar, squatted and opened out the basket.

'The government has decided to restore the Parthenon. It's much like a huge jigsaw puzzle. They find fallen pieces of stone, figure out where each fell from to rebuild each section. They carve out the missing pieces from new marble in a different colour to show what is original and what isn't. Not everyone agrees it should be rebuilt but I think it's a great idea. To me it's no different from replacing a roof when it leaks, on a more modern building. Now come and eat while we watch the sun rise over the horizon.'

The sky changed between grey, salmon through to bright pinks and purple while they munched on fresh buttered rolls, feta cheese, ham and sliced ripe tomatoes. Phoebe knew without a doubt this picnic would be one of her most vivid and pleasurable memories. Between bites, she moved to various positions to snap photo after photo. The change of shadows on various parts of the structure as the sky brightened was remarkable, each moment as awe-inspiring as the last.

While she sipped on delicious hot coffee poured from a thermos, Phoebe began to sketch. At first she did a detailed study of a small section of pillar but to get the sense of proportion, she outlined Nick with his folded body leant against the circular marble. Completely absorbed, she flipped to a clean page to draw a more detailed sketch of Nick alone. One arm was draped over a folded knee, his other denim clad leg outstretched. His eyes were closed and she wondered if he was asleep. Had he slept last night or had he lain awake affected by their kiss the same way she had been?

'What are you drawing?'

Phoebe jumped and glanced up. Nick was headed towards her. Heat shot up her neck to her cheeks at the same speed she flicked the page back to her previous sketch. Flustered by almost being caught out, she scrambled to shove the pad and pencil into her backpack. Shoot, how stupid to get caught. As fast as she moved, Nick was faster. He grabbed the pad and studied each picture. His eyebrows rose when he came to the one of him alone. What must he think of her?

'These are good, very good.' He closed the pad and held it out. 'Why are you so embarrassed about your sketches when you have to know you have talent?' He reached out and touched her cheek, which she knew must be a telltale bright red for it was a red hot incinerator from the inside.

'I'm not embarrassed.'

Nick laughed before he leant forward until he was so close she could smell his aftershave but also the essence of him. He smelt yummy. 'Liar,' he whispered before he turned away and returned to the remnants of their picnic. He began to pack all the bits and pieces into the basket. 'We need to leave before the security people arrive.'

Mortified, Phoebe wanted to run ahead to avoid any confrontation but couldn't leave him to pack up by himself when he had prepared all the food and given her such a brilliant outing. So she joined him with her mind in turmoil.

What could she say? Did he want an answer? While she packed, she didn't dare catch his eye. She was overjoyed when he didn't ask any more questions, which made her all the more edgy. At least if he made a comment she would know what was on his mind. He was so closed about so many things – like how he would go somewhere and not tell her where, although she was a guest and didn't have a right to his privacy but shoot, it made it hard, especially when he revealed last night how he had spent the night before discussing her with his aunt, Oh, how she wished she had more experience with this man-to-woman hoo-ha.

***

The descent was much harder than the ascent, with the slick dew still stuck to the smooth marble surfaces. With the basket in one hand, Nick led the way with one hand held out to support Phoebe in case she slipped or stumbled. Overnight, he had vowed to never touch her again after most of the night was spent in a state of uncomfortable semi-arousal. He had to go and kiss her, didn't he? But he never expected it to have such an impact. Never before had the kiss of a woman sucker-punched him but with Phoebe it had been so different. Even now he remembered the soft warmth of her lips which tasted like the sweetness of honey. And how she had responded. The kicker was the slight sigh of pleasure from somewhere deep in her throat moments before he managed to drag his head back. He had almost lost complete control at the soft sound. As a result, sleep had been scarce with the sensation of her body pressed against his a constant invasion in his dreams, which woke him every time he managed to doze off. In the end, he figured it was useless to remain in bed. He was up at three, preparing their picnic. All the while he snuck around the kitchen he gave himself a severe reprimand and promised himself he would never touch her again.

130

Now, necessity over-rode caution but her soft, warm fingers gripped in his much larger hand didn't give the area below his belt any relief. As far as he could figure out, the only way he could ease this torment was to take Phoebe to bed, which would never happen. She was too vulnerable and in no space for romance. She had just lost her father for Christ's sake and been jilted by her jerk of a fiancé. Add in the brutish soldier and his own stupid cousin. What did Stephanos think, to behave in such an outlandish manner? Darned fool hadn't thought, at least not with the head on his shoulders. He just let his crazed hormones get the better of him. Nick snorted. His own hormones were on a rampage but at least he was able to exert some control over his. What was it with this particular woman that had men, him included, panting after her?

'Ooh!' Phoebe called. Nick tightened his hold on her hand. She tottered and swayed in an attempt to regain her balance but still she slithered, the sole of her shoe unable to grip on a wet patch. She pitched forwards. Nick dropped the basket, reached out with his other hand and managed to grab her around the waist. On a long sigh, he drew her against his body. His breath faltered when his libido forgot all about his promise. Her mouth was mere inches from his. He inched closer. Damn but he wanted to kiss her again. He yanked his head back.

'I promised myself I wouldn't kiss you again,' he managed to stutter, 'but you make it hard for a man to keep his promise.'

Hurt flickered across her face before Phoebe dropped her eyes and masked her features. 'That bad, huh?'

What did she mean? Did she want him to kiss her? Then he remembered her words about being un-dateable. Was she so insecure about herself as a woman? He took a step back, more to preserve his sanity than anything else, but kept a hold on her when she wrestled to free herself.

131

'No, it was amazing. I didn't say I didn't want to kiss you but last night I took advantage of you. I kissed you on the spur of the moment to prove to your soldier boy you were unavailable to him. I don't regret our kiss. How could I when it was one of the best kisses I've ever had?' He smiled at her shocked face. 'But kisses wouldn't be enough. I would want more – much more. Right now, what I want isn't what you need.'

'What do you mean?' Phoebe struggled to move away. He eased his grip but kept a light hold on her arms.

'Right now you need a friend to care about and respect you. You lost your father a couple of weeks ago, the most important person in your life. To top it off a jerk dumps you…' he couldn't think of the right words to describe how he felt about what Brad had done to her. 'He sure didn't respect or care about you.'

Phoebe's head dropped. 'I know. He used me and I didn't love him. Deep down, I think I always knew it wasn't love.'

'Then why did you agree to marry him?'

'I'm not sure - spur of the moment and circumstances I guess. He asked me while I was in a frantic rush to find a plane to get home. My mind was in a turmoil. I was worried about Dad and I guess I figured no-one else would ever ask me.'

With such a forlorn face, Nick couldn't help but draw her into his arms. Phoebe needed a hug. He would give it to her, despite his misgivings. 'I have no doubt the right person is out there for you. You are a beautiful woman with a soft and generous heart. Now we had better get out of here.' He swung her around, picked up the basket and kept an arm around her shoulder all the way downhill until they reached the car. It took a monumental effort to force his mind to concentrate on anything other than the woman who was brushed up against him and what his body wanted him to do with her. It wasn't called platonic friendship. Nor an employee – employer relationship. It was more like a red-hot, sweaty session under the sheets but he doubted a single session would ease this need.

Thirteen

Phoebe ran her hand over one of the doorframes she had spent the weekend coating in gold paint. Not bad for an amateur. She ran a critical eye over the finish. It was smooth, glossy and even with no dribbles or brush strokes. Dad would be pleased. Her heart hitched when an image of her father flickered into her brain. He always smiled, even when he chastised her for some misdemeanour. Not once had he yelled at or struck her. He had been so perfect as a parent; always gentle in manner and voice but at the same time firm to ensure she never got away with bad manners or behaviour. He always took the time to explain his viewpoint but more important he listened if she had a problem or didn't agree with him. Her opinion always counted. They discussed every topic of contention and she knew it had taught her to think about consequences of any bad action she did. She always knew she was loved but he was never afraid to let her know how proud he was of her. Maybe it was the reason she was so picky with men. Would any man ever measure up to her father? She peered heavenwards and whispered, 'I miss you, Dad.'

Determined to not wallow in self-pity, she gave herself a shake and spun around to survey the main living area. It was almost finished and looked elegant, almost the opposite to what it had been before. A drop-sheet still covered the entire floor and would be the last item removed since workmen had to traipse through the unit in a continuous trail. It was a pain but with the carpet already laid there had been no other option. Anxious to leave early so she could pick up her order from a boutique bakery around the corner from Nick's home, she stepped into the main foyer.

The men from the second team of tilers were hunched on the floor to pack up their gear. Phoebe had spent the day with them to outline the details of the layout she wanted. Minor changes were made in the design to fit in with the more detailed measurements the men had undertaken. Anxiety ate at her while the three experts marked the floor with laser lights and chalked string lines to show where borders and different patterns began and ended. It was a pity a clear lane had to be maintained so people could get access to the unit they had to work on until next weekend when the strip would be filled in while no-one was there. Her eyes moved to the dozen piles of tiles already cut into accurate squares, all the same size. It would have been a lot easier to purchase smaller tiles but they wouldn't have been the exact colours as those inside each unit and it was imperative the colours matched to tie the areas together.

She was about to leave when she remembered the men didn't know how to lock up. After going through the details with them, she bade them farewell and left. With excitement thrumming she increased her pace until she was at the rate of a power-walk to get to her temporary home as quick as possible. An unbidden smile curled out from the corners of her mouth. When was the last time she had been this content? A frown replaced the smile. It had been the day she began her journey of exploration all those months ago. She gave a little skip, spun around on the spot in pure joy and grinned at a middle-aged couple until she passed them. The weekend had been fabulous. After the initial uncomfortable moment when Nick apologised for his kiss, they seemed to have reached some deeper level of friendship.

At first, disappointment hit when Nick said he regretted kissing her but when she thought about his reasons, she had to agree she did need time to mourn her dad and get over the cruel way Brad had dumped her. Once she accepted

Nick's logical words, unease in his presence vanished. And hadn't they had fun? Together, they spent both days of the weekend with a paintbrush in hand. Together, they painted all the skirting boards and doorframes of one entire unit. When Nick insisted he help, Phoebe taught him how to fill the brush with paint, wipe off the excess and how to spread it on the wood in a smooth coat without drips, runs and a first class mess. He painted the skirting boards spread on the carpenter's horses while she tackled the more difficult, vertical doorframes. Another smile broke out when she recalled some of the pleasant banter that had passed between them. Now she understood Nick's intentions of just being a friend, she wasn't so afraid to just be herself.

The warm camaraderie had continued at home while they shared meal duties, chatted while they ate and cleared up together. Saturday night she had been too tired to join him while he watched a science documentary on television but last night they sat together on the lounge, watched a romantic comedy while they munched on microwave popcorn. Now she had a much deeper understanding of who Nick was. A long sigh escaped. He was Mr Perfect even more now but he made it clear he wasn't interested in her in a romantic sense. Friendship, he said. Well she could do friendship. After all friendship was all she had ever had in a relationship.

She doubted whether she could extend friendship to his cousin, Stephanos. A shudder zig-zagged down her body at the memory of the moment he had come into work today. Her body had gone into flight mode, ready to move as far away as she could get without leaving the building. It had taken all her reserves to face the teenager and listen to his apologies. He had been sincere and contrite and Phoebe had forced her lips to be gracious in acceptance but still she made him promise to keep his distance and not be in the same room as her. It had been an awkward, uncomfortable few minutes. Deep-down, she knew she would never be able to trust him – but her distrust lived with her.

Determined to sweep thoughts of Stephanos from her mind, Phoebe forced a smile and swung into the little bakery where Nick bought delicious fresh continental rolls first thing each morning. Excitement buzzed while the few customers ahead of her were served.

'*Kalispera*,' she said when it was her turn, even though she was certain her pronunciation of the Greek greeting wasn't crash hot.

'Ah, Miss Phoebe.' The elderly baker beamed at her. 'Your cakes are ready.' He retreated to a back room but was gone for less than a minute. He carried a small cake box and placed it on the counter. 'What do you think?' he asked. There was a hesitant smile on his face.

Phoebe leant forwards, peered into the box and grinned. Nestled between scrunched pink tissue paper sat two small round chocolate cakes, decorated with butter icing and crushed nuts. On one was the number two in white and the other graced number six. A candle stood in the middle of each. Since it was her birthday, she planned to serve these after their main course. They never ate sweets as neither Nick nor she favoured too much sweet stuff but she figured her twenty-sixth birthday deserved a tiny celebration. Tonight it was more important since it was the first time in her life Dad wasn't there to celebrate with her.

'Beautiful.' She glanced up and smiled. 'Thank you, they are perfect.'

'You are very welcome and have a very happy birthday.' The man took care to close the lid. He even taped down the end so it wouldn't come apart. Payment made, Phoebe held the box in both hands and walked at a more sedate pace for the last fifty metres until she reached home. To ensure the safety of her little treat, she placed them on the ground to unlock the door. She peered inside and called to check Nick wasn't home yet. With a smile which seemed to have taken up permanent residence on her face, she placed the box on the lowest shelf of the fridge and retreated to her bedroom where she stripped off, dragged on her dressing gown and tied the belt tight. Since tonight was special she wanted to dress for the occasion. It didn't take long to sort through her clothes, an easier task now they weren't jam-packed into her backpack. Now they resided on shelves in a wardrobe, which meant she didn't have a constant wrinkled appearance even though shabby chic was fashionable.

Phoebe unfolded a black jersey skirt and held it in front of her to study her reflection in a stand-alone mirror which graced one corner of the room. Happy with the skirt, she sorted through her tops, her head to one side while she considered each. A soft cotton top in vivid purple won her vote. She grabbed clean underwear and headed for the bathroom.

Steam curled up the walls, misted the glass and embraced her body all the while she soaked muscles which ached from honest work and being on her feet all day. She wallowed under the pings of hot water jets then scrubbed until her skin tingled. A large soft towel dried her flushed skin. She wrapped the towel around her body to sponge down the shower cubicle to leave it clean and dry for Nick. To see if it was safe to scoot across the hall to her room she poked her head out the door and called his name. No reply. In her room she took her time to brush the freshly shampooed hair dry with the aid of a hairdryer. After dressing, she pinned up the front strands of her hair and left the rest to flow free around her shoulders.

Undecided as to whether or not add a trace of make-up, her hand lingered over the lipstick when more than one voice came from inside the unit. Huh? Who would be here? To find out, she crept across the floor and placed her ear against the door.

'Hurry, Nicky darling, we can't be late,' said a female voice.

Nicky darling? He has a girlfriend? Her innards clenched so tight Phoebe found it difficult to breathe.

'Phoebe,' called Nick.

Far out. What was she supposed to do now? Her mind like scrambled eggs, Phoebe flew across the room on tiptoe and dropped to the floor behind the bed at the same time a knock echoed against her door.

'Phoebe, are you there?'

Please don't come in. Just go away.

The door opened a crack. 'Phoebe?'

She didn't answer – couldn't answer. The last thing she wanted was to meet the girlfriend and have to explain why she had taken up residence in Nick's home but for the life of her she couldn't think why. Rational thought had abandoned her. Nick's steps became muffled as he walked away mumbling something in Greek but she understood one word – her name.

The woman answered in Greek before there was silence until the noise of a shower broke the silence. So Nick must be in the bathroom. Far out, what should she do? If she went out there now they would know she had been hidden away like a coward which would require explanations she didn't have. And it sounded like they were supposed to go out somewhere. Phoebe peeked over the edge of the bed. Nick had left the door ajar a few centimetres. Darn it. Maybe it would be better to stay where she was until they left. If they left.

With the decision made, she stretched out on her back as close to the edge of the bed as possible and attempted to unscramble her brain. Logical thought was needed. So if Nick had a girlfriend, why hadn't he told her? Because it was none of her darn business. Why hadn't they met? Maybe because Nick met up with his lover during the day and didn't have the guts to explain why he had another woman in his home with him. But it didn't make sense because the

140

girlfriend was out there and must know of Phoebe's existence since Nick had yelled out her name.

All of a sudden clarity hit. This was why he didn't want to kiss her again. He lied. After their kiss he'd felt guilty so made up some cock and bull story about Phoebe not in the right space to have romance. Nick was the one who didn't want the romance because he was already involved with someone else. Swine. Why couldn't he have just said? Not so perfect, Mr Kalameides. You just lost a Brownie point for telling porky pies.

'Has Phoebe come in yet?' Nick called. Shower no longer ran so he must be out of the bathroom. 'She has been here because her towel is wet.'

Oh, shoot.

Greek words answered him so Phoebe didn't have a clue what they meant. Maybe they were about her but she bet they weren't complimentary. Maybe they might laugh at her for being a gullible fool. There was another period of silence, which Phoebe put down to Nick getting dressed. Or was the girlfriend in the bedroom with him? What if they began… oh, shoot, Nick's bedroom was next door to hers? Every darn sound would carry through the wall.

'Hurry, Nicky, darling.' Phoebe jumped; the voice sounded so close. Was the woman in her room? The ability to breathe deserted her.

A door opened and closed. Footsteps sounded. 'I'll write Phoebe a note. It was supposed to be my turn to cook.' Nick's voice faded to a mumble the further he moved from her room. It seemed like no more than a few seconds later when the front door opened and closed. She remained where she was to make certain they were gone before she was game to leave her little hidey hole.

When she got to her knees she spied the photo of her father perched on the bedside table. Still on her knees, she reached for it and held it out. 'Oh, Dad, why does it hurt so much inside me? It shouldn't hurt. There is no romance between Nick and me.' But deep down, she knew she wanted there to be more for a little voice in the back of her conscience answered.

'Dear, God,' she stuttered and scrambled upright. 'I do want more.' Phoebe carried the photo with her along the passage. There was a hollowness in her stomach, as though a giant vacuum had sucked out all her innards. With the photo clutched tight, she wandered from room-to-room until she realised how stupid it was to just roam.

When she reached the kitchen, she stood at the bench and placed the photo in front of her. A torn sheet of paper held in place by an apple, sat slap bang in the middle, too obvious to miss. She picked it up and read the scrawled words.

Where are you Phoebe? Something came up and I won't be home for dinner tonight. My turn to cook tomorrow. Nick.

Phoebe snorted. Something came up. Right. Why couldn't he tell the truth? Mention how he preferred another woman's company? Didn't all men prefer someone other than Phoebe Helena Jackson?

When the surface of her eyes became gritty with an itch to weep, Phoebe screwed the paper into a tight ball and tossed it into the bin. Mr Not So Perfect Kalameides would not get the better of her emotions. With teeth gritted tight, she flung the refrigerator door open to search for some kind of food but paused at the sight of the cake box. Damn, damn, damn. Tears welled but she forced them to not fall. Determined to salvage a teeny shred of positivity from her worst birthday ever, she lifted the box, carried it to the bench where she took utmost care to ease out the cakes and set them on a plate. She had to hunt for matches but found a box at the back of a shelf in the pantry. After she'd set her father's photo behind the cakes, she lit the two candles.

'Happy birthday, Phoebe,' she yelled at the top of her voice and let the candles burn down a bit before she blew them both out with one breath which meant she had no boyfriends. So true, she thought when the old game came to the fore. How many breaths it took to blow out your candles indicated the number of boyfriends you had. One breath for her but she sure didn't have one boyfriend. So much for that old myth.

A kind of heavy dull pain settled in the pit of her stomach. To get rid of it, she yanked the candles out and dropped them into the bin. Determined to enjoy the moment, she sat at the table, picked at one of the cakes until it was all gone, but had to force each crumb down since it had turned into corrugated cardboard so dry she had to force each morsel down her throat.

Why was her gut so churned up? Could be because she had never been so alone on her birthday, she guessed. Unable to force another crumb into her mouth, she shoved the other cake back into the fridge, returned to her seat and stared at her father's photo. The memories of many of her previous twenty-five birthday celebrations rolled through her mind.

Unlike today, they had always been fun. Dad always made a fuss to ensure he had some kind of special surprise for her. For her twenty-first, he flew her to Paris where they dined in one of the fancy restaurants in the Eiffel Tower. For an entire fantastic week they explored the city.

For her eighteenth, he hired a small restaurant and invited as many of her associates as he could for a surprise party. Thinking they were about to have a pleasant dinner for two, she had walked in the door and recognised a table of her university friends. When she walked over to greet them, she spied another table of her father's closest friends. It wasn't until she noticed the third table filled with people they knew; it had dawned on her the entire room was filled with people who were there for her. She recalled the burst of happy tears before she'd laughed at her reaction and cried some more because she had been so overwhelmed.

There had been the princess party when she first went to school and the night at the roller-dome when she was a few years older. Somehow Dad always managed to have a cake created about her latest fad. Tears welled at the memories. She dragged the photo closer. Dear Dad, the best dad in the entire world. 'God, I'm going to miss you,' she sobbed with the precious photo held against her chest. Bereft, she stumbled along the hall to the bedroom, changed into the favourite of her father's T-shirts and flopped onto the bed. She took utmost care to set the photo as close to her pillow as she could get it, lay on her side and stared at the man who had given her such unconditional love. Much as she wanted him to, he was never coming back - ever and it hurt like crazy.

Fourteen.

It took time to drape the long curtain over her arm without creasing it. To make sure she didn't trip, Phoebe eyed the steps on the ladder and held the folded fabric to one side on an outstretched arm so she could climb with her free hand able to hold onto the rungs at each careful step up. Balanced, she began to slide the hooks already in the tape, into the corresponding eyelets on the rail.

'Phoebe, where are you?' She jumped at the shouted words but had to grab the rail for support when she began to sway. Why did the mere sound of his voice turn her innards into mush?

'In here,' she called back but continued to hook, more as a means to centre her concentration when an uneasy sensation squished around her gut and deepened. She figured she knew why he searched for her but as yet hadn't come up with a logical explanation.

'We need to talk,' came from behind her.

She slid her eyes closed for a moment. Lifted her shoulders, let them relax. 'Go ahead and talk, I'm all ears.'

'Can you come down here?' Nick sounded imperious.

'Not right now, I've just spent the last hour pressing all the creases out of this so I need to get it hooked up.'

'Last hour, hmm? Which explains where you got to so early this morning.'

Big mistake letting the truth slip out. Better not let on this wasn't the first lot of drapes she had already hung today. The sun had begun to peep through the blinds when she woke after yet another night of restless sleep. With no clue on how to face Nick, she dressed, crept out of the unit. Work would give her mind a rest from girlfriends and the jealousy it left in her gut. It had taken her several hours of tossing and turning to figure it all out. She had fallen in love with Nick and what she experienced had been pure green jealousy.

As nonchalant as she could, she took care to descend the ladder, dragged it along a metre and began to climb back up. From the corner of her eye she noticed Nick with arms akimbo and a face which looked way too displeased.

'You want to explain why you snuck out so early?' he asked.

'I didn't sneak.' Well, she did but he didn't need to know.

'When I got up I crept around for ages so I wouldn't disturb you. When you didn't come out for breakfast at your normal time I discovered I had kept quiet for no reason.'

Phoebe couldn't help a grin at the image of him on tiptoes around the unit while he ate breakfast and readied for work.

'I am glad to see you are amused.' She jerked at the voice right behind her. She hadn't noticed him move but now she could see dark brown loafers with a peek of white socks.

Phoebe slid in the last hook, twitched the gorgeous fabric and slid it along to ensure it moved without any hitches or snags. Now what? If she stalled longer it would be obvious she was unsettled and too scared to face him so she dismounted the ladder and took a few steps back to assess the finished product. 'What do you think?'

'I think your tactics don't work.'

She swept a hand up to indicate the curtains. 'The curtains.'

'Oh, they look nice.'

'Nice? You couldn't say elegant, or fabulous, or fantastic? All you can come up with is nice.' To her the word nice was such an insipid word, so to describe the effort she had put in to the creation of such an elegant bedroom as 'nice' was an insult.

146

'Phoebe, why are you so antsy?' Her shoulders were grasped and she was turned around so they were eye-to-eye.

'Maybe because I put my holiday on hold to help you out. Maybe because I spend all my waking hours in here working my butt off and all you can come up with is *nice.'*

Nick sighed, 'Okay, they look elegant, fabulous and fantastic and I more than appreciate what you are doing for me but right now I am more interested in a different topic.'

Despite his facetious comment Phoebe figured there was no way she would get any more work done unless she paid him some attention. She was equally as sure he wasn't about to leave until he said what he wanted so she wriggled free of his hold and took a few steps back to give herself space to breathe. Too close and the aroma of his aftershave, along with the unique, wonderful scent of Nick seemed to create an urge to get closer and plaster her body against him. Shoot, she had it bad but now she knew he had a girlfriend she couldn't afford to let him get too close or to let these sappy emotions she was so unused to have free rein.

'What is it you are more interested in?' She stared him right in the eye.

'What I found in my fridge this morning.'

Oh, darn, she had forgotten about the cake. She'd intended to bring it with her and toss it in a roadside bin on her way to work.

'You are interested in food rather than how this place looks?'

'Funny, Phoebe, very funny. This morning I open my fridge door to take out some milk and find a cute cake perched on a plate. I notice it has a number six on the iced decoration and upon closer inspection I spy a tiny round hole surrounded by a few drops of hardened wax.' He took one step closer. 'An intimate study in my garbage bin revealed two half burnt candles of the *birthday* variety.' Another step nearer and Phoebe edged backwards until she came up against a wall. 'It doesn't take a genius to figure out the number two was on the cake belonging to the second candle.' Two hands landed on the wall either side of her head. 'Why didn't you tell me it was your birthday yesterday?' His voice softened to almost a caress.

Phoebe's throat closed. She attempted to duck away but the hands dropped to her arms and held her in place. 'You weren't home to tell.'

Nick released a long, frustrated sigh. 'You had all weekend to tell me and I did come home but *you* weren't there.'

Phoebe dropped her eyes and mumbled into her chest. 'It's not important.'

Nick sighed long and loud. 'I disagree.' He coiled his fingers under her chin and hoisted her chin upwards. 'If it weren't important you wouldn't have gone to the trouble of getting the cakes, which would have been a special order. If I had known I would have ensured I was home. So, tonight, I will take you out somewhere nice… oops, you don't like the word nice - somewhere *fantastic* for dinner. I have to inspect a building out of the city today so won't be home until a little later than normal so let's make it seven. And wear clothes a little more *elegant* than baggy jeans and my ragged shirt.' He tugged on the shirt she still wore every day.

Since the heat of embarrassment incinerated her face and her legs had taken on the impressions of wobbly jelly because of his closeness, Phoebe yanked her body free. 'You don't have to.' In an attempt to find some breathing space she spun around and strode away. An intimate meal with Nick was not what she needed now she knew he was involved with someone else.

He followed. 'No, I don't have to, but I want to, so be ready at seven and let me warn you, sweet Phoebe, if you are not dressed for dinner, I will carry you out as you are, even if you are dressed in your pyjamas.'

He turned and left. The nerve of him, ordering her around like some two-year-old. She fumed as she spread the

148

next curtain over the ironing board and banged the iron down in a fit of pique. Bang, slide, bang, glide. It took her the entire hour of bangs and slides to work her temper into a more congenial frame of mind before the workers arrived. By then she was able to greet them with smiles and friendly banter.

All day she wondered what the girlfriend would think of Nick at dinner with Phoebe on the opposite side of the table. Would he tell her about his girlfriend? Unlikely since he never expanded on simple statements as to where he was going or what he was doing. He was a closed mouth on his private life; his business life also when it came down to the nitty gritty. Take today, he would be out of the city today but where, how far? Was it on the mainland or one of the hundreds of islands? She snorted. As if she had a right to know. But it drove home how she was no more than a convenient blip on his radar. He put up with her in his home because she was saving his neck. Free room and board for her expertise, even though he did pay her well, which was a huge bonus for she needed the money with an emptied-out bank account. Nick seemed to be content with the way things were as mere friends. It was she, who deep down, wanted more. And she couldn't understand where this desire had come from or why.

Still she had to drum into her mind how this was a temporary friendship, no, more like a temporary business relationship, while she stalked home. A fast power walk, rather than a pleasant amble, was needed to release built up angst. It was later than normal since Nick had intimated he wouldn't be back until late and she didn't need more than a few minutes to shower and dress. Elegant, he insisted. Well, Phoebe Jackson didn't do elegant. In fact she wouldn't have a clue how to.

A quick glance at her watch when she mounted the three steps to Nick's front door, told her she had thirty minutes to find an *elegant* outfit to wear. Might as well be what she wore the previous night since she didn't have a lot of choice. When you had to carry your wardrobe and bed on your back, the wardrobe wasn't vast. Phoebe went straight to her room, peeled off her clothes and scanned the room for the oversize robe Nick had lent her. Far out, she left it in the bathroom before sunrise so she could avoid another trip past his room with the chance of waking him.

Voices had her pause mid-stride. A female voice laughed and began to speak in Greek.

'Phoebe,' Nick called.

Her heart dropped to her toes and rebounded like a yo-yo at the thought Nick would open the door like he had the previous night and catch her in the altogether. Horrified, she scampered across the room and dropped to the carpet between the wall and her bed. This was becoming a such a ridiculous habit. Her clothes. She dropped them on the end of her bed. With her ears attuned, she slid her hand up and over the edge of the bed, tapped her fingers around until they reached the crumpled pile, snared them between thumb and forefinger and whipped the garments towards her. They landed where they fell. Could she get some of the clothes on before...?

The door opened.

She held her breath.

'Phoebe, are you in here?' There was a brief pause. 'Damn, where is the woman?'

Stark naked on the floor, she wanted to yell back but didn't dare for Nick would come further into the room. Given her luck this past month, his girlfriend would follow and wouldn't it be an interesting little scenario?

Muffled voices receded. Phoebe dared a peek over the bed. Of course, Nick had left the stupid door wide open. Before she had a chance to figure out what to do next, the front door opened and snicked shut a few seconds later, followed by complete silence.

Phoebe glanced at the clock. Her eyes boggled. It had been less than five minutes since she had walked into her bedroom.

Certain she was alone, Phoebe sat upright, dragged Nick's shirt over her head and shot across the room, down the short passage to the curtained window next to the front door. She peeked out. Nick held the hand of a petite woman as he helped her into the passenger seat of his car. When he moved to the driver's side, Phoebe could make out the features of his passenger. Black hair sleeked back into some sort of knot. She was beautiful with dark eyes and gorgeous burnished skin so typical of the native Greek women. No wonder Nick wasn't interested in Phoebe. Tall and lanky with plain brown hair, she didn't stand a chance against such beauty.

Phoebe doubled over when agony gripped her innards. She folded to the floor; her arms wrapped around her to hold together shattered emotions. He had forgotten their dinner date, which just proved how unimportant she was. Rejection hurt, as much now as it had in her senior year at school and like then, she knew she had to get away. How could she have let herself fall in love with Nick when her love would never be reciprocated? She paused, did a double take. Love? Had she really used the word love? Oh, darn it, she loved the man. How stupid could she be?

It was a struggle to get to her feet. Upright, she staggered back to her room, yanked open the wardrobe door and pulled her backpack from the top shelf. She began to stuff her belongings inside, not giving a damn about wrinkles and creases but she took enough care to ensure every item fitted.

All the while she worked it was as though she was stuck in a huge vacuum unable to function. It wasn't until every last item had been stuffed in she realised she was still naked under Nick's shirt and now had no clothes to wear. Frustrated, she yanked things out again, rummaged around with her hand and managed to pull out an odd assortment, none of which matched but who cared? At least she had clean underclothes, a pair of jeans and a decent top.

Numb with pain, she shoved limbs into holes, yanked, buttoned and tried to zip until she realised her jeans were on back to front. As many swear words she could think of were flung around the room while she tugged the jeans off again, twisted them around and tried hard to concentrate on the task until she had the zip up.

She scanned the room for any missed item while attempting to sort through the fuzz in her brain to figure out if any other item of hers was in any other room. Her sketchpad? No, she'd left it at work. Pencils? In her small backpack. Laundry? None, she had folded the clean clothes in the semi-dark of dawn.

Satisfied there were no more of her belongings anywhere else, she fed her arms through the small backpack to settle it across her chest. Next, she bent her legs with her back to the bed and wriggled her arms through the webbed straps of the big pack, gave a heave, paused and bent forwards to get the weight balanced on her back. She clipped and tightened latches, made her way to the front door and groaned under the weight. It had been over a month since she had carried this load. Now she wondered how she had coped before.

When a thought came to her, she paused. No way could she leave without some sort of explanation but to let on how much she hurt at his betrayal, was not about to happen. Her emotions didn't belong to anyone else but lived with her. If she was dumb enough to fall in love with a man who didn't want her love, it was her own damn fault, more so when said man already had a girlfriend and he told her, point blank, he only wanted friendship.

A note would have to suffice. She entered the inner sanctum of Nick's office cum third bedroom, found a piece of paper and thought hard about every word she wrote. Politeness and gratitude was a given. Poor guy had saved her from dire circumstances and hadn't committed any sin. It wasn't his fault she was so devastated. But it would be impossible to stay and be in such close contact when his very presence made her yearn for things she could never have and wasn't entitled to. Nick had a life she had interrupted. It wasn't his fault she had been stupid enough to lose her heart to Mr Perfect-who-belonged-to-someone-else.

Satisfied she had been generous and appreciative, she settled the note on Nick's pillow, turned and raced for the door, made sure it was locked and left. It wasn't until she had walked a block she dared to stop and wonder where the heck she would spend the night. She spun around, searched the area as though some boarding house would appear before her eyes. It took the trudge of another block before her mind cleared enough to come up with a solution. The units. No-one ever went upstairs. She could camp in one of the empty units on a higher level until she found a more permanent place. Water and power were connected. No tiles had been laid but there was a bath connected to drains so she would be able to bathe and rinse out her clothes. She could eat out and purchase small snacks for breakfast each day. Problem solved for the present.

Fifteen

Phoebe had never been so nervous in her life. It was as though her nerves had adopted a permanent twitch. For two hours already she had toiled away and it was now eight in the morning. Nick would arrive soon and would either be furious or happy she was no longer an impediment to his freedom. She bet on anger but he was the one who broke a promise and stood her up.

Too on edge to stand still, she began to pace but paused when the front door hissed open. Adrenalin surged, along with her heartbeat which increased to the rate of a super-fast train.

'Kalispera,' said Yiannis who preceded the two other painters inside. They always came together in the one vehicle. The traffic – they told her. 'Today the laundry?' he asked when all three paused in front of her.

A sigh of relief escaped along with a forced smile. These guys didn't need to know how strung out she was. 'Yes, thank you. After the laundry you can start in unit three. We can't paint the bathrooms or kitchen in here until the guys have finished laying all the tiles.'

'You have a colour chart for us?'

'Yes, I sorted the paint cans earlier. Each room has the cans required and there is a colour chart taped to one of the cans.' It had taken her all of the two hours she had been downstairs to sort through the dozens of cans and write out which colour was to go where. Serves her right for having so many different colours in each unit but the end result was worth it if she took into account how great this unit had turned out. The actual application of the paint didn't take long with three experienced men working as a team and since the units had recently been painted the only undercoat required was on the darker walls which would now be paler.

The men acknowledged her with grunts and tiny nods of the heads as they passed through. Phoebe hadn't even turned back when the door hissed again. The breath stuttered in her throat.

The new team of tilers traipsed in, with a cheery wave and mumbles of greeting before they set down their various lunch packs in the far corner of the reception area and set to work.

With a desperate need to keep her brain occupied, Phoebe re-examined the intricate patterns which had already emerged. She had already spent half an hour studying the large mosaics but the men needed to know she was interested in their brilliant work. The men were good, excellent, in fact. They'd managed to follow her plan without continual consultation with her. But George had said they were the best he had ever worked with. There were plain tilers, craftsmen and master craftsmen and this team of four fitted into the latter category.

With her nerves on tenterhooks, Phoebe racked her brain for more jobs she could get stuck into. She wandered through the almost completed unit until she spied a smudge on a window. An intimate clean of a few windows would go a little way to ease her tension. She collected a bucket of hot water, added a dash of methylated spirits and found a couple of soft rags. With the rags slung over one shoulder and the heavy bucket in one hand she stepped up a few rungs of a ladder.

'Where's Phoebe?'

Phoebe jumped at the loud voice but forced her arm to continue rubbing at the smudge which appeared to be paint wiped off with the back of the hand in pure laziness. Turps was needed but no way would she step down and go to fetch some. Nick sounded angry but she wasn't game to call out to him. Loud footsteps echoed. She sucked in a long breath.

'What's this?' Nick said in a voice that wasn't quite a yell but more of an order.

Phoebe glanced around. He held out her note. 'A piece of paper,' she said but had to swallow down the lump lodged in her throat.

'Now is not the time for smart comments from your sassy mouth.'

Sassy mouth? Was sassy good or bad? Phoebe rubbed a little harder but couldn't miss the cessation of all the normal chatter and work noise. Oh, this was just dandy. The entire unit was about to be a party to his anger and her humiliation. The rag was snatched from her hand.

'Down! Now.'

Uh, oh. She stiffened her spine and took her time to descend the three steps, pretending she was concerned about slopping water over the lip of the bucket, although it was no more than half full.

He waited, in silence; the silence intense and the tension so high it was as though it wanted to ping and jettison around the room.

The letter was thrust in front of her eyes: eyes she couldn't find the courage to raise. 'Do you want to explain this?' This time Nick's voice was soft but there was not an ounce of give in it.

'I thought it was self-explanatory. Do you want me to read it to you?' She grabbed the rumpled paper and winced at Nick's drawn in hiss.

'I know what it says but now I want an explanation for what it doesn't say.'

Dad always told her how a good method of defence is to not cower but attack instead. She lifted her head but almost backed away at the fire in his eyes. She blew out her cheeks, hefted her shoulders and eyed him. 'Like it says, I found a place to live.'

'You had a perfectly good place to live.'

Yes, she did – until the girlfriend made her appearance. 'We both know it was a temporary arrangement to live with you until I managed to get back on my feet. Now you pay me good money I can afford to be independent again. We can both get on with our lives without me getting in your way.'

'In my way? Phoebe, you were never in my way. And I thought we had a date last night.'

A snort of disdain fought to escape but she managed to hold it back with an uncomfortable cough. 'You said seven o'clock. I was ready, dressed in the most elegant clothes I possess, at seven. I was still ready after I'd waited half an hour. When you didn't come I figured you had forgotten so I decided to fill in time by moving out a day earlier than I had intended. I would have told you last night if you had bothered to turn up.' Anger wanted to rear its ugly head. It simmered under the surface but again she fought it back.

'I left a note for you to say I would be an hour late.'

'I never found any note.'

'It was on the kitchen bench where we always leave notes to each other, and to be clear, I would never not turn up for a date, especially one I looked forward to a great deal. What sort of a man do you think I am?'

Regret hit for her haste but at the same time delight simmered to know he hadn't forgotten. But there was still the issue of the girlfriend. He might never forget a date but he didn't seem to mind about two-timing his girlfriend and Phoebe could never countenance such behaviour.

'Why would I go into the kitchen if I was supposed to be dining elsewhere? I never went into the kitchen.' She wanted to add on about him with another woman but it would require too many explanations about her cowardice. And how could she explain how she had been there all the time, hidden away, stark naked, because there was another woman present? Awkward in every way.

158

Nick rubbed a hand through his hair. 'I'm sorry but we were late getting back so I came straight here to the units to pick you up. When I found the place locked up, I drove home the route you usually take but you weren't anywhere. We were so late I had to get Katerina home because she had and important function to attend so I figured I would leave you a note to delay our meal for an hour.'

Phoebe had stopped listening at the words *we* and *Katerina*. So they had spent the day together. The knowledge stabbed and tore like a blunt serrated knife. Now she was glad she left. Nick and Katerina could now spend as much time as they liked together and Phoebe wouldn't have to suffer this intense jealousy. It didn't sit well how she had allowed the green monster to invade, even though she'd never experienced it before, but she sure recognised the signs for what they were.

Her shoulders were taken in a firm hold. It felt so darn good when tremors of lust shimmied through her body. Shoot, but she had it bad.

'You left because you thought I had let you down?'

'No, I gave you the reasons in this.' She held up the letter which somehow was now screwed into a ball.

'I don't want you to be gone. I enjoy your company. Won't you reconsider?'

'I can't.' If there hadn't been someone else she would return like a rocket but when she had this intense emotional attraction to Nick, to return would give her more pain and heartache. Better to break away now while she still had some pride left and it wouldn't hurt so much when she left the country.

'How about dinner tonight, to make up for last night.'

She wanted to say yes. 'I have plans.'

'Plans? Is this with another of your imaginary friends?'

Adrenalin surged in pure anger. 'Imaginary friends. You sure know how to twist the knife, don't you? I might not be the sort of woman men want to take out but I sure as hell

159

don't need to make up imaginary friends. I have been invited to dine where I now live.' She jerked free and stalked away, ashamed of her many lies, but shoot, he sure knew how to tear her emotions to shreds. 'Now if you will excuse me, I've got a truckload of work to do and the sooner I get it done the sooner I can go play with my imaginary friends and get on with my life.'

'Phoebe, I…'

'Go to hell!' She ran - because she needed to get away. She yanked on the front door and tugged it shut behind her. A quick peek around and she fled in the opposite direction to which Nick's car faced. To ensure he wasn't able to follow, she ducked into the first little eatery she came across and hid away in the furthest corner from the doorway. A bookshelf of touristy knick-knacks and a large dusty faux philodendron hid her well. It was a great opportunity to eat breakfast since she hadn't eaten the night before.

***

'Phoebe!' Nick yelled as he struggled with the door. It wouldn't open. He twisted and yanked hard, almost tugged his arm out of the socket before he realised the little minx had twitched the security lock. By the time he figured out how to open the damn door and stepped outside, there was no sign of Phoebe. 'Damn woman,' he muttered under his breath while he strode to the nearest corner and peered along the street. She had him tied up in knots. To find her gone last night had sent his innards twisting like the winds of a tornado and the debris settled in an uncomfortable pile in the pit of his stomach, which resulted in another sleepless night while he wracked his brain as to why she would leave with a damned note which was all polite and proper, sappy with appreciation and glowing words: none of which he believed. There had never even been a hint of her moving out; no arguments or disharmony. He thought they had been

160

getting on so well. The weekend had been one of the best he had ever spent with a woman. He snorted at the memory of how often he had to fight the continuous urge to drag her into his bed or kiss her senseless.

So why did she manage a mysterious disappearing act every time he wanted to speak with her over the past two days? And how come she hadn't seen his note? They always left memos in the same spot and every day she hit the kitchen first the minute she arrived home. Every day she dropped the infernal bag she carried everywhere with her, filled up a glass with water and drank it down in one go - until last night. He scoffed, the sound a cross between a snort and groan.

With his mind in a turmoil, he walked the block, peeked down each driveway, in windows and behind shrubs. It was the second time she had condemned him to reside in purgatory and both times because she misunderstood his words. He snorted. She rarely gave him a chance to explain what he meant. Instead, she chastised him before he even got half the words out.

He stopped and leant against a brick fence. Why was she so touchy about dates and friends? It had to be insecurity. He set off again to continue his search while thought tumbled. Some awful incident must have happened in her past to make her so sensitive; something which dug deep with hurt. The fiancé? He didn't think so because she hadn't wept buckets about his defection or seemed upset after the initial disbelief. In fact, he got the impression she had been relieved the idiot had ditched her. He didn't believe for one minute her fanciful story about why she left. She left because she believed he had stood her up. Which meant she needed to find a bed on the spur of the moment. Hotels! He would search nearby lodgings.

Happy he figured a solution, Nick quickened his pace and returned to his car. He was about to turn the key when he glanced up at the units. He doubted she would have cooled

161

down enough to return, but he checked regardless. With no sign of her, he rang his office to cancel the day's meetings. He sighed. Again. Since Phoebe had arrived on the scene the impeccable orderliness of his business had been shot to pieces. He kept finding the slightest excuse to cancel meetings, knock back excellent deals, nit-pick on minor details, and somehow spent too much time seeking out Phoebe – just to spend a few minutes with her. The need to check on the progress of the re-decoration was the excuse each time. And why not? His reputation depended on units worthy of inspection by the prospective buyer but deep in his gut he knew it wasn't the real reason.

A long, deep sigh escaped his lips as he drove away to search for hotels and boarding houses within a two-kilometre radius. He wanted her. Badly. And he couldn't have her. His shoulders slumped. Maybe she had done him a favour by moving out. With her out of sight maybe she would also move out of his mind. Fat chance.

Sixteen

She had been hiding from him - for three interminable days and it had driven him nuts at first. He thought about the fruitless day he spent knocking on doors of bed and breakfast places, hotels and boarding houses, even after he'd extended the radius to five kilometres. The wasted and frustrating day had meant the necessity of back-to-back meetings for the next two, which resulted in no free time to visit the units between the hours of nine and five. He frowned at the memory when he'd swung by the units before and after work at various times in an attempt to catch Phoebe but each time he was told, 'Phoebe has been but has just stepped out.' It hadn't taken him long to figure out it was a deliberate ploy of hers to not be in the units between eight and nine each day or after five in the evenings, his usual time to check on work progress. She wanted space: he had given it to her, but no longer.

He drew his car to a halt against the kerb and smiled. She was in there now for certain. A phone call to Loukas Novros from the new tiling team had confirmed Phoebe's presence. But not for long. Nick was about to kidnap her. The tilers needed the weekend to complete the entry floor without the presence of any other workers. Tiles today, grout tomorrow.

To make sure Phoebe wasn't on the lookout for his car, he parked half a block away, out of sight of any of the windows. On foot, he made his way down a laneway, wove between the dusty potholes and mounds of dirt. He shoved a gap in the temporary corrugated iron safety fence and strode into the completed underground car park of his building. After dusting off his shoes he paused and studied the two secure parking bays for each unit, alongside a decent sized storage facility for items like bicycles and sporting equipment. It hadn't cost much to build them but they were a strong positive feature when the units went on the market. He should know since he had lived in various units in his adulthood: none of which had sensible storage space.

It took a minute to find the right key to unlock the security door. When he reached the stairwell he trod as quiet as he could as he rose. If Phoebe heard him, she would skedaddle. He paused halfway to listen. She was discussing the floor with the men. When she laughed a shimmy of pleasure wound across his shoulders. Damn but he missed her. He crept higher, increased his pace the moment the floor came into view for there was no way he could hide his presence now. Good, her back was turned which gave him a chance to get closer. Loukas spied him and raised his hand. Phoebe twisted her head around.

'Kalimera,' said Loukas.

'Morning,' said Nick, a second before he noticed Phoebe's lips tighten. The lady wasn't pleased she'd been caught but too bad. Her twitchy nerves were obvious but he figured the nervous edge would persist while she waited for him to mention the way she had moved out. Well she could wait until the world ended for the topic wasn't on his agenda today. Instead, he would act as though life was normal and Miss Phoebe Jackson was in for more than one surprise over the next forty-eight hours.

'The floor looks fabulous.' Nick turned to give the floor a close inspection but kept between Phoebe and her escape route. Even with the still bare two-metre strip from the front door to the unit door, the design looked incredible.

'You don't mind if I steal Phoebe from you?' Nick reached out and grasped Phoebe's wrist. A wave of heat swept through him followed by a tightening of the gut.

She pulled back. 'I have work to do.'

He didn't ease his hold as he eyed her. 'Loukas has already told me he doesn't want any workers here today, which includes you.' He grinned at the scowl she sent Loukas's way. 'I have a surprise for you and we need to leave now.'

***

Phoebe held her breath at the warmth from Nick's hand when it settled against the small of her back. Unsure how to react, she forced her body to relax and let her breath expand in her chest: a chest which ached with need. She didn't understand why she was so uptight. Nick didn't know how fond she was of him. He didn't know about her shame or about her jealousy. He didn't know friendship wasn't all she wanted. She gave herself a mental shake. She wanted more from him: more than he would ever give her and she just had to accept it would never happen.

Gentle nudges led her to the top step which led underground, where she paused 'Where are we going?'

'To my car.'

'Smart, then where?'

Nick chuckled and gave her a gentle shove. They began to descend; their steps echoed against the concrete walls. 'You have seen nothing other than a few sections of the city, and Athens isn't what Greece is all about. So today we will visit one of the islands.'

Excitement shimmied through her belly and went further. A detailed exploration of some islands had been her original intention when she first compiled her itinerary. Most on her father's recommendation. When they reached the bottom step, she darted her eyes around. So far there had been no time or reason to venture down here. 'Are these bays for the tenants?'

165

'Yes, two bays each.' One hand indicated towards a large shed-like structure. 'And there was enough room to give each unit a large secure storage area.'

When they continued on towards odd, coloured sheets of iron, Phoebe became mystified. They reached a gap.

'Through here.' Nick leant on a loose sheet, widened the gap and yanked the sheets together after they passed through. His hand returned to her back, exerted pressure to indicate which way she was to turn.

'Why didn't you park out the front?'

Nick leant forwards and laughed. His hot breath fanned her ear. 'So you could manage one of your vanishing acts the moment you spotted my car? Not this time. I spotted you when you peered out the front window when I arrived.'

What could she say? He was right but no way in the world would she be game to admit it. Not concentrating, she tripped and glanced down as Nick's arm slid around her waist and tugged her close.

'Careful.'

She was so caught up in her thoughts while they made their way along a laneway she hadn't noticed the uneven slabs. Concentrate, she ordered her brain but had to skip to step over another uneven patch.

They rounded the corner onto the pathway. *Click, click.* Nick pressed the remote to his car. He opened the passenger door and stood aside. Always the proverbial gentleman, which she liked. Too many guys these days didn't have a clue. She scoffed. Brad for instance, had never stood aside for her and was always first through the door. Shoot but she had been a fool. But it was the way people were brought up. Sad really. She supposed it was one of the shortcomings of the feminist movement. Equal rights etcetera, but she enjoyed it when a guy showed respect and was protective. It gave her the sense she was important to someone and was wanted. Wrong thought. Nick had a girlfriend and didn't want Phoebe. But Nick was just Nick – thoughtful and well -

gentlemanly. Such an old-fashioned word but it felt so darned good even though it would never last.

Unfamiliar with the scene outside, she assumed they were on their way to the ferry terminal, Phoebe gazed at the passing scenery while Nick drove. The silence began to unnerve her but she didn't know how to break it. It took too long before she realised she recognised a few features: a grove of eucalyptus trees alongside the newish freeway. She twisted her shoulders towards Nick. 'Are we headed towards the airport?'

He smiled. 'Yes.'

'I thought we would go by ferry.'

'Quicker by air, which gives us more time to sightsee.'

This conversation felt safe. 'Which island are we going to?'

'Naxos.' He paused. 'I've missed you, Phoebe.'

Why, oh, why did he have to bring up topics she had been doing her darndest to avoid? This was what she didn't want to discuss because he would ask questions to which she had no answers, or at least none she wanted to divulge. Too scare he would notice the heat from the inside of her cheeks, she turned to the side window.

'Where are you living?'

Darn it but he was going to give her the third degree. 'Near work.' Well, it wasn't lie – well, maybe a weenie white lie.

'Hotel?'

At least she could answer this question with honesty. 'No,' she said to the window.

When he laughed in response her head twisted around of its own accord. He stared straight ahead.

'What's so funny?'

'You are. But I don't see what the big deal is. What does it matter where you live or why you wanted to leave? You are a mature adult who wanted independence. I understand. You wanted your own space? Fine by me but to be

167

unavailable every time I drop by can't go on. Apart from the fact I am your boss, I needed to tell you about today, but since you made yourself unavailable you now have to spend the next two days with only the clothes you have on right now.'

'Two days? But…'

Nick laughed. 'Yes, the entire weekend.'

Far out. A range of emotions hit at the same time. Chagrin, confusion, embarrassment and his supercilious tone unnerved her. 'I need clean clothes.'

'We can buy what you need. I packed a new toothbrush for you along with a few basics and since you are so fond of a T-shirt to sleep in, I have one of mine for you.'

Her blood heated. Oh, my. The thought of his aroma wrapped around while she slept sent hot pulses to places she never dreamed could be so sensitive to a mere image.

After he parked the car and retrieved a small travel bag from the boot, Nick led her to an inter-island departure lounge, his long strides almost impossible to keep up with. His haste gave her the impression they didn't have a lot of time to wait for he strode to a customer service counter and handed over some paperwork. So he already had the tickets.

'Come,' he beckoned, turned and strode towards a large door with *departure* written over the top in letters large enough she couldn't miss them. She had just about had enough of his lord and master tactics so she planted her feet and remained where she was and watched him disappear through the opening. But it wasn't Nick who returned. Her jaw gaped when his brother appeared with a concerned frown spread over his face.

'Are you coming?' he asked.

Stunned, Phoebe planted her hands on her hips and stood her ground. 'Why are you here?'

'Nick hasn't told you?'

'Told me what?'

Alexos muttered under his breath in Greek, reached for her and grasped her wrist. 'I'll explain as we go but we must hurry, the plane is ready for take-off.'

Even though she tugged hard, the grip around her wrist didn't ease. She scowled at Nick's grin when he stood aside to let her board before him. Gentleman, my foot. Darn man was enjoying this.

It wasn't until they were seated and buckled in Phoebe folded her arms and set her face into the fiercest look she could muster. 'I don't care who tells me but I insist someone explain what the hell this is all about? If we were sightseeing, Alexos wouldn't be here.'

Alexos leant across the aisle. 'We think we may have found your fiancé.'

'Think? And don't call him my fiancé. Jerk, sounds much better.'

'A man fitting the description you gave us left a hotel in Santorini without paying his bill but he used another name. We tracked him to Naxos where he booked into one of the better hotels under yet another name. I need you to give us a positive I.D. so we can arrest him.'

'Why wasn't I told about this?'

Alexos shrugged his shoulders and indicated with his head towards Nick who was seated next to her against the window. Phoebe turned around and raised her eyebrows.

'How could I tell you when you made yourself unavailable every time I tried to track you down?'

'I was there every day while the men worked.'

'And I was snowed under with meetings every day and am certain if I had found the time to turn up at the units at *any* time over the past couple of days, you,' he tapped her on the end of her nose, 'would have stepped out for some mysterious errand.'

She knew her guilt was obvious by the way Nick smiled and how her cheeks flamed from the inside. She didn't dare raise her hands to her face to gauge the heat but instead

169

yanked the emergency chart from the pocket in front of her and pretended a studious study of every word even though it was impossible to make out a single letter.

Seventeen

Nervous wasn't an apt word to describe how Phoebe felt but she was too uptight to think of a better word. Her innards were doing somersaults and there was a hard and huge lump lodged in her throat. It was ridiculous to be so scared for Nick stood right beside her and Alexos had gone ahead and was now somewhere inside. She rubbed her sweaty palms down the front of her dress.

A dress, for goodness sake. When did she last wear a dress? And it was so short, leaving her skinny legs exposed all the way from the toes, which peeked out of strappy flat sandals, to halfway up her thigh. She was almost naked. Even her shoulders and arms were bare except for the narrow straps which barely held up the skimpy amount of soft cotton fabric. A shiver wanted to take control of her body at the memory of Nick taking her into a fashion-wear shop, where he flicked through the racks, unhooked dress after dress and plonked them into her arms. To add to her humiliation he had dared to examine each garment after she had put it on. At Nick's insistence the sale's assistant had flung the privacy curtain back each time Phoebe had struggled into an outfit. He nodded or shook his head after an intense study of her from head to toe each time. How embarrassing. Even worse was the addition of luxurious underwear which had appeared soon after a lengthy conversation, in Greek, between Nick and the assistant. To top it all off, he had insisted he paid the bill for three brand new outfits, his birthday gift to her.

Now, here she was, dressed in next to nothing, about to front the bane of her recent life, Bradley Evans.

171

'Are you ready?' When Nick swung an arm around her shoulders and gave a little tug, she shuddered, not from fear this time but because every time Nick touched her, her body seemed to explode in pleasure and want, which was why she had made sure there had been so little contact with him. It was easier to not see him at all than have him so close – especially when he was unavailable to her.

No, she wasn't ready, she wanted to say. 'Yes, about as ready as I'll ever be. Do I have to do this? What if he's not in there?'

'The officer who has followed him for the past twenty-four hours said Brad was at the bar.' Nick leant closer and whispered in her ear. 'How about we show him you haven't been bothered about his obnoxious behaviour?'

Nick's hot breath sent waves of shivery pleasure to every extremity. Heaven forbid, this was not good.

'Huh, how?'

Nick eased her closer, not that her body let her resist. 'Just follow my lead.' With an open palm, he shoved at the swing door of the beachside taverna and muscled Phoebe across the threshold.

What did he mean by follow his lead?

With his arm still in a firm hold around her shoulders, he forced her a few steps inside, spun her around, dropped his head and his lips melded with hers. Oh, my! Her blood surged and boiled while her traitorous body melted and plastered itself against Nick's hard length. His lips were soft and warm yet firm as they super-glued against her mouth. A quiet groan rumbled from his chest moments before his tongue ran along the seam of her mouth in a blatant request to seek entry. Despite the way her brain screamed 'no,' her mouth argued, won, and opened of its own accord.

It took too long, yet not long enough to come to her senses. He has a girlfriend, her conscience managed to recall. Phoebe forced her lips away. 'Why did you do that?' she stammered, her voice not sounding at all like hers.

172

With his mouth still inches from hers, Nick grinned. 'Well, first and most important because I've hankered to kiss you again since the first time.' He drew away further. 'It is also because those cute lips of yours always beg to be kissed and I couldn't resist a moment longer.' His arms drew her closer. 'And third, because we are being watched by someone who deserves to be taught a lesson.' His head swooped down again.

This time his kiss was longer and deeper. She resisted, but her mouth argued, softened, opened and he took full advantage of her submission. Swept into the realm of sensual bliss, Phoebe lost all sense of time and place. Staggered by the depth of her reaction, she found the strength to draw back when a little niggle in her conscience telling her she shouldn't do this, turned to a sharp stab – he had a girlfriend.

'It gets better and better,' murmured Nick with a smile 'Do you think we might have convinced the jerk?'

The reality of what had just happened blossomed into a brain which had lost all reason. Phoebe jerked away. What was she doing – and in a public place full of people? Her eyes darted around the room. The air whooshed from her lungs when she spotted the man who watched them from across the room. Was he always so loose skinned? Their eyes caught and she knew the moment comprehension dawned on Brad's face. It was obvious he had just recognised her. A stunned look turned to a frown seconds before he swung the almost full glass up onto the bar. When the frown turned to horror he grabbed his wallet, twisted around and ran but managed a few steps before Alexos loomed in front of him, his badge held high.

'It's him, now I want to get out of here,' Phoebe grated and turned away, desperate to get out of this heel hole.

Nick tightened his grip on her shoulders. 'No stay. You need to sort this out.'

She went rigid. 'No way. I can't face him, not now.'

'Let me do the talking but apart from the money he stole, he owes you an explanation and an apology.'

A deep groan rolled up from the pit of her stomach and rumbled out. This might get ugly. To date, she had never heard any form of apology escape Brad's mouth for any reason. Shoot, why hadn't she figured this out before? Had she been so infatuated with the mere idea of a man being interested enough to remain with her for four months of travel that she had been blind to his faults? But she had no experience to compare him with - until now. Nick was the epitome of the type of man she wanted. But now she had found the right man, he was unavailable. Typical.

With her body anchored against Nick by his arm, she had no choice but to walk beside him. They wove through the patrons who sat at small square tables laden with various dishes of Greek cuisine and carafes of wine. Her stomach threatened to rid itself of the coffee and Baklava they had enjoyed after the clothes-buying spree. Even though she had to swallow down rising bile, they kept on, one scary step at a time. By the time they reached the bar, Brad had his arms handcuffed behind his back with what looked to be a plain clothes officer each side of him. Both men were dressed in the same casual wear of the many locals and tourists she had seen on the island.

Alexos rifled through Brad's wallet, inspected each card and slip of paper he came across and kept a couple of items out, which he placed on the bar. The atmosphere buzzed with conversation and she was certain every eye was fixed on her: had followed her journey to the gallows.

Alexos glanced up. 'Phoebe, can you confirm this man is Bradley Evans?' The serious tone of his voice startled her but she figured this was serious business and now was not the time for casual conversation. She figured he wouldn't even want her to acknowledge she knew him as Nick's brother.

'Yes.' She coughed to clear her throat when the word came out as a shivery squeak. Shoot but she was so nervous. 'Bitch.' Brad hissed.

'Excuse me?' Such venom from Brad startled her. Never before had he shown such a nasty streak. Well, maybe to leave her with his hotel bill was pretty nasty and there was the small fact of how he was the one who might have stolen her money but right now she couldn't be certain.

Brad stepped towards her, right into her personal space. 'You are a frigid bitch,' he spat before an officer yanked him back so hard, Brad stumbled then hit the bar. Bottles and glasses on top rattled.

Phoebe froze but Nick laughed at the same time he gave her a little squeeze. 'Are you for real? Phoebe is the most sensuous, sexy and gorgeous woman around.'

When her cheeks turned into an instant inferno, Phoebe swung her head sideways to find herself staring into eyes burning with passion. Oh, my.

Nick shot her a quick smile then turned back to Brad. 'On the flight from Australia, Phoebe slept in my arms all the way.'

A bomb detonated in her cheeks.

'As soon as we collected her backpack from the hotel she moved into my townhouse with me. We have lived together ever since.'

Phoebe now understood what it felt like to combust instantaneously but all Nick said was true. What he didn't say meant a whole heap more but she could see why Nick said what he did. Brad's stunned face told a different story. Revenge had a very sweet tinge.

'I don't believe you,' Brad snarled. 'Phoebe doesn't have the guts to get off her Arctic high horse.'

Phoebe saw red when a surge of anger bristled and raged. The bastard deserved to receive some of his own medicine. Staring him the eye, she straightened her spine. 'Everything Nick said is true. He is far more a man than you could ever hope to be. You are a snivelling wimp who tries to suck women into your seedy web. I am so glad I saw you for what you are. I said yes to your proposal to get you off my back with your continual, not so subtle hints about how much cheaper it would be to share a room. I knew money wasn't the issue but more of a way for you to get me into your bed. It was so darn obvious. Do you honestly believe I would be stupid enough to marry you? While I was home I had plenty of time to think and see you for the kind of person you are. I led you on when we spoke on the phone while I was home. I had no intention to continue to travel with you after I'd met a real man. All I needed was my backpack. Living with Nick has shown me what a real relationship is all about.' She lied through her teeth but it sure felt good to pay the creep back and even better was his stunned face.

Brad hissed a split second before he surged forward and lifted a leg ready to kick out at her.

In an instant, Nick spun Phoebe aside and positioned himself in the line of fire but the kick managed to slash mid-air. 'Don't you dare threaten my woman.'

His woman? Oh, my. If only it was true.

Alexos laid a calming hand on Nick's shoulder. 'Take it easy, Nick.' He held up a small card. 'Phoebe, do you recognise this?'

The blood drained from her face at the recognition of the small plastic card. Thoughts surged and tangled themselves in her mind before clarity came forth. 'You did steal my money. Why would you be so mean to me?'

'I stole nothing.' Brad yelled and struggled to free arms which were held tight. The other two officers gripped an elbow each and brought Brad's struggles to an end. His face said he lied. His eyes dropped, his Adam's apple bobbed and a pink flush stole up his neck. Bradley Evans blushed?

'We have a record of the exact time and place of every transaction made from this account since the day Phoebe returned to Australia. We also have security photos of the person who made those transactions. You even smiled for the camera.' Alexos sounded so officious yet there was a hint of smugness.

'You never told me,' Phoebe glared at Alexos. Why hadn't they told her about their discovery? She had a right to know.

'We collated all the details two days ago and it seems my message never reached you.' Alexos raised his eyebrows in a silent question but he turned up the corners of his mouth in a sort of half smile.

He knew, darn it. Just how much had Nick said to him? She bet it had made an interesting little chat. Mortified, Phoebe focussed back onto the present conversation and realised Brad was being arrested.

'Unfortunately for you,' said Alexos to Brad, 'the legal system here is not as lenient as it is in Australia. You will spend time in a Greek prison until your court appearance where you will be forced to make financial restitution to all the parties you have robbed. Apart from Phoebe there are three hotels I know of with a claim. I will make enquiries to see if there are any others. My advice to you is to contact family members back home to have the money repaid before your court appearance if you want a lighter sentence. And let me add, local prisons are nowhere as luxurious as those in Australia.'

Brad looked so horrified Phoebe had a brief hitch of sorrow towards him. Life in gaol wouldn't be pleasant, even less so in a foreign prison. His face crumbled at the same speed he dropped to his knees. It was a shock when he turned his face up to Phoebe and sent her a puppy dog look. 'Phoebe you can't let them do this to me, you can't press charges.'

Stunned, she couldn't believe her eyes or ears. Incapable of uttering a single word, she stared at Brad. He looked and sounded so pathetic. She didn't know what to say. He deserved to be punished but could she let him wallow in some foreign gaol?

'Phoebe isn't the one who is laying the charges,' said Alexos. 'I am. You broke Greek law. I am an officer of the law. At this very minute I have two officers searching your room and your belongings. You need to pray we don't find any other untoward evidence for bail is not easy to obtain here in Greece, especially foreigners who might think they can flee the country. Let's get out of here.' Alexos inclined his head towards the front door.

Nick placed one arm around Phoebe's waist and pressed into the small of her back to force her around. Oh, how embarrassing. It was as though every customer in the room had turned into stunned statues, all of which gawped – at her. It was stupid to think she was the centre of attention for all eyes remained on something behind her as she walked through the room but it sure felt as though they were trained on her. She supposed it was a rather spectacular lunchtime floorshow.

***

All he could think as he shepherded her outside was how Phoebe and the moron never shared rooms the entire time they travelled together. The news pleased him a great deal, but had they slept together? It made sense they had for there must have been some sort of physical interaction between them for Phoebe to agree to marry the man. But she deserved much better than this cold-hearted, pathetic cad.

'Phoebe, please, you can't let them take me away. You owe me.' At the sound of the whining voice, Phoebe stilled and jerked around so hard, Nick felt as though she had wrenched his arm out of the socket.

'I owe you?' Her tone turned the air into instant icicles and sent a shudder of fear through Nick. Man was he glad it wasn't him she was mad at. Three simple words which usually meant a thank you but the way Phoebe let the words roll it wasn't a compliment. He tweaked his shoulder to check it was still joined to his body the way it should be and turned to watch but kept close enough to intervene if needed.

'What do I owe you?' Phoebe narrowed her eyes and stretched tall with her hands on her hips.

Thank God the punk was still held a safe distance away, thought Nick.

'Well, Jeeze, Phoebe, I traipsed around all those blasted gardens and waited interminable hours while you *oohed* and *aahed* and drew copious pictures. Talk about boring with a capital B. I followed you around for four months, spending all my savings while I waited for you to mellow and where did it get me?'

Phoebe's mouth gaped and eyes widened in shock. Instead of her usual blush which rose with such ease, the blood seemed to have retracted from her face in an instant and now left it ashen.

'You traipsed around after me?' she squeaked before she stepped forward, her face a fierce scowl.

As Nick closed the gap he tensed in readiness.

'Listen here, Buddy,' said Phoebe with one finger jabbing at Brad's chest. It must have been hard for Brad winced.

'You talked me into having dinner with you, *after* I explained why it wasn't such a clever idea because I was about to go overseas for eight months. And I paid for my share of the meal when you were too measly to pay after you talked me into a date. It was *you* who insisted you wanted to join me on my study holiday even after I detailed my itinerary. *You* agreed we would both pay our own way in every aspect: travel, food, accommodation, entertainment and incidentals so neither of us was indebted to the other for a single cent. *You* also agreed it was not an option for me to share a room. I barely knew you for heaven's sake. You also

179

agreed we could go our own way if either one of us thought the togetherness bit didn't work out.'

Nick was proud of her, especially when the other man cowered when Phoebe stepped even closer and invaded the man's personal space with a belligerent pout on her mouth.

'Not once did you mention you wanted to part company and go your own way. Not once did you say you wanted to change the situation and besides, I traipsed after you every time you wanted to spend countless hours in nightclubs and pubs where you drank and caroused until you acted like a first class idiot. If you spent all your money it is because you filtered it all through your kidneys with the copious amount of booze you shoved in your mouth. In the top and out the bottom.' She flapped her hand in the direction of his mouth before it indicated the area below his belt.

Nick swallowed a snort, stunned at her words.

'And then,' Phoebe continued her tirade, 'you asked me to marry you. A man does *not* propose if he hates the company so much.' Phoebe stepped back and wheezed in a breath; her chest heaved. 'Oh I know why you proposed and it wasn't with the intention of a happy ever after marriage. You thought a proposal would get you into my knickers. Why do you think I took so long to sort and pack my gear? Why do you think I wasted even more time in the bathroom? Idiot!' she spat, spun away and hissed at Nick under her breath, 'Can we please go?' Without waiting for an answer she stomped down the two steps and stalked along the cobbled pathway.

After catching Alexos' eye and receiving a nod, Nick chased after her, caught up and kept pace. He didn't have a clue what to do. He wanted to place an arm around her shoulders and tug her close but her demeanour shot out definite vibes to leave her alone. Instead, he decided to stay close and be there once she stalked off her anger. It seemed she made a habit of pounding off frustration and insecurity and right now, he guessed her insecurity was at an all-time

180

low. Good to know now he had figured it out. Her passage took them along the edge of the road which hugged the water's edge. As she strode, Phoebe muttered to herself with the occasional unpleasant comment and a few not so lady-like words which were far more audible. He wasn't certain who she was mad at: him, herself or the ex.

They stepped onto the road to pass a trio of young fishermen who sat on small round stools immersed in intimate studies of their fishing nets to find any signs of damage as it was coiled. The stench of fishy aroma had his nose twitch. It must have affected Phoebe as well for she made a wide detour onto the road until they were past the stench when she swung back. They reached the boardwalk that led towards the ferry terminus. Phoebe turned sharp left. Nick had no choice but to follow, fearful she might fall amongst the variety of small sea-craft; she was so close to the edge. Most boats were the traditional bright painted wood but a few more modern steel and aluminium run-a-bouts bobbed amongst the rainbow of colour, all attached to colourful buoys.

Phoebe stopped so sudden Nick barrelled into her. He grabbed her upper arms as she wavered. 'Sorry,' he said and immediately dropped his hands, unsure whether she would appreciate his touch. He had never been so uncertain about what to do with a woman.

'I'm a complete idiot aren't I?' Phoebe said with her eyes staring directly into his for the first time.

How was he supposed to answer such a question? He cast his eyes around and caught sight of several long wooden benches in front of the ferry gate. He indicated with his right hand, 'Why don't we sit here for a moment?' He didn't give her a chance to reply but palmed the small of her back and guided her across the jetty planks. On closer inspection the seats looked ancient but still sturdy. The thick slats had weathered to a pearl grey but had been worn smooth by years of constant use: too smooth to carry splinters.

'First, Phoebe, you are no idiot. The one person I would give such a moniker to is Bradley Evans. Second, why did you agree to marry him?' Nick eased one arm along the top of the seat behind her, still too afraid to touch.

Phoebe sighed with her eyes studying the water which rippled with the slight breeze. It took her several seconds before her eyes lifted and she gulped several times. Long seconds when Nick wondered whether or not she would answer.

'I thought we got on well and figured it would be the only chance I would ever have of marriage.' She turned her head away as though embarrassed by her confession.

Her honesty stunned him. Why would she think such an insane concept? Snippets of past conversations raced through his mind. *Un-dateable* stabbed to the forefront. Maybe Phoebe was more inexperienced than he thought.

'You never slept with him, did you?'

Her body stiffened. 'None of your business.' Her chin hit her chest but he spied a splodge of red on the small visible section of her cheek.

'True, but from your conversation back there,' he wavered his hand in the direction of the taverna, 'I am certain it was the gist of the tongue-lashing you gave young Bradley. You hinted the reason he proposed was to get you into his bed.'

What sounded like a strangled groan came from Phoebe's direction before she lifted her head. 'It was a conclusion I came to after the hotel incident. When he proposed I thought he loved me. He said he did. Like a fool, I believed him. But now it is obvious it was a ploy to keep sweet with me while I was back home so he could empty my bank account at the rate of the $1,000 euro limit a day. Which makes me a first-class idiot.'

Nick dropped his arm to rest on her shoulders and dared to tighten his grip to give her a hug. He wanted to draw her closer, much closer. He wanted to absorb her pain so she didn't hurt any longer and to give her all the good things she deserved.

'You were taken in by a smooth, callous leech. I am sure you aren't the only woman this man has preyed upon and you won't be the last. Think positive. The jerk will spend time in prison to pay for the crimes he has committed since he arrived in this country and more important, you are free of him. Now, I hired a car for the afternoon so how about we toss aside unpleasant thoughts for a while and spend the rest of our time here exploring the island. I know of a few spectacular sights you might enjoy and we could even seek out a few village gardens. I promise I won't find them boring.'

It was a pleasant surprise when she turned to him and sent him the barest of smiles. 'Sounds perfect although I figured we'd be returning to Athens now scumbag has been arrested.'

'We could have returned on the afternoon flight but I didn't think you would want to be on the same flight Evans will be on. Alexos is taking him back to the mainland today.'

A shudder wove across Phoebe's shoulders before she peeked at him. 'Good point, thank you.'

Eighteen

Exhaustion had set in to the extent Phoebe's eyes hovered closed the entire time Nick drove them from the airport. It was a mammoth fight to keep them open. There wasn't much of Naxos they hadn't explored over the past thirty hours which resulted in little sleep. The amazing experience had been much better than she had expected from her studies of the Greek islands and with Nick as her guide, it had made the experience even more exciting. With him able to speak the language they had gained access to a couple of private gardens where she had studied the layout and speak, through Nick's translations, with the owners. It had surprised her how delightful and welcoming the people had been.

She thought about her favourite garden on the far side of the island. The small plot of a few acres had been in the family for generations. The grove of ancient olive trees supplied fruit and oil to family, friends plus regular café's and shops for years, which gave the family a steady income. Next to the grove stood a line of a few different varieties of citrus trees, several rows of grapes, both red and white and a lush vegetable garden with an intriguing system of open trenched irrigation. The soil was rich and friable where it shouldn't have been, given the bedrock but generations of dug-in humus had built it into a paradise most home gardeners would be jealous of. Nothing went to waste. Unwanted stems and leaves were laid as mulch between new plants to protect them from the harsh sun and retain moisture. After harvest, the rotted mulch was dug into the soil to enrich it for the next crop. And they had crop rotation down to an artform.

What warmed her heart was how, even though the people were poor compared to Sydney standards, they were happy and content with their lives. They could afford the basic necessities of life through hard manual labour and a well set up barter system. They had few luxuries but were so content with their humble lifestyle. It was a subsistence life in the traditional villages but there were none of the stresses of life in a bustling city where people never stopped to appreciate the simple things, had to have the best of everything but still weren't happy when they had them. She could live this more humble type of life.

When she noticed they were almost in Athens, Phoebe forced her eyelids apart and straightened. 'Just drop me off at the units. I want to see the entry hall.' It had taken her ages to come up with a logical reason for Nick to leave her at the units. Worry had kept her awake last night when her body had screamed for sleep, for she knew Nick would be the gentleman and insist on taking her to her new home. He was that type of guy.

'Good idea,' said Nick with a chuckle. 'Did you enjoy your little nap?'

'I wasn't asleep – just rested my eyeballs.'

Nick laughed. 'If you weren't asleep how come you didn't answer when I asked you a question?'

She peeked at him. A wide grin spread across his face. 'Oh, umm, what did you want to know?'

He laughed again. 'Whether or not you wanted to inspect the entry floor before I took you home.'

'Oh.' Shoot, how to get out of this mess?

The rest of the journey was silent. While she mulled over ideas on how to get away, Nick concentrated on a safe passage through hectic traffic. So many drivers ignored the traffic lights, shot through intersections at the last second. The locals were used to the kamikaze driving but it scared the bejesus out of her to the extent she would never drive in Athens, even if she was begged. She couldn't figure out where people parked their cars during the day for there never seemed to be anywhere near as many parking spaces as there were vehicles.

When Nick pulled against the kerb right in front of the units, Phoebe still hadn't come up with a solution. She shot from the vehicle, grabbed her daypack from where it was stowed next to her feet and went to the boot to retrieve her new purchases which she had managed to pack into the one large paper bag. She grimaced at the flash of memory from earlier in the morning. Uncomfortable wearing a dress, she donned her old jeans for the day's adventure. Before she managed to cross the lounge area of their two-bedroom suite, Nick had called her to stop. 'No jeans,' he insisted and threatened to peel the denim from her body if she didn't change into one of her new outfits. His stance, when he began a purposeful prowl towards her with a determined glint in his eye, had given every indication he would carry out his threat so she had retreated and changed.

'Leave those.' Phoebe jumped at the growl from right behind her. She clenched her fist around the cord handles, took a deep breath but eased her fingers open. She could always get her clothes at a later date. Better to not give him any clues about her plan to elude him – somehow. She had to, for she was certain Nick would be a true gentleman and insist on walking her to the door of any abode she said she was staying at. If he did, and he would, she would be in a real pickle. But there was no way she would leave her backpack so she slung it over her shoulder and backed away from the car.

'You can leave your backpack as well,' said Nick.

'No way. I already lost one debit card along with all my money. All of my essential paperwork, including my passport, is in here so I keep it with me at all times.' She stepped past Nick and headed for the front door of the units but frowned when she realised it still hadn't been painted. Tomorrow. First on the list and second - she would purchase a few potted bushes to place on each end of every step to give a more welcoming appearance. Conifers: large enough so they would be too heavy to steal but trimmed into similar shapes to give a classical elegance. The type of plant that could withstand little water and lots of heat. It was a task she could do with ease and it would give her joy to work with plants again.

When she reached the top of the stairs she had to fumble around in her bag for her set of keys but Nick beat her, reached over her shoulder to insert his key in the lock.

'Allow me.' He twisted the doorknob before pushing the door inwards. His touch sent a wave of awareness through her innards. And of course, Mr Perfect stood back to allow the lady in first.

She couldn't help the unseen roll of her eyes and tiny smile as she stepped inside the dark foyer, reached up to the wall and switched on the light. The sight in front of her brought her to a standstill. Even though there was still a skim of dried grout over the tiles, the floor looked way better than she had imagined.

'You are a genius.' Nick moved to her side and slung an arm around her waist. 'I never thought these units could be this... I can't think of the right word. Elegant isn't quite right. Maybe classy.'

'You need to give credit to the tilers.'

'Oh, I will but you created this magnificent design. This is beyond impressive. I am more than thankful I wasn't able get a business class seat. I might even consider a visit to your young Bradley to thank him for being such a jerk.' Nick tightened his hold and gave Phoebe a hug.

He must have felt her tense for he eased back a fraction. She prayed it was because he thought it was the mention of Brad that had her on tenterhooks but her body managed to go on high alert every time Nick came anywhere near her. All weekend her nerves had been on edge, her blood heated and surged while her innards clenched, like they were right now. The last thing she wanted was to be reminded of what a fool she had been. And she was even more foolish to allow her passion for Nick to take such a firm hold. She had to keep reminding herself he wasn't available.

Embarrassed at the accolades, she eased from his hold. It had taken her a few years to learn how to accept kudos with grace but she could never understand what all the fuss was about. She didn't have any special talents. Colours just came together in her head and somehow they worked when applied. But interior design wasn't what gave her the biggest kicks. To create beautiful green, living spaces from a neglected weed-infested patch of dirt was where she received her biggest thrills.

Even though she was delighted with the way the entry hall had come up, Phoebe moved around the room pretending an intimate study while she attempted to calm her traitorous body and rid her mind of thoughts of Nick and how close they had been over the weekend. It made her wonder how faithful Nick was to his girlfriend. The very fact he didn't even baulk when he kissed Phoebe on more than one occasion, and he regularly touched her in what she regarded as intimacy, indicated less than faithful behaviour: another *not so perfect* mark to him. She savoured the memories of his arm slung around her waist and shoulders, the many hugs and times they stood so close with more than one part of their body touching and how those touched parts seemed to scorch whenever it happened.

'Let's inspect the display unit.'

Phoebe jolted out of her daydream. When did he move so close to her again? Shoot, but she must keep alert.

'Okay.' She turned, stepped away and hurried across the foyer, to the unit's front door, now painted the softest of gold with the panels picked out in burgundy. The unlocked door opened with ease and she kept on, determined to keep as much space between them as possible.

Much to her chagrin, Nick took his time in each room, studying walls, trim, curtains, tiles. He asked continuous pertinent questions as they went and kept moving close to her in the process. The unit was almost complete, even the tiles. All it needed was a good clean and the hardware such as mirrors, towel rails, light fittings and toilet roll holders, to be attached.

They entered the last room; the kitchen Nick's phone rang. He eased it out of his shirt pocket and flipped it open. Now, Phoebe thought, she had her opportunity. She made out she would give him privacy by turning her back and retreating. As soon as she was out of sight, she ran. 'See you tomorrow,' she yelled at the same time she grabbed the front door, opened it and allowed it to slam. In an instant her pulse thrummed at a frantic rate. She spun around and sprinted for the stairs, bolted up them three at a time until she reached the next floor, where she waited in earshot with her chest heaving and her heart in imitation of a drum tattoo. While she listened for movement from Nick, she tried to even out her breaths. Would he think to come upstairs?

Nineteen

Mid-conversation, Nick spun around when Phoebe called out. Damn, where has she gone now and why didn't he even notice her leave? 'Phoebe, wait!' he called then said into the phone, 'I'll call you back.'

With a curse, he dropped the phone on the marble bench and went in search of Phoebe. He had just reached the unit door when the building's heavy main door snicked shut. A quick yank, the door opened. With frustration rising, he strode across the newly laid marble of the entry hall and pulled at the main door. She couldn't have gone far in such a brief time. From the top of the steps he searched both ways along the street and frowned. No Phoebe. Several swear words escaped under his breath while he bounced down the steps to the pavement and turned towards the corner. She had to have gone around the corner for there wasn't a soul in the street. When he rounded the corner he met up with a young couple hurrying towards him. A quick glance beyond the couple indicated no Phoebe. He spun around and searched the opposite direction. A mother pushing a pram, an elderly woman bowed under the weight of three shopping bags which overflowed with groceries, and a businessman with a newspaper tucked under one arm were all headed away from him but there was no woman dressed in the sunny yellow dress he had coerced Phoebe into wearing.

Frustrated, Nick called after the couple, who had now passed him and spoke to them in Greek. Both shook their heads. The woman denied seeing anyone let alone a woman of Phoebe's description.

All he could think of was to drive the nearby streets. He glanced at his building. Lights were still on. It took less than two minutes to switch lights off and secure the building. Once in his car he circled the block, scanned driveways, buildings and yards as he drove. No Phoebe. There was little choice but to widen the search which he did with his mouth screwed into a thin line. He kept to a slow pace so he could peer both ways along streets at intersections while searching another block in each direction. It was as though the woman had vanished into thin air.

'Damn it, Phoebe, where are you?' he muttered as he pulled against the kerb. With the motor still running he leant forwards, the fingers of one hand drummed a restless tattoo on the top of the steering wheel while he thought. Why was Phoebe so evasive about where she now lived? Was it because it was so bad? If so, why did she leave his place at all? Sure, there was a misunderstanding because he left his note in the wrong place but was a forty-five-minute delay enough of a reason for Phoebe to be so disillusioned she was desperate to find other accommodation?

He paused on the thought about the time. He had been home at six forty-five when they were due to leave at seven. There had been no sign of Phoebe yet she claimed to be ready at seven. Not possible for she said she still waited thirty minutes later and fifteen minutes after the time she inferred, he was back. Even though Phoebe was not one to take forever to ready herself for any event, unlike many women he had dated, there was no way she could have packed all her gear and be gone in under fifteen minutes. And she couldn't have showered and dressed in the few minutes before seven. None of this made sense. Had she lied? Maybe but she was a straight shooter, sometimes too straight. So what had spooked her?

He let his thoughts go to Phoebe's general demeanour. It was obvious she was insecure about the dating game. Somewhere, sometime, someone had let down. Evans?

Maybe but he travelled with her and even though they didn't sleep together there must have been a relative closeness for Phoebe to have agreed to marry him. No, someone must have hurt her in the past.

Whenever they were together she showed no signs of inhibition or uncertainty. The weekend had been brilliant, apart from her nervousness at meeting up with Evans, which was understandable. Even he had been on edge. From then on, she had been ebullient and carefree, laughed with ease and had been enthusiastic about every sight and adventure they had experienced.

He frowned when he recalled her request to drop her off at the units and thumped the steering wheel with a fist. He hadn't noticed at the time but she had gone quiet after he mentioned he would join her to inspect the new floor. Hmm, she tried to take her new clothes and seemed miffed when he told her to leave them. Lord, but he was dense. Now he knew why she had wanted them but it didn't explain why she didn't want him to know where she lived. Why?

Nick blew out his cheeks on a long sigh. There was no need to keep searching. If Phoebe was so intent she didn't want to be found, then it was a useless exercise to search for her. Another breath huffed out. Frustrated, he settled back into his seat, checked the side mirrors and pulled back onto the road. He had three meetings tomorrow but somehow he would find a way to steal a couple of hours to have it out with the elusive Miss Jackson to find out what she was up to and why.

As he turned into his driveway, Nick remembered the aborted phone call from Costas who said he had posted an important message which required immediate attention. Taking care to park, he turned off the engine and went to take out his phone. The pocket was empty. The kitchen bench. He had put his phone down. Should he go back? Darn it yes because for Costas to say it was important then it was vital.

193

Nick reversed onto the street and retraced his route; minus the extra detours he'd taken in the search. Even though he knew it was useless he couldn't help but let his eyes search from side-to-side in the hope he would spot a flash of yellow. The new clothes he insisted she buy had given Phoebe a sophisticated elegance but he was certain she had no idea how beautiful she was in clothes which weren't baggy and covered as much skin as possible. The way she fidgeted by tugging the hem down and hitching up the top, indicated how awkward and uncomfortable she was about revealing so much of her svelte body. Did this need to hide her assets have anything to do with her emotional insecurity? It fitted. Had she been abused or even raped? A shudder wove across his shoulders at the thought and he vowed to find out the truth.

When Nick spied a dim trace of light from the second floor of the units when he got closer, he frowned and eased against the kerb on the opposite side of the bitumen. He must have left a light on, maybe the stairwell. Any light from there would creep upwards. He eased from the car, pressed the remote locking device and jogged across the street, keeping to the shadows so he wouldn't be seen.

Darkness pressed against him. His skin twitched at the eerie atmosphere: an eeriness that heightened after he thought back for he was certain he hadn't left any lights on. He took the stairs two at a time, keyed the lock and twisted. Downstairs. Of course! Phoebe didn't leave via the front door. She went down. It must have been the garage door he heard snick shut, which was why he couldn't find her in the street. Sneaky little witch.

With held breath, he shoved the door open, glanced at the stream of light that snuck down the stairwell creating staggered shadows. Puzzled, he paused. Maybe Phoebe hadn't locked the garage door and intruders had entered the premises. It was possible since the rear security fence hadn't yet been installed. If he could get in and out via the temporary fence then so could intruders, although the door to the inside should be secure. Maybe not if Phoebe went out that way. To avoid any noise, he toed off his shoes, tiptoed across the floor and paused in front of the elevators. Soundproofing in the lift-well ensured the elevator was quiet but in this pressing silence maybe the stairs would be a better option.

He crept to the stairwell and began a stealthy climb. The light brightened as he rose, making it easy to see, which negated the possibility of hidden human forms jumping out at him. The first floor landing held no intruders but, just in case, he tested each door as he circled. All secure. He paused before climbing higher, listened for any movement or whispers. There was nothing of value to steal up this high. All construction was completed, as was the plasterwork. He blew out a harsh breath when he remembered the boxes of unattached fittings. Was someone pilfering the hardware? It wouldn't be the first time theft occurred on one of his sites but he thought this building was secure with internal deadbolts.

Unsure and a little afraid, he slowed, took one step at a time, paused on each to force each breath to remain shallow and controlled. There were no objects stored on the stairs to trip over so he kept his eyes trained upwards. The light didn't seem to be bright enough to come from the entry hall so maybe one of the units had been left open or maybe forced.

Expecting a sudden rush of some human eager to escape, Nick took his time to ascend the final few steps. Tense nerves twitched before he dared to let his head rise above floor level. Light spilled from unit four in the rear corner. Clever for it was the least likely to be seen from either road.

To ensure he wasn't seen, he sidled around the perimeter with his back against the wall. With a held breath, he stuck his head around the open doorway. His breath stuttered and eyes boggled at the sight of an almost naked Phoebe on an opened out sleeping bag. She was leant up against the wall with one long leg stretched out and the other bent at the knee. A sketchbook rested on her bent thigh like paper on a lectern while a pencil swept in arcs against the page. His eyes travelled the length of her from the bare toes, along the unblemished smooth skin of her legs and over a hip. A mere strip of coffee coloured lace trimmed with cream satin peeked at him. She had on the lingerie he bought at Naxos and boy, had it been a fight to get her to accept his gift, but God, it suited her.

He swept his eyes higher. Her slender waist was bare but the arm holding the pencil hid her breasts. He wasn't sure if he was disappointed or glad. For once, her hair wasn't restrained by a piece of plain white elastic but flowed loose, the front hiding her face in a sweep forward. A goddess was an apt description. He had already sussed out there was a gorgeous body kept hidden underneath the baggy outfits Phoebe insisted on wearing but reality far surpassed his imagination. His blood thrummed, heated and headed south, forcing him to shift to ease the pressure behind the zipper of his pants while he fought a battle with his mind to centre on anything other than what he wanted to do with the woman. Despite the thinness of the sleeping bag, to stretch Phoebe out along it with him on top sounded like an excellent idea. Maybe if he took her to bed it would cease this instant effect she had on his libido every time he spied her.

Time to have it out with her. Nick straightened. 'Well, this explains a lot,' he called.

There was a loud shriek of fear. Phoebe levitated and twisted around at the same time. The pencil flew across the room and bounced twice while the pad hit the wall with an echoing splat.

'What are you doing here?' Phoebe gasped with a fierce glare speared at him and her splayed hands flung over her heart. Her shoulders heaved, probably because he had scared her half to death. Good, she deserved to be afraid.

'Well, since my name is on the title deeds to this property, I figure I have a right to be here.' He stalked towards her. 'You, on the other hand, are what we call back home, a squatter.'

When he neared, he noticed her eyes flicker in fear, which delighted him for she owed him a lot of straight answers. Phoebe began to back up when she realised he wasn't about to stop. When she hit the wall he planted his hands against the plaster, one either side of her head to hem her in.

'I have one simple question, Phoebe Jackson, and I want the truth. Why?'

She flinched, dropped her head. Oh, no way, she wasn't getting away with pretending shyness. Nick curled the fingers of one hand under her chin and forced her head up. 'No hiding. We will stay right here until I am satisfied with your answer and don't dare spin me some namby-pamby story. Why did you leave a perfectly comfortable bed and mod cons to camp out on a cold concrete floor?'

When Phoebe squirmed and tugged her head to gain freedom, Nick's conscience tweaked but he wasn't about to relent. Instead, he tightened his hold on her chin to keep them eye-to-eye. They were so close her breath whispered against his cheek every time she exhaled. He absorbed the essence of her. She smelt like fresh air and wildflowers, which did not help his still aroused body. Thank goodness she couldn't drop her eyes downwards. It was obvious she was embarrassed for a blush rose up her neck before her cheeks reddened. 'I've got all night, Phoebe.'

She winced, gulped and her eyes flicked from side-to-side as though she sought some place to which she could escape. He pressed his body closer but kept a fraction shy of her hips for pure self-preservation. 'Don't even think about it. The sooner you tell me the truth, the sooner I release you.'

Her eyes slid closed. 'I was in the way.'

Nick reeled backwards at her whispered words. It was the last thing he expected her to say. 'In the way? When did I even infer you were in the way? This is the second time you have intimated you were in the way. You have never been in the way. I enjoyed having you stay with me.' He leant down and picked up her discarded dress. 'Put this on.'

Mortification sprang from her face the moment she glanced down and her state of undress registered. She grabbed the garment, grasped it against her front and fled into the next room. While she was gone Nick began to gather her belongings and shoved them into her backpack. There weren't many items to pack which indicated she packed everything away each morning and hid them in a cupboard in case someone ventured upstairs. He was rolling the sleeping bag when Phoebe returned. She shot across the room, dropped to her knees and fought to unroll the bag.

'What are you doing?'

'Taking you home. You can't stay here.'

Phoebe turned her head away but not before Nick noticed her bite her lower lip. 'Then I will go to an hotel.'

Nick grabbed Phoebe's hands to still her. 'You haven't answered my question yet. What drove you away from my place? Did I do or say something to offend you?'

She shook her head. 'No, of course not.'

As he stood, Nick drew Phoebe upright with him. 'Then please explain?'

Like a stunned guppy, her mouth opened and closed several times without a sound apart from a few frustrated sighs. It was obvious she was more than agitated by the way she roamed the room fidgeting with anything she could find to fidget with before she faced Nick from the other side of the room.

'If you and I were a couple, how would you feel if I had some strange man come to stay with me?'

Mystified at this skewed fantasy, Nick wondered what the heck he was supposed to say. Honest was best. 'I wouldn't like it but knowing you, there would be some logical explanation as to why this mystery man had appeared on the scene but I can't see what this has to do with you taking flight from my place since I don't have a romantic interest at the moment.'

Phoebe's jaw gaped. 'Oh, come on. What about "hurry Nicky darling, we can't be late"?'

There was one person who got away with calling him Nicky. 'Are you talking about Anna?'

'Anna? I thought her name was Katerina.'

Now he was confused. 'Katerina is my assistant.'

Phoebe screwed her face. 'I thought your assistant's name was Tina.'

'I fired Tina.'

'You did, why?'

'Several reasons. First, she was rude to you.'

Phoebe laughed. 'She thought I was a threat. Aussie girl wants to meet up with you the day after you return from Australia? She thought we had been in an intimate relationship back home.'

At the sudden unusual heat to his cheeks, Nick turned away until he was sure he had it under control. An intimate relationship with Phoebe sounded like a brilliant idea which had his libido on the rampage once again. Damn, but this woman turned him on something fierce. He walked away, daring to speak over his shoulder until he could bring his libido under control. 'What you just said is the second reason. I originally hired Tina because I wasn't attracted to her at all. She certainly isn't the type of woman I could ever be interested in. Especially her age. I am not keen on boss/employee romantic liaisons. When you pointed out she was, how did you put it…?'

'Had the hots for you?' Phoebe grinned.

'Yes, then she had to go.'

Phoebe snorted rather indelicately. 'You can't fire an employee because she is enamoured with you.'

'No, but I can fire her if she forges my signature on a legal document.'

'Oh.' Phoebe paused. 'The interior design contract? She forged your signature?'

Nick sighed. 'Yes, the woman concerned was her sister-in-law.'

'Nasty.'

'More than nasty. Tina could end up in court and serve time in prison if her sister-in-law presses charges in order to get paid for work she wasn't contracted to do. I can't have an employee who resorts to forging my signature.'

'So Katerina is your new assistant.'

'Katerina agreed to fill in until I can find enough time to advertise and interview new people. She was my former assistant until she married Alexos.'

'Katerina is your sister-in-law?'

Nick smiled at Phoebe's stunned face, her eyes wide and jaw snagged open. 'She is but she's also four months into her first pregnancy and Alexos is not happy she's gone back to work.' A sudden thought crashed into his brain. 'Hang on a minute. If you heard Anna - you must have been at home.'

Phoebe spun around. Nick strode across the room and grasped her shoulders to twist her back around. 'I called you. Why didn't you answer or come out?'

'Well, what do you expect? She called you darling. What was I supposed to do? You think I wanted to intrude on a relationship. I was living in your house and you brought home a girlfriend. It was rather awkward.'

Nick grasped her chin. 'Do I detect a hint of jealousy there?'

Phoebe blushed. 'No, of course not.'

Nick put on a sad face. 'You could have boosted my ego a bit and said yes.'

Phoebe pulled away and snorted. 'As if you need your ego boosted.'

'I don't know how to take your comment. Now can we get one thing straight? Anna is not my girlfriend.'

'She called you darling.'

'Anna calls everyone darling, including her mother and she will call you darling as well. Anna is my sister.'

Phoebe's eyes popped. 'Your sister!'

'Yes, she rang me during the day to see if I would have dinner with her fiancé and his parents so I could get to know them. I came home in the hope you,' he tapped her on the end of her nose, 'would join us as my dinner partner so I wouldn't be the odd one out. I wanted you to meet Anna and thought you might enjoy a night with other people.'

'Oh,' The redness returned in a rush but Phoebe dropped her head to hide it.

Nick grinned. 'Yes, oh. Now, since we have cleared up all your misconceptions about my non-existent love-life will you come home with me? I promise you there is no woman lurking in the background. I can assure you I would never have asked you to stay with me if I had a romantic interest. I would never do such a thing to a woman, nor would I put you in such an awkward situation. It would show a total lack of respect and respect for one's partner is of utmost importance to me. If I did have a partner I would have put you up at my mother's place.' Relief surged when Phoebe nodded her agreement and bent to gather the few remaining items.

Twenty

'We have a problem.'

'What now?' Phoebe muttered with eyes closed. Her shoulders lifted and fell for the umpteenth time. With her eyes still closed she turned to Yiannis. Already it felt as though the day had been forty hours long and it was not long after ten. Final touch-ups had taken much longer than expected but she was happy with the progress they had made each day. The display unit was complete except for a final clean. To protect the carpets, the plastic was yet to be removed but would be after lunch when the industrial vacuum cleaner she had hired would be put to good use.

She was even more pleased with the number of rooms in the other three units which now sported new coats of paint. Even though all the tiles weren't finished, the prospective buyers who were to arrive first thing tomorrow morning, would be able to visualise the finished appearance of each unit.

'What's the problem?' Phoebe asked when she dared to open her eyes but one glance at Yiannis and she figured it was a major hitch and not a teeny-weeny problem. His face held a worried frown.

'There's not enough of the Dado paper. We are a roll short.'

'Short, but I measured it three times to be sure we had enough. Let me check.' Phoebe followed Yiannis to the entry where she swept her eyes around the walls. The strip of paper that delineated the two colours on the walls caught the eye and tied the colours of the floor and walls together – until she reached the main wall. Oh, God! The strip ended halfway between the front doors of the two units. It couldn't be on a wall which wasn't the first thing customers would see. Oh, no! People would walk into the entry and there, right slap bang in the middle of their line of sight stood a gaping chasm.

'Five rolls,' she said. 'I ordered five rolls.'

'There were four.' Yiannis squatted, picked up the crumpled bag with the logo of the wallpaper company, peered inside and withdrew the docket. 'It says five, but I swear there were only four.'

'Maybe it fell out.' Phoebe grasped the paper and read it for herself although she didn't doubt what Yiannis said.

'I searched. Stephanos is going through the rubbish in the skip bins outside and Stavros is searching amongst the supplies for the other units but I am one hundred percent positive it isn't there.' He pointed to the lifted Sellotape still attached to the edge of the bag top. 'This wasn't opened until today and when I opened it there were only four.'

Phoebe pressed her hands against each side of her head to try to concentrate. Her mind had turned into the twisted clothes in a gigantic tumble drier. Her father had always maintained every problem had a solution so she had to come up with a solution, quick smart. They had less than twenty-four hours before the units were to be open for inspection by a bevy of invited prospective buyers.

Think, woman, think. She eyed the wall. Maybe they could peel off what was there and paint a line. No. Not enough time and it would be obvious there was a humungous stuff-up. Not the effect they needed to give purchasers confidence in the décor. She caught a glimpse of the paper bag and docket still in Yiannis's hand. There was an imprint of the company name. She smiled. There was also the phone number. 'Can you phone them to see if they have another roll?'

The frown lines disappeared from Yiannis' face. He tugged at the mobile phone clipped to his belt. Phoebe held out the paper while Yiannis dialled. A few moments of Greek dialogue, a glance at the docket to get the design name and number and a huge grin spread across the man's weathered face. 'They have three rolls.'

Relief surged through Phoebe. 'Wonderful, order all three in my name.' A frown replaced the grin when she recalled where the shop was situated. Miles away and out of the city in what they call back home a light industrial area. Nick, she needed Nick to drive her. 'Can I borrow your phone?' she asked, and grimaced at the thought she still hadn't bought a sim card for her own mobile phone. But when had there been the time? Phone in hand, she dialled Nick's number and swore under her breath when it went to voice mail. She left a message. Five minutes later she left another, then another and another. Frustrated after a full hour of no return call and no arrival of Nick through the front door, Phoebe prowled around while fairy-floss brain cells figured out which man they could do without for at least two hours. The painters were frantically finishing rooms; oil-based enamel on the woodwork, which couldn't be left or it would spoil and leave a hard line which would take even longer to sand away. And it would have to be re-painted again, which would take up even more time. The tilers were fixing the mess in the *black hole* so it no longer gave the impression the unit belonged to a really cheap, nasty brothel. The carpenters hammered, drilled, sawed and attached essential hardware. The sole person without a million tasks to complete was her. She grabbed her bag, the paper with the address, told Yiannis where she was going and fled.

There was not a cloud in sight but a summer breeze rippled through the air, which made the walk sort of pleasant. The reason for the walk soured the atmosphere. Phoebe sidled along the sidewalk with a watchful eye on the traffic for a vacant taxi. It took too long to hail one but at last she sat huddled on the rear seat drumming her fingers on the armrest while the driver negotiated a way through what seemed to be the worst congestion she had seen so far in Athens. It was as though the entire population wanted to use the same few roads. She kept taking a peek at her watch but the minute hand never seemed to move yet time raced by faster than a bullet train. It was already after eleven. Her mind scrabbled to calculate how much time to get there, to get back, how long to apply the Dado and how long it would take to vacuum carpets, wash and polish tiles and mirrors, plus dust and wipe down skirting boards. Another week would just about do it.

Her jagged nerves were about to ping apart when she recognised a few of the shops in the light industrial area she had visited with Nick eighteen days prior when they purchased the million and one items needed to turn a catastrophe into classy accommodation. She was happy with what they had achieved in such a short time but it was the buyers who would make the ultimate decision. If they loved the décor they would put in offers to purchase. If they didn't like it, they would walk away and Phoebe's reputation would be in the bottom of the holes she dug in gardens to plant trees. Huge holes for mature trees, not little piddly indents for seedlings.

When they neared the wallpaper emporium, Phoebe studied at the meter and yanked a pile of euros from her purse, then tripled the amount to give the driver an incentive to wait the ten minutes needed to make her purchase and also to pay for the return trip.

The second the taxi veered against the kerb Phoebe reached over with the wad of notes. 'You can wait?' she asked.

'How long?'

'Five minutes, ten at the most.'

At the driver's nod, Phoebe shot from the car, ran inside, barged past a young couple holding hands and a man in white paint-spattered overalls. She reached the counter to be met by an empty space. She searched the area with her eyes.

The solitary staff member she could spy was with a well-dressed middle-aged woman and a book of samples. A groan erupted. Phoebe knew how long it could take for a customer to flick through samples while they decided which one they liked best and changed their mind over and over. Next they would amble through another book, followed by several more and again change their mind another umpteen times.

At a string of Greek words, Phoebe spun back to the counter. 'I don't speak Greek,' she said to the wizened old man, 'but I phoned and had three rolls of Dado put aside in the name of Jackson. Here,' she pulled the old docket from her pocket, 'this pattern.'

The man smiled and reached under the counter. He placed a paper bag in front of Phoebe. She checked the innards, smiled in glee when she recognized the pattern. Thank the good Lord for small mercies, she thought and opened her purse to take out the amount required. She could quibble about how she had already paid for five rolls and received one short of her order but it wasn't worth the time for the few euros.

Transaction complete, Phoebe hurried outside and stuttered to a standstill. Every parking space was occupied except for the one where her taxi was supposed to be. Mystified, she peered both ways along the street. The taxi must have moved but there was no taxi to be seen, parked or otherwise. And she paid the driver to wait. An inelegant scoff escaped. Why would he wait when he already had triple his fare and could be off to pick up another passenger to make even more money? It was a dumb thing to do. Wonderful, now she had to find another taxi and pay again.

Furious with herself, she set off, trawling the edge of the sidewalk with her head skewed around to search the tops of cars for an unlit taxi sign.

Her feet still hugged the kerb twenty minutes later when she realised there was a sudden dearth of traffic. Mystified, she paused and peered ahead. There were no vehicles in sight nor were there any pedestrians apart from her.

Ever so slow, she turned back around and searched the length of the street the way she had come. One sedan was parked against the kerb but from the amount of dust and grime coating the enamel it had been there for at least a hundred years. She turned back and grunted when her foot slipped off the edge of the kerb. There was a sharp wrench up the outside of her ankle before her shoe gripped the bitumen. When she planted her foot on solid ground, her ankle gave way. She stumbled, hopped and grimaced when a spear shot up her leg.

The day had already done its best to turn from awful to ghastly. Now it laughed at her. It was all she needed to not be able to walk. Phoebe took a tentative step and groaned at the sting under her ankle bone. She wriggled the foot around and gasped each time the newly damaged flesh twinged and shot an immediate message to her brain – her ankle wanted to remain stationary. To relieve the stab of pain, she knelt on one knee, rubbed at the sore spot and fingered each tiny bone around the tender area until she could conclude it was nothing more than a sprain. She could handle a sprain.

She struggled upright, hobbled the first few steps, found the most comfortable way to place her foot and continued her journey. When she rounded a corner she spied an elderly woman dressed in a navy long-sleeved dress, perched on a wooden bench next to a bus stop. A bulging bag of groceries rested either side of her.

A bus: she could catch a bus into the city centre which would both save time and give her injury a chance to rest. From there it would be easy to find a taxi or even another bus. Happy with the idea, she settled next to the lady. Up close the cotton dress was faded and frayed in places but the pleats were pressed knife-edge sharp. Obviously a poor but proud woman.

'Kalispera,' said Phoebe with a smile at the woman.

'Kalispera.' The voice sounded tired but continued in a rapid staccato of Greek with hands flung about to emphasise the meaning but even with the expressive gestures Phoebe could make neither head nor tail of what the woman said.

'No Greek,' said Phoebe when the woman paused to take a breath, 'I speak English.'

The woman grasped Phoebe's left hand and twisted it over. She pointed to Phoebe's watch. Time: the lady wanted to know the time. Phoebe leant closer to hold her watch within the lady's line of sight. The woman shook her head, counted off twelve on her fingers, shook her head again. On one hand she held up one finger and pointed with her other hand to the post of the bus stop. What was she trying to say? Twelve... no... one... no... bus stop. Bus at twelve. But it must be well after. One peek at her watch told her how long after twelve it was. It was almost one. Had this woman been waiting well over an hour? So where were the buses and come to think of it where was any traffic or pedestrians? It dawned on her this road was as barren as the previous one. The lady next to her was the only human she had seen for some time. It was weird: as though some UFO had flown over and sucked up all signs of human life.

Mystified, Phoebe stood and studied the metal sign attached to the top of the post. She skimmed down the list of times. As far as she could make out there was a bus about every thirty minutes, the next due at one so she settled back down to wait.

When the minute hand on her watch reached five minutes after the hour, an uncanny restlessness settled into the pit of her stomach. Already, she had been away too long. Unable to sit a moment longer, she began to pace along the pavement, stopped, turned and paced back, not only to test her ankle but for something to do.

Some unusual-shaped leaves on a bushy shrub behind the fence caught her eye. She ran a gentle finger over the small branch, studied the serrated edge and fine veins. She'd never seen the plant before and wondered if there was enough time for a quick sketch, for the shrub was pretty with variegated greens ranging from cream through to emerald. It would make a fabulous feature plant.

Maybe a quick sketch would do. She eased her arms from the straps of her bag, but paused when she became aware of a loud rumble. Phoebe cocked her head to one side to listen. Couldn't be a bus. If it was, it was one sick vehicle. It sounded more like chanting voices and they were getting louder by the second. She half-turned at high-pitched shouts. A siren joined the cacophony. Police or maybe an ambulance, she thought but still swung her bag from her shoulders and undid the leather strap that held the flap down. Maybe there had been an accident. It would explain the absence of vehicles if the roads were blocked by emergency vehicles.

Two pencil strokes and the leaf shape became outlined. A slight curve swept down the middle and the central vein appeared. Leaning closer, she counted the lateral veins which branched out in pairs, copied them onto the paper. Each tiny serration curved out then tucked under like the end of a tick.

'Dios!' the old woman called out.

Phoebe twisted her head around to see if she was all right then glanced the way the woman stared. A vast number of people poured around the corner like the surge of a tidal wave. Continual chants and yells increased in volume. They appeared to be armed with long sticks and an odd assortment of weapons they must have picked up along the way and they were headed towards her. What the devil was going on? An object flew through the air. She ducked. It thudded against the pavement about a metre to her side. A broken brick edged with dried mortar.

Adrenalin surged through her veins. With her heart acting like a thunderclap, she shoved the pad and pencil into her bag and flicked her eyes in all directions in a desperate search for somewhere to hide. The horde streamed down the road like a lava flow, filled the bitumen and pavement in a heaving mass of yells and screams. No way could she find a path through. Her body tensed when more objects flew through the air. Most were rocks and bricks.

The old woman screamed. Phoebe leapt towards her. Common sense told her to flee but there was no way she could leave the woman to fend for herself; she was way too frail. The woman stood, wavered then lurched towards the ground. Blood spurted from a gash on her cheek. In an instant, it began to spread and drip. Again Phoebe was certain she'd been transported to some surreal world while she ran until she reached the woman and knelt by her side. This could not be happening. This is a tourist city – these riots didn't happen. To make a liar of her, the crowd surged like a tsunami and were mere metres away when Phoebe figured there was nowhere to go but under the slatted bench. 'We must get down,' she yelled at the same time she grabbed the woman and dragged her to the side of the bench where she pushed and shoved until the woman rolled to relative safety under the slatted boards.

With little room left, Phoebe squeezed and wriggled to get her body as far under as she could but the solid bench legs made it impossible to fit which left her arched back protruded at her shoulders and hips.

The crowd surrounded them in a surge. Eardrum splitting yells and chants rattled Phoebe's eardrums while feet thundered past. Phoebe pressed closer to the trembling body she held tight with one arm. Her other arm was squashed around her bag which pressed into her chest. To make it even more unpleasant there was a vile odour of stale urine and a much worse stench which she didn't want to think about.

A clutter of boots ran over the wood above them. Phoebe grunted when a heavy object landed on her hip. She squeezed tighter and was rewarded by a hefty kick in the small of her back. The breath whooshed from her lungs. A thought shot through her mind about meeting her maker sooner than she wanted but not before her kidneys were ground into mincemeat.

It was impossible to tell if the whimpers came from her or the woman so she bit her lip, screwed her eyes shut and prayed for divine intervention. She lost count of the number of times she was trodden on or kicked before police sirens cut through the air. There was a sudden lull in the shouts for a few brief seconds before it rose again in a rumbling crescendo. It felt like forever before the swish, scrape and thuds of footsteps petered out, the voices softened with distance and the sirens ceased.

The silence was sudden and profound.

Phoebe dared to lift her head a few centimetres to search the area. She ducked again when a police car swooped past. It was another five minutes before she was sure the danger had passed. She couldn't hold back the gasps at sharp electrified bolts of pain at every movement while she wriggled free. With a final surge, she lay flat on her back, certain she had been torn apart. With her eyes shut, she sucked in a few breaths and eased them out before daring to ease sideways, scramble onto all fours but had to grit her teeth at the pain. Another two cars with blue and red emergency lights flashing sped past while she took utmost care to roll the woman from under the bench.

'Are you all right?'

A pale face washed with tears and streaks of red stared back at her. Phoebe's heart twisted at the stark terror etched amongst the pallid wrinkles.

'Let me help you up,' said Phoebe. She managed to stagger upright, with her breath held against the agony. It hurt even more to bend at the waist to grasp the woman under her arms. A wave of nausea swept through her. She swallowed down the rising bile, held her breath while she helped the lady to her feet. Aged limbs were not cooperative but after a few staggers and groans the lady stood on shaky legs. Phoebe gripped the lady's arm to steady her. The once meticulous laundered dress was covered in unmentionable grime and wisps of grey hair stuck out every which way from what had been a neat, coiled bun at the nape of her neck.

Phoebe brushed at the worst patches of dirt and eased the woman onto the bench. The groceries were gone. Phoebe eyed the pavement in search of them. Fruit and vegetables were scattered piles of mush. A couple of cans had rolled away but survived. What appeared to have been sausages wrapped in white butcher's paper were flat splotches of bloody flesh ground into shredded paper.

Another sedan with a portable blue light sped past before brakes screeched and the car shuddered to a halt. A crunch of gears and the vehicle reversed back to them. A door opened then slammed. Footsteps neared. Male Greek words sounded. Phoebe struggled to turn towards the voice, wincing at the effort.

'Phoebe?'

Startled at the sound of her name, Phoebe twisted around and peered at the owner of the voice. 'Alexos!' Boy, was she relieved?

'What are you doing here?'

'We were waiting for a bus but it never came.'

She cringed when Alexos eyed her up and down. 'Are you hurt?'

If she said yes there was no doubt in her mind, he would send her to a hospital which would take forever and she didn't have time. 'I'm okay but I need to get back to the units as soon as possible. But this lady needs medical attention. She was hit by a missile.'

Alexos turned to the woman and gave her the same scrutiny he had bestowed upon Phoebe. He spoke in Greek before turning back to Phoebe. 'She says you saved her life.' He reached out and slid a strand of wayward hair behind her ear. Shoot, but she must be a mess. She sure felt a mess and stank to high heaven.

'I don't think so but she lost her groceries.' Phoebe released the death grip she still had on her backpack and fished around for her purse. She took out a couple of notes, grasped the woman's hand and pressed the money into her palm. The lady shook her head and tried to give the money back. Phoebe wrapped the lady's fingers around the notes.

'Tell her it is my gift to her. By the state of her clothes I don't think she can afford to lose her groceries so I would like to help her. Please?'

While Alexos passed on Phoebe's message she examined her own clothes. There was a bloodied rip on one knee, her clothes were filthy with smears of gross black and brown that stank and every part of her body hurt like blazes every time she tried to move but she didn't think any bones were broken.

'She says thank you and you are an angel.' Alexos smiled as he brushed some unmentionable from Phoebe's brow. 'I will organise a car to take you to the units but I have to go. I am supposed to take photographs of damage and of those doing the damage.' He frowned. 'Are you sure you are not hurt?'

Phoebe didn't dare tell the truth. 'I will be fine but I must get this wallpaper back to the painters.'

It wasn't an option to not move even a millimetre during the twenty-minute drive. Phoebe's body had seized up. It was a monumental struggle to get limbs to carry out the simple act of alighting from the rear seat of a sedan. And she stank! A sigh, a gulp but still she winced at the simple movement of her head to thank the officer who had to be way too young to be in uniform. It was a slow process to straighten, every centimetre torturous but at last she was upright. After the police car drove off, Phoebe searched both ways along the street and was relieved when Nick's car wasn't in sight. She could hand over the rolls of dado then scoot… well, maybe not scoot, more like stagger home for a shower and change of clothes. Since she had already wasted so much time, another hour wouldn't make any difference. There was no doubt she would have to spend half the night cleaning in any case so she might as well be clean and… she sniffed but regretted it when her stomach recoiled at the sour stench, fresh.

There weren't many steps to climb but it hurt like blazes to lift her right leg and even more to put her weight on it every time she rose. Once up, she paused to get her lungs to work as they should, with even, gentle breaths and not staggered gasps. On a final long grunt, she straightened her back and shoved her shoulders back. Any sign of injury would no doubt be reported to Nick if he ever managed to show up. It took great effort to force her body to move in a normal gait after she pushed at the door and stepped inside.

Yiannis turned from the two trestles where he had trays and rollers set out ready for the wallpaper. He frowned all the while his eyes swept up and down.

'Don't ask,' Phoebe said. She unzipped her bag and withdrew the package. 'Can you get these up before you go home?'

'I'm asking,' came from her left.

Nick, where did he come from? Ignoring him, she forced a normal gait towards Yiannis and kept her face a mask in an attempt to ignore the stabs of a spear at each movement. Far out, but she was beyond sore.

'What are you doing here?' she shot over her shoulder in the vague direction from which his voice had come.

'You rang - five times,' said Nick, his voice so close Phoebe knew he was right behind her.

'I rang hours ago.' She handed the package to Yiannis who opened and closed his mouth several times to say something but instead, shrugged his shoulders after a lengthy stare over Phoebe's shoulder.

Phoebe cringed. 'There should be plenty this time,' she said to Yiannis with a forced smile.

'I was in a meeting and had my phone turned off,' said Nick. 'I came as soon as I was free. Now would you mind explaining why...' his phone rang. 'Excuse me a moment.'

Feet shuffled before footsteps faded. A door opened. Good he had gone into one of the units. She had an opportunity to leave. She managed a step.

'Yes, she's here,' Nick said so clear she figured he hadn't shut the door. 'She looks as though she's been dragged down some back alley and through a swamp but she is here.'

Phoebe turned and limped towards the front door.

'She what?' Nick yelled a split second before his shoes moved faster and came closer while he spoke in rapid Greek.

Phoebe quickened her pace and grasped the doorknob. A large hand reached over her shoulder and shoved the door shut again.

'You, Miss Jackson, are not going anywhere,' Nick said in her ear and to the phone he added, 'Alexos, I will call you back.'

Darn it. Trust Alexos to blab. Phoebe dropped her hand and braced herself.

'What on earth were you doing anywhere near the student protests?' Nick asked as he grasped her shoulder and turned her around.

Phoebe sucked in her breath at the pain then simmered at the implication. She managed to get her hands on her hips without so much as a grimace. 'Well, I was desperate for a bit of excitement so figured I would wander the streets until I found an army of idiots who thought it was fun to destroy whatever they came across.' She glared at him. 'How was I supposed to know the local students weren't happy with their campus?'

'It's funding cuts they aren't happy with and details of where and when they were to protest has been on the news for the last few nights.'

Phoebe cocked one eyebrow. 'This is the news you watch each night which is spoken in Greek?'

It was a shock to see Nick blush. 'Sorry, I didn't think. Remind me to translate for you. The public were warned of the route of the peaceful protest but it wasn't anywhere near here so I didn't think it necessary to warn you.'

'Peaceful?' Phoebe squeaked out. 'Give me strength. If that was peaceful then I would hate to see the Greek version of a vicious riot.'

Nick reached out, tweaked the same lock of stray hair his brother had and clipped it behind her ear. 'You saved a woman's life and Alexos wanted to know if you were hurt.'

'All I did was help her get out of the way and I'm fine. I need a shower and change of clothes.' Phoebe turned towards the front door.

'I'll drive you home.' He swung and arm around her waist with one hand and reached over and opened the door with the other.

A gasp she had no hope of holding back, slipped out when Nick brushed against the spot she had been kicked.

Nick dropped his hand. 'You are hurt, show me.'

'I'm fine. I need to hurry. There is still so much to be done before tomorrow. This entire floor has to be cleaned yet.' She knew she blathered at a blistering pace but she needed to divert Nick. The continual jolts of pain indicated there was more than one wicked bruise in places hidden from view.

Somehow he managed to pin her against the door. She hadn't been aware he had moved but here she was. Her back kissed the fresh painted wood with a hand either side of her head. He hadn't touched her, yet the warmth of his body did a fantastic job of setting her nerves on fire. She wanted him closer but fought back the impulse to plaster her torso against his and not because it would hurt too much. The unique scent of him did dastardly things to her innards. His mouth... those sexy lips were so close; lips she had already learnt from experience, would turn her to mush.

She forced her eyes upwards from his mouth. Even the dark bristles that shadowed his beard-line sent a tremor of yearning through her. Her eyes met his. He stared at her. He grinned. Shoot, did he know how much he affected her? Was there drool on her mouth or did she have a sappy face?

'Like what you see?'

Heat shot through her veins, up her neck then further. On the inside an inferno had whooshed and set her alight.

His grin widened. 'Interesting. I'll pursue this later but right now - turn around.' He twisted his fingers in the air.

She stood her ground with a fierce glare.

'So, you want it the hard way, do you?' said Nick. He dropped his hands to her shoulders. His touch was gentle as he twisted her around so her back was to him. He lifted the

218

corner of her T-shirt in the exact place where she had been kicked. How did he know?

A harsh expletive was followed by a long hiss as more of her shirt was lifted. 'Damn it, Phoebe, why didn't you tell Alexos you were hurt? You should be in hospital.' He twisted her around again and squatted in front of her.

Mortification slammed into her when he lifted the hem of her shirt and tucked it under her breasts to give the front section the same scrutiny with his mouth screwed into a thin line. He poked a gentle finger at the rip in her jeans, rubbed the smear of blood on his own shirt and glanced up at her. 'I am taking you to an emergency room.'

Phoebe sidled away and yanked down her top. 'We don't have time. This place has to be thoroughly cleaned before tomorrow.' She grasped the doorhandle and yanked.

'I don't give a damn about tomorrow.' He slammed the door shut. 'Your health is far more important. These bruises and scrapes are serious. There could be internal bleeding. You are in my employ and just like any other employee hurt whilst carrying out their duties, I insist on having a doctor check you out.' He sounded irate and determined.

'But the cleaning, I'll be fine.'

Nick snaked one arm around her shoulders and turned her back into the room. 'The cleaning will get done even if I have to stay up all night to do it myself but right now you and I are about to visit a doctor.' He paused at the trestles. 'Tell me what else needs to be done so the men can do as much as possible before they leave.'

Phoebe sighed. There was no point in arguing. 'If they can pack away…' she indicated the trestles, 'maybe upstairs, and roll up the black plastic over all the carpets. Get rid of all the tools so this entire floor gives the appearance it is ready to be moved into. With everything hidden away it will make it easier to clean.'

'Right, you wait here.' He turned away, took three steps and swung back. 'Don't dare move from that spot. It is

219

already taking every ounce of my willpower to suppress how angry I am right now. It wouldn't be wise to defy me.'

Phoebe winced then stared after him. He began to issue instructions in Greek while he tracked down and found each of the workers. She wondered if she could test his words and go to the other side of the room. Yiannis caught her eye. He seemed to be concentrating hard on rolling air bubbles from a new strip of Dado. But his shoulders quivered. The darn man was laughing. 'Not funny, Yiannis.'

Yiannis turned and tried, with little success, to wipe the smile from his face. 'He is upset because you mean a lot to him. Nickos was worried about you. He has been pacing around here for the past three hours. He rang the shop. They said you had been. When it took so long for you to return Nickos went to search for you.'

Three hours? And he went to find her? Oh, my. But she didn't think Nick cared as much as Yiannis intimated. Then she remembered how Nick had told his men they were an item to protect her from any more harassment. He would have to pretend concern, she thought as she wandered towards Yiannis for a closer inspection of the Dado strip. She ran a finger along the new join. Perfect. Then she noticed the faint chalk line hugging the underside edge. Yiannis had done a professional job. He used a tape to measure from the top of the skirting board and the white chalk would brush away. She recalled her father being furious when the line had been marked in thick pencil, which was impossible to clean off without leaving a mark. 'Great work, Yiannis.'

'You moved!'

Uh, oh. 'Only to tell Yiannis what an expert he is.' She grinned at Yiannis then tried to scoot back to her spot but could manage nothing more than an awkward limp, which incurred a scowl from Nick. Her ankle hurt, as did her hip and worst of all was the small of her back.

'I hope the doctor admits you to hospital,' mumbled Nick. He took a gentle hold of her elbow and ushered her towards the stairs where he took her weight while they descended one slow step at a time.

She had been stupid to not check the underground car park. 'If he does, I will check myself out. There are no bones broken, I am still upright and breathing. Bruises heal and the cut on my knee is only a scrape.

'You are the most exasperating woman I have ever met,' said Nick at the passenger door he held open and raised his eyebrows at her awkward movements. Getting into a car was harder than it had been getting out a few minutes earlier and no matter how hard she tried to disguise her restricted movements, she couldn't.

Twenty-Two

'Told you nothing was broken.' Phoebe paused before taking the first step upwards. She really, really, did not, ever, want to hoist her body up any more steps. They had to wait two hours before she had been poked, prodded, x-rayed and sewn up. The time had given her innards a chance to find every torn, strained and bruised cell, each of which still sent painful messages to her brain to insist she needed to stretch out on a feather-soft mattress and not move for an entire week.

Beside her Nick snorted. 'Your right ankle is strapped; you have three stitches in your knee and at least a half of your body is either black or blue. You wince whenever I touch you, yet you say nothing is broken. So how come your face gives the indication those three steps are Mt Everest? Here let me help you.'

Nick moved so fast Phoebe didn't have a chance to resist. One second she was standing and the next she was in his arms being carried. It still hurt where his body brushed against bruises but not having to use muscles was certainly less painful. She had no choice but to slip her arms around his neck to maintain balance. Her eyes closed at the scent of his nearness. His hard muscles tensed against her softer curves which sent her a sense of warmth and security. How wonderful it would be to stay like this for hours. The aroma of a trace of aftershave, mingled with Nick's male essence, enveloped her. Her face was so close to his she could make out each individual spike of his day-old beard. She was tempted to melt against him but before she could settle her feet to the ground at the top of the steps. He reached around to twist the doorknob and it opened without the key.

Phoebe was mystified when Nick shoved at the door. Why would it be open? His warm palm pressed against her shoulder to urge her forward so she stepped over the threshold and paused. Three strange women stood side-by-side facing them.

'Sorry we are so late,' said Nick 'This is Phoebe.' He took her hand and tugged her towards the older woman. She was dark haired and tallish and despite her years, had an elegance about her.

'Phoebe, this is my mother, Eleni.'

His mother! What was going on? 'Mrs Kalameides,' Phoebe acknowledged with a slight nod of her head.

'Please, call me Eleni.' When the woman smiled, her face lit up. Phoebe recognised Nick's smile.

'My father would never allow me to address someone from an older generation by their first name. Relatives were aunt or uncle and others were Mr or Mrs,' said Phoebe.

Her hand was grasped. 'Your father was a man with good values. I prefer Eleni but if you are uncomfortable with my name you could tag on an Aunt or Tia, as we say in Greece.'

'And I'm Anna.' A younger and shorter version of Nick's mother stepped forward. 'You said she was pretty, Nicky darling, but Phoebe is gorgeous.'

Nick laughed while the dreaded heat burned her neck and rose. 'Told you,' he whispered against her ear. 'And this is Katerina,' he added louder with his hand indicated towards the final woman.

Phoebe recognised the petite woman from the car. Up close, she was stunning and although dressed in jeans and a loose cotton top, her beauty belonged on the front page of some famous and expensive women's magazine. Even though she had showered and changed into fresh clothes, Phoebe felt like a first-class frump compared to Nick's family. There goes the newfound confidence she had begun to build with Nick since he convinced her he was not involved with any other woman in the romantic sense. The past few days had been perfect. Now she no longer crept around to avoid contact with him. She had relaxed and enjoyed the hours they shared. He was such a fun person to be with. With her defences down she laughed at his dry wit and got involved in clever banter about such a wide variety of topics, which showed how well-read Nick was. The spooky part was how it was so similar to the repartee she had always enjoyed with her dad. But now, in the presence of such class, her confidence took a nosedive. All of a sudden it dawned on her she was way out of her class and there was no way Nick would be interested in her.

'Your dinner is ready in the kitchen,' said Anna. 'Come.'

When the women turned towards the completed unit, Phoebe held back and grasped Nick by the arm to still him. 'You want to tell me what is going on?'

Nick smiled. 'This is our cleaning crew. I rang Mum while you were with the doctor, to ask if she knew of a cleaning company. After I explained our problem she told me to leave it to her. I presume they have already started since we took so long to get here. But first, we need to get some sustenance into us.' He slung an arm around her shoulders to urge her forwards. 'If I know you as well as I think I do, you haven't eaten since breakfast.'

Phoebe slammed her lips together so she didn't have to answer but grinned to herself. Darn man knew her too well, which delighted her in one sense for she had begun to understand Nick might care for her a tad, but now? After realising how outclassed she was? Not a chance. She had been living in la-la land.

She studied the kitchen bench as they neared it. Cling film undulated over two dinner plates loaded with an array of finger food. She recognised yummy vine-leaf wrapped dolmades, quartered tomatoes alongside lumps of feta cheese. Oh, how she loved the fresh Greek feta. Next to it were orange segments, black olives - ugh, she still hadn't acquired the taste for olives. And there were two buttered soft bread rolls. From where she stood she couldn't make out what the other items were but they sure smelt yummy.

'We've eaten,' said Anna, 'and finished vacuuming in this unit. Katerina is on vacuum detail. Alexos threatened dire consequences if she did any heavy work. I am polishing glass and tiles while Mum is tackling the floor tiles. Now what else needs to be done? Oh, and there is the seat you asked for.' Anna nudged Nick and waved a hand in the vague direction behind them.

Phoebe turned to spy a fold-up outdoor lounge covered in a grey and burgundy striped mattress, laid out in the middle of the dining area. It didn't take a genius to figure out what it was for. No way. But it sure looked so inviting.

'I can see your mind turning,' said Nick, 'and yes, you can issue instructions from the lounge but you will not do any physical work apart from eat and rest.' His arm slid around her waist. When her breath hitched at the pain he moved it higher. 'This is why you are to rest.' He edged her towards the lounge. 'Now sit.'

'And if I refuse?' Some perverse voice seemed to just spurt from her mouth.

Nick sniggered as though he found it hard to not laugh out loud. 'You have a choice. Lie here where you can see everything is cleaned to your exacting standards or I take you home and put you into your bed.'

Darn man. He knew as well as she did what she would opt for but no way would he get it all his way. 'Bully,' she hissed at the same time she sank down and sat on the edge.

Nick squatted in front of her and eyeballed her. 'Maybe you see it as me being a bully but I see it as caring about your welfare,' he said. He lifted her legs, twisted her body around then gave her a gentle shove until her back rested against the upright back. He stood and moved to the bench where he fidgeted with the stubborn cling-wrap until it came free. Returning to her side he handed her the plate. 'Eat enough for *me* to be satisfied or, Miss Stubborn, I will sit here and feed you.'

'Leave the girl alone, Nickos,' said his mother.

Thank goodness someone had come to her rescue. To make sure he left her alone, Phoebe made a show of picking up one of the dolmades and exaggerated the action of slowly taking a bite. It was delicious but no way would she show her enjoyment in front of Nick. Let him think she ate under protest. She would thank the ladies later – in private.

'Any specific instructions?' Nick asked between bites of his own food. Leant up against the bench, he kept an eye on her while he ate.

'I am sure the women of your family don't need me to tell them how to clean.'

His mother laughed. 'Well done, Phoebe. About time my son met his match.'

Inside, a warm glow bubbled up and exploded. She took a real liking to Eleni.

'Hey, whose side are you on?' Nick grinned.

'Phoebe's,' came back in a chorus from the three women.

'And so am I.' Nick dropped his plate onto the bench and squatted in front of Phoebe. 'You risked your life to save a complete stranger today and got hurt in the process. I am immensely proud of you but at the same time am angry at myself and deeply ashamed for not being there when you needed me.'

Phoebe opened her mouth to protest but Nick placed one finger on her lips to hush her.

'I made a poor judgement call today. I should have ensured I had no meetings booked on such a critical day. It was my place to be at the units to cover last minute hiccoughs but I wasn't. So cut me some slack here. The

226

doctor recommended forty-eight hours rest and to keep your ankle elevated as much as possible.' He turned puppy dog eyes at her and smiled. 'I am doing my best to atone for my sins by ensuring you follow the doctor's orders. Now, I will check if the men moved all their tools and other bits and bobs upstairs. Is there anything else you think might need to be done?'

'I had the idea to leave two or three tiles laid on the floor or against the wall in all the untiled areas. I labelled all the boxes with the unit number and where each tile is to be laid. For example, unit four, en-suite floor, wall and trim. Your customers can get an idea of what the finished unit will look like. I am certain most of the painting has been done on this floor.'

'I'll see to it.' He ran a finger down her cheek. 'Now rest your ankle.'

A shiver of pure pleasure followed his finger trail. Nick walked away. She eyed his back and wallowed in the sensation while figuring she could acquiesce with grace since resting felt darn good. So she settled back and nibbled while everyone else bustled around. Guilt simmered for not being able to pull her weight but figured if she attempted to get up and help, Nick would carry out his threat and take her home.

Twenty-Three

When she awoke to an eerie silence, Phoebe shook off the vestiges of sleep and stretched. She couldn't recall closing her eyes or even the heaviness of drooping eyelids. Someone had draped a rug over her; it must have been Nick for she recognised it as the one from the boot of his car when they picnicked at the Acropolis.

With utmost care, she thrust the blanket aside, eased her legs over the side of the lounge and creaked upright. Good grief, her body was too sore to move but she needed to visit a bathroom. Her legs acted like jellified rubber at the first couple of steps. Afraid she might fall, she slowed to concentrate on each step. She was almost at the bathroom when she realised it had already been scrubbed and polished for the next day's display. Upstairs: there were toilets upstairs. All she had to do was to make it up to the top.

It hurt at each step but she staggered across the unit, crossed the lobby towards the stairwell but paused at the thought of climbing. The elevator was for once, far more appealing so she changed direction.

'She's a lovely woman, Nickos,' came from behind the ajar door of the unit next to the elevator.

'Yes, she is,' said Nick.

'Do you love her?'

With a hitch in her breath, Phoebe came to a standstill.

'Excuse me? What gives you such an idea?' Nick sounded as though the question had stunned him. Phoebe's heart plummeted. If he was stunned then anything more than mere friendship had never crossed his mind.

There was a mocking feminine laugh. 'You have rung me every day since you arrived back here in Greece and every second word out of your mouth has been Phoebe.'

'Has not.'

'And I see the way you look at and touch her. You care about her.'

Phoebe's hands flung to her mouth.

'Of course I care. Phoebe put her holiday on hold to create this masterpiece and got hurt because I didn't think and put other business first. I owe her a great deal.'

Phoebe's innards tensed in despair. Gratitude. All he felt was gratitude. Those kisses, the banter, the closeness on the lounge with his arm hugging her tight, and the soft caresses - were all just gratitude.

'So you're not interested in her romantically.'

'Jeeze, Mum, what is this? You know I don't believe in all that love mumbo jumbo and Phoebe has to leave soon so what is the point?'

Breathing had become impossible. Her body seemed to have forgotten how to expand her lungs. Listening in was never right but Phoebe's feet were super-glued to the spot. Despite the tension and now knowing the truth, the old familiar sense of inadequacy surged. Just like every other man she showed any interest in, Nick didn't want her. She wasn't good enough.

'You will and I think Phoebe means more to you than you care to admit.'

'Not going to happen, Mum. Phoebe lost her father a few weeks ago, for God's sake and the jerk she travelled with treated her so bad. The last thing she needs is pressure from another man.'

'Which means she has nobody who cares two hoots about her. Maybe another someone in her life is what she needs. I know I wouldn't have survived your father's death without you four. I was desperately lost.'

'Mum?' Nick sounded exasperated. 'Enough. I'm going to see if the girls have finished.'

A gasp slid from Phoebe's throat. She was about to get caught at the elevator while she waited for the doors to open. She bolted across the tiles and forced her legs to climb even though her eyes glassed over with a sheen of unbidden tears at the pain. Footsteps echoed on the marbled lobby the very second she reached the landing. She spun around the corner then leant against the wall with a held breath. Shoot, she shouldn't have moved so fast. It hurt. And so did her heart. It hurt a lot. She was such a failure as a woman.

When the footsteps ceased and muffled voices rose, Phoebe crept step by painful step up the next section and managed to reach the bathroom where she flopped onto the pedestal with her hands over her face. It was an effort to suck in lungs full of air while she fought a bout of tears. Why, oh, why did she allow herself to fall in love with Nick? And she knew it was the real thing. It wouldn't hurt so much if it weren't real. It sure never hurt inside like this with Brad's defection. The only thing that suffered then was her pride for being duped. She had even been relieved, despite him stealing her money. In fact the loss of the money was worth it when it showed what a mealy-mouthed jerk he was.

But this... this soul wrenching pain? What could she do to alleviate it? She sure couldn't bear much more time in the vicinity of Nick. Home – she had to get home to Sydney. There was no way she could continue her journey of exploration through Europe, not now she had so little money and not when she was so overcome with this emptiness and being so alone.

'Phoebe!' The yelled words from below startled her. Shoot, how could she bear to face him? And his family? She had to pull herself together. Phoebe made use of the facilities, doused her face in cold water and swiped away the moisture with the bottom of her shirt. She swept both hands over her hair to ensure it was neat, straightened her clothes but with no mirror, it was impossible to see if she had managed to rid her appearance of all the signs of desolation. How did one hide utter despair?

'Where the hell are you?'

'Up here,' she called back before contorting her face into various poses to get the finer muscles to work and ease the tension. Next, she forced her lips into a smile, turned and made her way through the unit. Nick's footsteps slammed on each step at a rapid rate. He had to be running. He reached the top the very moment she pulled the unit door shut.

'What the devil are you doing up here?' A frown creased his forehead.

Her heart beat at a frantic pace. Somehow she had to pull this off. 'Can't a girl even go to the loo in private?'

A stunned look came over his face. 'But why up here?'

She forced her feet to step as normal as she could towards the elevator. To use the stairs would take her close to Nick, besides, she really, really, really didn't want to ever have to go up or down another step. 'Up here hasn't been scrubbed and polished for presentation.' She pressed the elevator button and sent a prayer skywards for him to just go away.

He didn't. Of course he had to come and stand right next to her so she could absorb his unique, wonderful scent. He had to brush against her so his warmth sent her innards on a flight path straight to her womb, which clenched. He had to palm his hand on her hip to guide her into the open elevator which had to arrive right then. His gorgeous sexy body had to press into hers all the way down. As if his conversation with his mother, a conversation she had no right in being a party to, hadn't caused enough excruciating pain, now he had to torture her even more. What did she ever do to deserve this agony?

And, of course, there was his family all lined up with expectant faces, waiting at the bottom, facing the open elevator. 'Give me strength,' she muttered under her breath, but she stepped out and began to walk, ignoring everyone.

'Where are you going?' Nick was right behind her.

'Obeying he who must be obeyed,' she said and kept walking with the intention of returning to the lounge she had been ordered to rest on. But it wasn't there any longer.

Shoot. She stood staring at the vacant spot. 'Where's my bed?' It was a stupid question, she knew, but couldn't think of anything else to say?

'We have finished and are about to go home.'

Like an absolute idiot and completely flummoxed, Phoebe turned and retraced her steps until she came face to face with the line of three women who had turned around and once again faced her. She had to thank them so scrambled around for the right words in a brain that had turned into mush.

'I can't thank you all enough for the fabulous food and for coming to our rescue. I imagined I would have to spend the entire night with a polishing rag. And it was lovely meeting you all at last. My guilt is strong for not helping you.'

Phoebe suffered several minutes of gushes, apologies, hugs, and all those frivolous girlie air-kisses and meaningless chitchat she didn't understand, with as much grace as she could muster. She felt stupid and so inadequate. It all made it obvious she didn't fit in with this family. At last, the three departed.

'Are we going?' she said after a lengthy silence.

'Don't you want to inspect the finished product?' asked Nick.

She did. She was proud of what she had achieved in so short a time but there was a greater need to get home so she could lock herself in her room and stay as far away from Nick as possible. It hurt deep inside to be so near what she could never have when she wanted it so desperately. First task in the morning would be to book a flight home. 'I know what it looks like. I spent between twelve to eighteen hours a day working on this and am positive your family don't need me to check on their cleaning abilities.'

Without a clue as to what to do next, she headed for the front door, opened it and stepped outside. Far out, more steps. Her battered body protested at the thought of having to work its way down more steps. Her ankle sent out several extra strong throbs, her knees locked straight and her sore muscles rebelled by making their presence felt. An urge rose to walk home so she didn't have to be in close contact with Nick but as quick as a flash it was negated by the thought of the exercise, so she heaved oxygen into her lungs, suffered the pain of descent and stood by the passenger door of Nick's car.

It took a few minutes for Nick to douse lights and lock up. 'What's got into you?' he said as the click of the remote unlocked the doors.

'Nothing apart from the sensation a humungous road roller has run over me fifty times and turned me into a physical wreck. I am desperate to go home and stretch out.' Guilt flared at voicing her fragility. She never admitted to such weakness but heck, the day had been extra-long and arduous. Oblivion for a month sounded pretty darn wonderful.

Twenty-Four

'Dig, Phoebe, dig,' she chanted in rhythm with the press of the shovel into the ground, the heft of a sod of dark dirt and turn it over. All she had to do was one shovel at a time. What happened elsewhere didn't matter. She either had to keep toiling or curl up and die. Life would go on; she kept telling herself. All she had to do was buckle up and work away the pain. Until now, she had never believed in the concept of a broken heart but now she knew better. And it did hurt in a pain that sucked out not only every cell of her body but also her soul.

Desperate for a break, she paused to catch her breath, glanced back at yesterday's turned over garden bed, scowled then set her mind to what she wanted to achieve today. The gentle slope of the plot of her family home ended in a dense mass of foliage, the taller trees dating back to when the home was first built almost a hundred years ago. New buds still glistened from the overnight rain, which had left the clay-based soil, heavy and cloggy. Some new leaves had lost their tenacious hold and lay scattered everywhere like large glossy green confetti.

While the tempest outside had raged she had been snug and cosy in her bed. Many century-old houses were cold and draughty but when you had an illustrious interior decorator as a father it meant this house had been renovated with the addition of thick insulation. The modernisation hadn't detracted from the 1900's style. To not have followed the style would have been sacrilege and appear stupid. Her father had put his soul into renovating their home to his exacting standards. Now it belonged to her. Now she could renovate the garden, a job she could undertake until it was time to restart her career. Already, there was paperwork for three tenders sitting on the desk inside. Already, rough estimates for each had been done. All she needed now was the will to work out final figures and submit the tenders. But her will had taken a leave of absence, along with happiness, and joy and any positive part of life. Loneliness sapped her soul.

While she rested aching shoulders, Phoebe eyed the garden. The wide avenue along the front of the property was almost traffic free. Unusual for a weekday but maybe the weather had enticed people to take a sickie to clear up after the fierce winds and lashing rain of the night. It reminded her of the empty streets in Athens the day she was mobbed.

Oh, far out, why did she have to think of Athens? With another wave of despair, she dropped the shovel, folded to the ground and ignored the damp that pressed through the denim of her ragged jeans. She hugged bent knees and rested her chin.

Athens. Nick. She hadn't heard from him but Alexos had sent her an email with numerous details about how he had deposited three quarters of her stolen cash into her Cashcard account. It had been folded in the clothes in Brad's backpack then kept as evidence until Alexos had made a submission to have it released and returned to Phoebe. She was grateful but didn't much care at the moment. It was still there as euros. Maybe, when she finished the painful job of packing up Dad's belongings and had set the garden to rights, she could go back to explore Spain and Portugal. But there were the tenders still not finished and she wasn't in the space to begin a new project. Everything was still too raw.

A willy wagtail landed a couple of metres in front of her and began to hop and run in the search for bugs. Its shiny black tail flicked from side-to-side each time it paused before it scampered to peck at some unseen bug where it paused again. The tiny bird eyed her, puffed out its white chest, lifted off and flew to another spot. There had been a similar bird at the Acropolis, on the search for delicacies whilst she and Nick had savoured fresh ham and cheese rolls. Drat, Nick again.

Nick. Her thoughts had been consumed by him the two entire weeks she had been home and as much as she drowned herself in physical labour, he wouldn't leave her alone. She wondered how he reacted when he discovered she had left a day earlier than she had told him was her departure date. It had taken four days of emotional agony before she had been able to get a flight home.

She grinned. To fill in the time she spent the days in the décor shops to choose carpets, paint, drapes and tiles and put together palettes and samples for the other floors of the unit complex. She had told a heap more lies - told Nick she had spent the time exploring various parts of the city when in reality, she worked frantically to pull together ideas as a way of keeping her brain cells away from thinking about her heartache. The day of the flight, she waited until he left for work before a mad scramble to lay all the samples out on his lounge floor before the taxi arrived to take her to the airport for the journey home.

Nick would have come home expecting her to be ready for a farewell dinner but to face him while they dined in some fancy restaurant was something she couldn't do. She didn't do pity dates. His words were still vivid in her brain.

'Just to prove you are not un-dateable, let me take you to dinner before you go.' His invitation had hurt beyond any pain she had experienced before. She still didn't understand why his words had buckled her at the knees but it had confirmed all she had overheard and knew as fact. He wasn't interested in her in any way apart from having saved his neck. It had been deliberate to agree to the time, when she knew it was two hours after her plane departed.

Tears welled. Before they could fall she fisted them away. It was almost impossible to believe she still had any left after the bucket loads she had wept over the past two weeks. More than she had done in her entire life. They seemed to just come and wouldn't stop – more so at night. Night was the worst. The few hours when she wasn't busy seemed to drag despite her physically drained body begging for sleep.

'Dig, Phoebe, dig,' she muttered. She rose and bent to retrieve the shovel. 'Ugh!' She flicked off the slimy slug which had made a cosy home under the handle in the short time it had been on the ground. Slugs and snails abounded in the chemical free garden but so did native birds who feasted on the bounty.

With tense muscles, she settled her muddy boots apart in a comfy stance then swung. Dig, heave, toss. Dig, heave, toss. She kept at it in a steady rhythm, ignored the runnels of sweat that streamed down her face, back and between her breasts. It wasn't until a sound which shouldn't have been there, caused her to pause and rest the blade edge on the ground. She straightened and glanced over her shoulder.

'Nick?' He stood leant up against a veranda post, one knee bent and arms folded over his strong, wide chest. His eyes were on her. Sure she was hallucinating; she closed her eyes, used the back of her hand to wipe away the drips of perspiration then bent and swept the tails of her dad's old shirt over her face.

Still hunched over, Phoebe twisted around. Oh, God, he was still there. Blood began to thunder through her veins. 'What are you doing here and how did you find me?'

He straightened. 'Well, what a nice hello. Finding you was easy since Alexos had a copy of your details. As to why I'm here…' he stepped off the veranda and with his eyes still on her, began to advance. 'I came to retrieve something you took with you when you left. And I believe you owe me a dinner date.' He stopped just out of reach and shoved his hands into his pockets.

237

'I took only my own belongings – nothing of yours.' Her innards had done a darn good job of tying themselves into intricate knots in the brief minute since she had spied him.

He frowned then grinned. 'Technically, it does belong to you but it has been rather difficult to live without it.'

Now she was confused. 'You're not making sense.'

A shiver wound its way across her shoulders when he reached out and fingered her hair. 'You cut it but the new style suits you.'

'I figured I needed some kind of make-over to make me more attractive to guys.'

His hand stilled, his face grimaced. 'Did it work?'

'Not yet but I've not been out to any social functions yet to find out.'

'Good.'

'Pardon?'

'Well it saves me from being arrested and put in jail for punching some guy's lights out for daring to take you out.'

Her heart stopped before it kick started again with a hefty wallop. 'What do you mean?'

He laughed, ran a shaking hand down his face and through his hair as though frustrated. 'The last two weeks have been hellish.'

Not half as hellish as hers she thought.

He paused and glanced to his right before catching her eye again. 'I was peeved at the way you left. And your note was full of hogwash. Pity date? You have a bad habit of interpreting plain English the wrong way.' He shook his head but his hand shot out and grasped her chin. 'I can't believe you thought such a thing. I invited you out because I very much wanted to enjoy a pleasant meal in candlelit surroundings – with you. I wanted more than a date. You have no idea how hard it was to keep from dragging you into my bed each night. I have to admit I thought it was only sexual attraction that had me panting after you, desperate for more than I was entitled to. But after you left

I realised it was much more than sex. I missed you, sweet Phoebe. My house is like a mausoleum without you.'

He eased his grip then ran a finger down her cheek. She shivered, loving his touch but every cell in her body was on alert. Hope soared but she was scared spitless.

'It took me two days of hell and arguments with my conscience to figure out what this love business is all about.'

Phoebe couldn't hold back the gasp which escaped.

He smiled. 'It's knowing in here,' he took her hand and held it against his head. 'And here,' he moved her hand to his heart and held it against his chest. 'Every night I go to bed I want to hold you in my arms and when I open my eyes each morning I want your beautiful head on the pillow next to me.'

He lifted her hand and planted a soft kiss in her palm. Her heart convulsed.

'It's knowing I can't lose you, that I want you to be the mother of my children and how I don't want to spend another moment of my life apart from you.'

He moved nearer, reached up and brushed away the tears which somehow flowed down her face. Until then she had no idea she was crying.

'I never believed in the concept of love but Mum kept telling me it was because I hadn't met the right woman yet. She said I would know when it happened.' He leant forwards, brushed his mouth over hers, which sent her blood careening like Formula One speed cars. 'She was right. Now I know.'

He cupped her face. 'You are the right woman. I love you, Phoebe. It was my heart you took with you when you left, which left me with a gaping and unbearable painful hole.'

Phoebe dissolved into tears of joy and plastered her body against his. His arms swept around her, tugged her so close she could feel his heart beat in time with hers. She snuggled her face into his shoulder. It felt like she had just come home.

'Can I take it from your reaction you might feel the same?' He murmured against her ear.

Pulling back, she nodded. 'Yes, oh, yes.'

'Wow, such a relief. I thought I would have to beg and cajole and spend months wooing you in the hope I could get you to fall in love with me.'

She sniffed, wiped away some of the grot with her fist and smiled. 'It sounds pretty old-fashioned but I wouldn't mind the wooing bit.'

'I thought it might appeal so how about tonight? Do you think you could stand putting on an outfit a little more elegant than your dad's shirt and the rattiest pair of jeans ever to exist and join me in a romantic meal? They do candlelight. I checked.'

'Sounds wonderful.' She swiped at her face again. 'Far out, I'm a mess.'

Nick used his thumbs to wipe at a few stray tears. 'You take my breath away every time I look at you regardless of what you wear, even smeared in mud.' He grasped her hand, dragged her up onto the veranda then led her around to the front door where a huge bouquet of red roses was propped against the painted wood.

'I wondered if you were a flower person before I remembered your profession. Then I became worried about whether or not you liked them cut or preferred a living plant. There was only one way I would find out.' He retrieved the cellophane covered flowers and held them out.

'They are gorgeous, thank you. I can't believe this. A man has bought me flowers.'

'You've never received flowers before?'

'Oh, yes, but only from Dad. Never a...'

'Lover?'

Heat rose. She dropped her eyes. 'No.'

Even though she still held the bouquet, Nick grasped her hands, took a step back. 'This is awkward but I need to ask this.'

'Oh, oh.'

He smiled. 'From the conversations we've had, I get the impression that you haven't had much experience with men. You know, intimately.'

'Sheesh. Am I a virgin? No but it wasn't a pleasant experience and no it wasn't with Brad.'

'Good to hear you never slept with that piece of scum. Not so good to hear your first time wasn't pleasant. We'll have to do something to remedy that but,' he paused, caught her eye. 'Do I want to make sweet love with you? Definitely but only when it's okay with you. We can take it slow. I love you Phoebe.' He leant forwards, pressed a kiss to her brow.

Overcome, it took her a few seconds to reach up to kiss him. 'I love you, Nick, which is why I had to come home. It was too hard to be with you, when I was in love with you and knew you didn't feel the same.'

His kiss was long, warm and gentle but told her so much.

'Leaving was the right thing to do. It gave me the jolt I needed. And believe me, it was a billion-volt shot. One which brought me to my knees. The thought of not seeing you again…' He shuddered. 'But no more running away when insecurity hits. And I know you are insecure with men, not that I blame you. Any time you are unsure about some issue, we talk about it. Okay?'

'Okay.'

'Now do you think you could invite me in? It appears I have a lot of wooing to do and I am certain what I have in mind isn't suitable for public scrutiny.'

She grinned. 'I like the sound of that but this door is locked from the inside. I've had a couple of unpleasant visitors.'

Nick stepped back. 'What sort of unpleasant visitors?'

241

'Brad's parents. They have begged me to drop all charges against Brad. Says I'm lying. Their darling little boy wouldn't do such things even though I pointed out it wasn't me who laid the charges.'

'How bad were the parents?'

'Nasty enough I threatened to call the police if they ever came here again. It appears Brad didn't get bail.'

'No. He's been locked away for three years. There were two other hotels he scammed. The proof of his stealing your money was indisputable. The parents, according to Alexos, refused to pay restitution.'

'Seems to run in the family. But enough of that scumbag. We have to go in the back door.' Phoebe spun around and led the way along the veranda.

'Nice property. Nick kept his arm around her waist.

'Thank you.' She opened the back door. It was uncanny but she was certain she floated inside.

'Wow, it's gorgeous in here,' said Nick. 'But even more gorgeous is the woman who lives in it.' He tugged her close, wrapped his arms around her. 'Now, let's see what we can do about getting this wooing business started.' He grinned, searched her eyes, dropped his head and took her mouth in a searing kiss.

She could handle all the wooing he could manage and then some.